THE BARBER'S COLLECTION

R. CONRAD SPEER

~

a novel

atmosphere press

A highly entertaining collection of stories in which Speer demonstrates an amazing gift for language and imagery. He is particularly adept in revealing a character in a few pithy lines of dialogue, a talent which is both admirable and amusing.

~ Lyn McCauley, author of *Early Release*

The voice is at times lyrical, at times jagged, but always distinctive and in touch with not only the lands that it inhabits, but also their spirits. The longer pieces are tragicomic, while the shorter ones ... are haunting. And the personifications in "When Elephant Got Dealt" are diabolically humorous. Speer demonstrates a wide range and great versatility in these stories.

~ Suman Mallick, author of *The Black-Marketer's Daughter*

What an interesting, surreal mix of stories. From baseball to woodpeckers to a children's tale. Speer has an eye for detail and place. One of my favorites was "Farm Family Affairs" – sparse and haunting. Highly recommended.

~ Thomas Rooz Bazar, author of *An Expectation of Plenty*

An intriguing and exhilarating collection of stories. Perhaps my first foray into the Canadian consciousness – it feels different but not alien. Speer's attention to detail is superb, best illustrated by the first story, "Woodpeckers of Triangulum." The same story registers a low-key humor, a humor which consistently appears throughout the collection.

~ Robert Castle, author of *The Hidden Life*, *A Sardine on Vacation*, and *Berthcut & Sons*

To C.E. and G.W.

Book I

Veterans of the Axis, Accidentally

Nuthouse nine

*S*ome *quick trims and a few major cuts,* Cal thought as he turned the ignition, starting and revving the engine of his prized pastel blue Buick Electra. He inched out of the driveway, proceeding with caution until passing the overgrown periwinkle hydrangeas obstructing his view of the sidewalk and street. *But first, the clubs.*

If he was asked to take a sort of official position on Mondays—or at least his Mondays, seasonal Mondays, the Monday of today—it would be: Long after the sunup cockcrow was when the sublime summer day began in town, when some perceptible bustling with commerce was underway on Main Street, in a kind of formal sense. While it might be even later, it was certainly no sooner than that, when Cal could get to his essential business of opening the shop and providing those vital services to any placid gentlemen in need. However, before the general grogginess could shake itself loose, for that requisite sobering up to take hold, another key matter of leisure would have to be attended to first, notwithstanding the kiln-levels of smothering heat already settling in the early morning atmosphere.

In the final moments preceding the punctual rising of the Sun, he exited the small town proper carrying such an excitement about him that it was causing a mild daze in his head with an almost bit of a blur in his sight. Driving down the steep grade of the big hill parallel to the river, Cal soon discovered the thick smog—originating in part from the raging forest fires in the north, the smoke conspiring with patches of dense fog hovering over the water—was blunting the typical first bright pink colours in the sky, turning the eastern horizon into a dusty mauve. He approached the oxidized steel bridge towards the bottom of the hill—a horizontal derrick-looking span to the southwest and perpendicular to his current pockmarked road—which crossed a channel to a little island before the second section of the bridge put the driver in another town altogether. Nearing the distorted yield sign posted at the entrance to give bridge traffic heading north-easterly the right-of-way, Cal eased his foot off the gas, slowing it down enough to ensure he would not get t-boned by any errant oncoming traffic originating in haste from the neighbouring town otherwise still sound asleep across the murky river.

Continuing the standard drive straight ahead, crawling forward to pass by the fading yield sign, Cal saw a police car at the other end of the bridge, stopped on the island, lights flashing away as if a glittering mirror ball at dawn. He rolled through the intersection at a slow enough pace to see the active police car parked diagonally across the road. The cop was positioned as if to halt traffic going to or coming from either direction, for what he assumed was some minor accident, a likelihood of someone having hit a white-tailed or mule deer, or some such other common enough disturbance during the night. *Although being so close to the institution, you sure can't discount that,* Cal thought, methodically considering the proximity, measuring out the distance in his head, giving the area a brief scan as if to confirm his quick calculations. *There's been so much mad commotion out here as of late and all, could be anything of the sorts. Nothing would surprise me, not anymore. It can't.*

Cal's mind was wandering back to the hospital and its

patients, returning to those thoughts from when he rolled out of his messy bed not quite an hour ago, the police car having refocused his concentration on what sort of absurd tumult he might come across today. At the same time, place, and excessive temperature of seven days ago, the first few holes were quiet until the inevitable hubbub set in during his outing of last week, this weekly ritual, this activity, this golf.

On the fourth hole, he saw a right naked and aged male patient attempting a surreptitious climb out of the crisp candy apple red parking lot dumpster, bringing along an unsound kite made of filthy garbage bags and broken twigs, then running off at full speed by the side of the main road, in some desperation, trying to create his own unlikely aeronautical breeze in the dead calm of the stagnant morning air.

On hole number six, he saw a rather pretty female patient, a young woman wearing the issued all-white outfit, smiling in an apparent nirvana-like bliss while sitting cross-legged in a bed of marigolds, giving the pleasant flowers a joyous sniff while uprooting and proceeding to eat them, nibbling like a rabid bunny, from the dazzling orange petals right through the green leaves and stem to the dirt- and worm-covered earthy roots.

And on hole number lucky seven, he saw a most familiar face; the man wearing his woolly parka and winter boots in the one-hundred-degree heat, thus also sporting an inherent and profound stench about him, while on a frantic search for some trivial treasure on a festive—if repetitive—date of absolute and fantastical fiction.

The butterfly police were successful in nabbing all three of those ornery patients last week; as harmless as each of them was in reality, these ostensive offenders, on the lam, even if still on the grounds and not more than fifty feet away.

I haven't seen Mr. Sanders yet this summer, roaming around, looking for his tasty chickens to spice up. Nor Johnny Johann, keeping up his phony post-war schtick of innocence. Cal continued contemplating on which of the regular gems of patients he might encounter wandering about the grounds today, and the possibility of those new guests he could welcome to the asylum and the town in his own unique way. *Come to think of it, I haven't seen Yuri either. Nor Leon. Nor a bunch of those hordes of other bastards. Although I suppose if anyone is locked down and drugged up real good these days, it's those guys, considering everything going on: Their brutal crimes, pathetic conditions, the need for more guinea pigs to test hopeful new methods on. But unless he kicked the bucket in the last week, I'll see the Skunk for sure. After that, it's a bit of a crapshoot, I guess.*

Gathering the Buick's speed back up and returning his attention in front of him, Cal carried on, driving on what became a windy little road snaking along the river. A thick canopy of foliage transformed the curvy path into a verdant tunnel, with only wisps of sunlight poking through the lime green elms above and down to his windshield, creating disorienting patterns of flashing light as he cruised ahead on the incongruent asphalt beneath. For another mile, he began climbing and coiling up a second hill, the lesser incline which led right onto the resplendent grounds of his tranquil destination.

A well-known and long-time resident-patient sat on the side of the road about half-way up from the bridge, patching up his little stone wall with a sloppy pail of mud, maintaining an original section he had built there decades earlier. The driver gave the busy bee a polite wave and an approving nod, to no response from the journeyman mason, as if Cal were a mere dragonfly that had flown past him. After a final stop at the centre of the grounds—to ensure no wayward residents were running about, out in front of the grand institution and next to the green of his final hole—he turned into the empty joint-use gravel parking lot right across from the tee box of his first hole, managing to park in a perfect spot under a cluster of thick ash trees offering the sole respite of shade in the area for his already overheating vehicle.

Cal's glorious bright and early Monday morning escape ritual, exercise, and fact-finding mission started when a nice first melt was underway—something he claimed, but it was when the snow was all gone, if the muddy puddles were not yet evaporated in full, sent back into the hydrological cycle above. The golf would continue until the first significant snow fell once again, and stayed; the worst season was a late start in May through a wrap in August, while the best could be as much as a good run from around the end of March through to as late as November. However, the calendar as planned out saw an invariable disturbance on either end—or in the middle, or both—by the notorious and terrible weather gracing these vast plains. The notoriousness made for tired and painful local clichés that could not be avoided no matter how hard one tried. These included the popular classics such as:

"If you don't like the weather, wait blah blah, change blah blah—heh!"

"There're two seasons here: One yada yada, other yada yada—heh!"

"It's hotter than a blank... It's colder than a blank... Heh!"

But on this fine day of his, out here on the course today: *There's no snow, wind, or rain, for which about to complain. Nope, not today.* Today—and this week, this month, summer—the area was graced with a stifling and unlift-able Death Valley-esque heat baking the land. This was the complaint: The southwestern-style desert scorch was not welcome here, not any longer.

First hole:
Park and walk… and knock

While not making a habit of taking set appointments during his course of normal business operations back in town, one had been requested for this day, and by a rather important client. Last Friday, an appointment with his physician was penciled into the calendar for this Monday, one that would soon kick off the workday and the work week, for all parties involved. For Cal, this meant he would need to get moving if he were to expedite the upcoming round, thus creating a window to accommodate the good doctor and his exacting schedule in less than three hours.

As the first one out on the golf course today—it being so early, so hot, and so much crop in the area either still being harvested in the fields adjacent and beyond, or hauled to the local elevators or the regional mill or maltster—Cal opened the driver's door of the reliable azure Electra, taking care with a slow step out, then digging into the front pocket of his light turquoise plaid shirt for a recently hand-rolled cigarette. He struck a match to light it up while basking in the absolute peace of this hour at this place, reflecting on the beauty of nature and the grace of humanity in his times and locale, concentrating his gaze on the vast architectural marvel that was the main building. The institution itself was the heart of the grounds, and it was even the nucleus of the town and region if Cal and his fellow citizens were being honest with themselves, whether they liked it or not. Cal was honest, he knew it, and he liked it. He loved it.

Everything else around the building also brought about a thorough fascination with Cal, as if the central structure were the Sun and all the other smaller buildings were its planets and moons, sundry infrastructure like tables and chairs as asteroids and comets, random items as space junk. Under a constellation of large elm, ash, and beech trees, he stared at the wide circle of scarlet Adirondack chairs, arranged there for outdoor staff breaks of the institution employees, even if often usurped by mischievous patients. The cigarette hung from his open mouth, the tips of his clenched and almost light golden beryl teeth were showing some lustre through the forced smile, breathing with gentle puffs, inhaling through one intake, venting out another orifice.

Cal opened the trunk and began struggling to hoist the golf bag out, using all his strength and leveraging what he could of each lightweight muscle for the task of apparent difficulty. On success, he propped up the bag in the gravel only to return to the trunk, retrieving those uncooperative loose balls and tees that had made their escape on the short ride over. Once the items were placed back in the bag—safe and sound, the zipper pouch secured this time— he slammed the trunk door of the vintage machine back down, grabbing and heaving the bag over his shoulder, heading towards the glorified club house meets drink stand meets fee hut meets clapboard shanty, all in the same fluid motion.

Without missing a step or taking an extra breath, he walked a steady long pace up to the still-closed wooden payment window and banged on it with the side of his fist perpendicular to his knuckles, knocking three times in an equal pattern and force. While he waited for not more than an easygoing five seconds, Cal stared at the absurd broken rooster weathervane atop the shack, managing a lopsided swivel as it was creaking away on its rusty tin perch. On not receiving an answer from the first knocks, he pivoted around one hundred eighty degrees on his heels and did the identical hammering on the bright cherry red door of the shack, which was positioned adjacent to the window. Again, no answer.

His lack of success was no surprise, for Cal knew this to be the case, just as it was last Monday at this exact same time, and again the week before that: It was too early in the first morning of the work week—and much too hot—for anyone to be manning this booth on the golf course. *Let alone an imbecile from the institution*, Cal thought, *even if the lazy worker lived right behind the hut in that immense brick building.* And so, he proceeded over to the first tee box, setting himself up for the hole and the round. Not wanting to waste any further time this morning, Cal teed off on the first hole, then used an iron of a lower number, a different iron of a higher number for a chip, and a putt, putt, and a putt, resulting in: A not so bad and, all things considered, maybe even respectable double bogey to kick off the weekly round of golf.

Second hole:
Thirst is unaware of any season

Testing his patience, Cal had been waiting to use the new object with a certain desperation, this cutting-edge product. Back in town, at his shop and his home, he had wrestled with an uncontainable excitement over the past several days, waiting for the order to arrive in weeks past and then having picked it up from Jim's hardware store mid-last week. And today, early this morning, he did not want to blow its good first use from the outset, waiting until this second hole where he was sure to maintain a greater focus, warmed-up and with an improved serenity. Here he stood, on another albeit longer par four, the impressive new tool of the trade housed in his golf bag, the moment itself present, with him and for him, this being where all the intense anticipation had led and was now peaking. *This is the undeniable climax of the morning and of the week. At least so far, but it's still quite early, a long way to go yet…*

On the tee box at hole number two, he was already sweating and burning, and so fast, so early. *It must be a hundred degrees already.* He was considering if the heat of the day had cooled off even one little bit overnight. While the fog was lifting and the smoke was drifting, the air in the sunny skies above remained dry and dusty. With a full wall of caraganas and willows behind and on each side, forming a scraggy horseshoe around the back of the tee box, Cal looked the distance down the second fairway. He found his grip, taking three proper and complete practice swings off to the side: Fast, slow, fast. A few inches off his tee, he stepped forward with serious conviction, looking down to admire how the ball was placed with such perfection on the small white tee, which in turn was placed so without flaw on the spotless patch of shamrock green grass. He looked down field to the flag on the mustard-coloured stick in the hole, again looking down to the ball and letting it go: The new Wilson driver, in action at long last. It let off a beautiful and elusive sound, something like a metallic ping merging with a solid oaky thwack. The ball lifted, lifting, straight, shifting, right, final hard right, curving just off, from the reasonable and healthier fairway grass into the long, thick and tick-infested grass on the edge of the rough—but at least a solid one hundred and fifty yards out.

The drive on this second hole was a great success for Cal, so he could not avoid smiling to himself, thrilled as he reached down to collect his tee. But the tee was long gone in this now russet patch—gone along with a clump of turf, larger than the width of his new oversized driver head. The jovial grin dissipated. Even with a humbled look and a more stoic façade, Cal could not help but remain giddy with this new driver and this first more than respectable drive to christen the club. He could move to eliminate the replaced and now obsolete former club by throwing it into his backyard scrap heap of a graveyard of other retired items and failed objects—a cathartic chore for later.

On collecting his bag and having taken not five steps forward off the tee box, out of the bushes shuffled something, or someone. At first sight, it appeared to be a naughty patient, grumbling about, scratching its way through the slight hole in the shrubs, bent over, this hunchback of the caraganas. Nearing the exit of the scrub, it was moving forward like a boxer with arms up and hands in front, with head back, down, and bobbing along, trying to avoid the sharp scrapes to the face they would otherwise invite from the prickles of the thorny branches. On closer view, this individual was wearing a beat-up and soiled baseball cap, tattered mechanics overalls, and covered in an exterior layer of a dense but frayed parka, albeit left unzipped and open in the front. This person was also wearing heavy yet shabby work boots. Cal knew, or at least gathered, that they were also used as winter boots for the patient—plus regular shoes. One all-purpose pair for all-weather situations—multi-climatic conditions for all of confined life out here at the asylum, even if the footwear was also beaten to total hell, as if worked away at by a coppersmith in a hurry.

The patient's clothes, boots, and skin were layered from head to toe in a grimy and greasy substance, all reeking of body odour, oil or fuel of some kind—petrol with a side of fresh cut grass. As Cal understood it, the scent of a mowed lawn can smell either good or bad, and the more positive type of grassy affair was a scent he knew well, one explained to him in extensive detail some time ago by a former French doctor at the hospital. It was a description Cal would never forget, even though he knew nothing of France and even less of wine.

However, this grassy smell in the presence of Cal this morning was not the olfactory-pleasing bouquet of fresh cut grass in the form of some fitting and wonderful aromatic Sauvignon Blanc—the best bottles being from the good French Doc's region of Sancerre, he would have others know. Cal was told this meant white wine, or some kind of white wine, and with absolute certainty a one-of-a-kind great some kind of white wine—the top of the pinnacle, those precursor grapes. No, this was not quite it, even with said recent grass clippings having a universal presence in this current place. This was not quite the fragrance, the exquisite scent of some sort of marvelous French wine—not at all, alas. What was fanning itself through Cal's nose was something more of a putrid and decomposing, methane-releasing, heave-inducing, ageing and browning grass piles in the sunshine sort of a sickening scent.

And because Cal knew that good smell and that bad smell, and he knew the explanation from the good Gallic doctor as told to him as it related to the exact same aspiring groundskeeper of a patient back then... Cal, of course, knew the patient at hand, discerning it right as this man escaped from the tangles and prickles of the hedgerow, as the disobedient fellow was working his way through and trying to regain a more regular and upright posture, somewhat. But today, the sickening stench was not just that of the wine snob-pleasing freshly trimmed grass, nor only of the withering grass smelling no better than a mangled mammalian corpse festering away in the heat, scavengers circling about. *If only*, Cal thought. No, beyond the aroma of wine and reek of death, it also gave off the unmistakable bouquet of: Piss. *Out on the golf course, nothing like the smell of urine in the morning, tainting the dew-fresh air.* If it was a hint, it was a hurricane. And it was the patient's own piss, as sure as the sky was presently blue. A true cornucopia of smells from hell. All of these, along with the other distinct trademarks, blew right at him in the gentle breeze, surrounding Cal in a concussive stink. That meant he knew with precision who this was. *This patient here. This vagrant anywhere else.* If not quite each and every time, the visit did occur most often, in some manner or another, while Cal was golfing a crack of dawn solo round just like on this fine Monday morning of today.

It was the skunk, or 'the Skunk,' as he called him, which was suitable enough. Cal reflected that perhaps skunks had redeeming qualities of some sort, such as with the potential value of their fur, and with their being kind of cute creatures, like little black and white plush toys for children, mini pandas or some such. Or at least the smell was an inherent part of their being; their biology and evolution made them what they were today, and the classic skunk smell was consistent, manageable, and from a reasonable distance might not even be that unpleasant to the human nose of afar. However, Cal's skunk, the Skunk's odour of today, was as it often was: It was of a foulness so pure and with some extra effluvium thrown in on this special occasion.

The sad aroma of the Skunk saw wild seasonal variations depending on the weather patterns, adapting to any shift in climate thrown at him, the unwarranted levels of apparel needed for the acclimatization, and the minimal frequency of bathing and grooming on the inside. And then, Cal believed, there was the issue of the psychiatrists being in cahoots with the pharmacists, propounding their theories of the day, married with their contemporary chemical formulas, concoctions of good and bad, insulin and snake-oil, and all the other elixirs as drugs imaginable in between. *If that stuff messes with their heads, it must mess with their bodies too, their smells.* Cal paused to consider this as if a philosopher contemplating the deep meaning of the present waft of noxiousness. *It must have something to do with their minds, and sweat glands, secretions. And I suppose it's the mental hygiene the staff are so absorbed in anyway, not the physical as much.*

The Skunk had been at the hospital for as long as Cal could remember, residing here at this place since he was dropped off by somebody or other years ago, family or otherwise. Cal did not know how the institution of old used to dress them up, whether so thick and cozy or not, but his overriding consideration was on imagining what the drugs did to this patient's brain to make him think it was so cold outside in such an objective and extraordinary heat. Cal wondered whether this patient would have behaved like this—with his absurd winter wardrobe in the irrepressible summer warmth—from his original condition, before and without whatever drugs they had him pumped full of today, before the other treatments, so many years later. Beyond the parka, and whatever events and ghosts were long behind him, the Skunk was thinking 'safety first,' wearing his winter work boots, which Cal believed a great irony, as he had never seen him do any actual work around the grounds, whether as a voluntary task or otherwise. *But still, you never know when you'll stub your toe on the soft grass. Or trip over some light clover. Lazy prick.*

"Hi, hi there. Hello. Beautiful day, day out," said Fred (aka the Skunk), approaching Cal with caution as he came shuffling forward, covered in burs and bringing his awkward physical mannerisms along with him. He looked up, first to Cal's eyes and averting his gaze, darting from Cal's eyes to his feet, and then back down to Fred's own feet—his dirty, grassy, pissy all-season boots. "Can't beat a day, day like today. On the, the golf, golf course. Here. Today."

"Sure can't," said Cal, grumbling while giving Fred a once-over look of incredulity as he attempted to hold his breath, which he managed to do for a few mere seconds, trying to be covert. But then it was right out there in the open as Cal gestured his disgust to Fred, that he, the Skunk, reeked in a horrible way, followed by Cal's explicit yet somewhat authentic gagging, as well as some fake and a bit of hyperbolic coughing and choking into his elbow and shoulder, as poor Fred did smell so terrible, on some other monumental scale of unpleasantness.

"And can't beat a day, day like today, today when it's your, your birthday," said Fred, attempting a frenzied smile. "It's my birthday. Today. Birthday."

This was also patented Fred: Fred's birthday was today, each and every single day, three hundred and sixty-five days a year—and three hundred and sixty-six days a year, every four years. If Fred was breathing, it was his birthday. If you ran into him on the grounds, whatever day the true calendar held, you might as well start singing 'Happy Birthday' to Fred and blow out his candles for him before the inevitable accosting and celebratory soliciting began. Although Fred was never looking for cake, not this merry skunk...

"Well," said Cal, in a congratulatory tone, yet without any of Fred's genuine, if odd and nervous, excitement. "Happy birthday, Frederick!"

Cal was in a good mood and did not feel like confrontation—prodding and provoking Fred—even if it was the normal course on the course, just for a bit of unadorned fun. While the result of the antagonization could be quite amusing to him during the given moment at hand, the entertainment value would pay dividends to Cal for many months to come, if lucky. The guys at the shop loved the twisted humour of Cal, and he liked to keep his material real and fresh—as real and fresh as the manicured course with the mowed lawn on the grounds and all-over poor Fred, the Skunk.

"Thanks, thanks man, sir. It's a good, good day, sir. Say, say any chance, chance I could borrow, sir, I could get some change, a little bit of change, to buy a, a pop for my, my birthday? That'd be a great present, a happy one. Pop. And it's so hot. Hot out here. I'd really, I would appreciate that, like that. Such a nice, nice gift. Change and pop. It's so hot. So some pop."

Cal was still thinking about his new club, feeling the craving coming on, needing to give it another swing on the next drive. He was wanting to head into the rough and get chipping out of it, but Cal figured he would still have a little bit of fun, since he was here and the opportunity had presented itself in this proactive way, as if it came to him on a silver platter. Cal felt himself in a crisp if uncharacteristic mood since he rose this morning and this was too great of a prospect to pass up, even if he had to breathe through his open mouth like a caveman for a few more minutes, huffing and puffing as he tried to maintain a bit of distance from his fellow Neanderthal—albeit this much more uncouth one, unclean and unrefined as he was—the Skunk.

"Frederick," said Cal, querying him in a gentle monotone, exhaling with enthusiasm. "I thought you said it was your birthday last Monday when I was out here? You told me one week ago—one week ago today, in fact, right about this time of day, same heat even, but it was out on seven. You told me then that it was your birthday, and I gave you some change for a pop that day, remember? You don't recall how hot it was back then, last week? How in the hell do you have two birthdays so close together? It's inconceivable. I'm beyond flummoxed, Fred. What gives?"

"Oh, oh. Oh, that wouldn't have been me, no. Not me," said Fred, taking a defensive step backwards, which was a positive move in the right direction for Cal as well, even if as a coincidence. "No, no. Today's my, my birthday. But there were guys here, a couple guys here, they, guys who they, that they had birthdays here last weekend, here. We had parties for them, for them inside, so I imagine one of them. Them, I imagine. And I look like one of those, those guys, a bit at least. Quite a bit. And same, same glasses even. Yeah. Same boots. Boots. Funny, funny thing," said Fred, spitting out an uncomfortable chuckle.

Continuing to have fun with the richness of crazy Fred's false story of innocence, but ramping up his own phony anger a notch to see the reaction and the unfolding thereof, Cal went at him while attempting, in concurrence, to return his focus to the game at hand, speeding up his walk now to move the play forward and past this second hole.

"Freddie, you're lying to me. You're right full of shit, man, top to bottom. It's not your happy frigging birthday today, not at all," said Cal, as he paused, posing with an ambiguous yet thoughtful look and crooked smile. "But Fred, I like you, I do. You're a good guy, no question. I can see that—I know that. So I'll make you a deal, alright? A fair one."

"Well, OK," said Fred, pausing with greater concern and becoming further lost in his own world of a most particular and singular attention. "Well..."

"Listen, it's a good deal for you, Fred—trust me on this

one," said Cal, as he fleshed out his idea on the fly. "I'll give you a little bit of change, for your birthday today, so you can go and buy a nice ice-cold soda pop for yourself—you can cool yourself down in this here heat... If—shush, ssshhh—if: If you go burn what you're wearing. Take it all off and burn it in the dumpster, behind the shop in back over there, the one with that apricot-coloured paint. You can borrow my pack of matches here. Take a bar of soap down to that creek—that little one right there, off the third green, by that flag there, isn't too much water flowing through it this time of year, but you'll find a little pool of some, I'm sure. Go down there and scrub that skunky shitty, rotting fish stench off every inch of your body. You'll have to find your own soap somewhere, that chalky stuff they issue you, I guess—wish I had a bar of soap on me to give you, but I don't have that with my golf gear. Anyways, then go down over there. The grass, dirt, piss, diesel, kerosene, whatever else you've got on your clothing—go and torch it, OK. I bet it'll burn real quick. We got us a deal or what? With this agreement, everybody wins, Fred!"

"Oh, oh, I can't, I, I... We get bathed in there," said Fred, pointing back over the caragana hedgerow towards the building. As he began rocking back and forth on his feet, becoming more flustered by the second, it seemed like each word of Cal's made Fred flinch on the inside; then he would twitch it out as an external reaction, as if he were being shocked. "We're not allowed to go near, near, in that creek, and, and, I can't. I can't. It's by the, by the, by the... It's by the big smokestack, so we can't, we can't go near there. The smokestack. Nowhere near there. Never ever. Ever. Never. And it's my, my birthday, and it's so, so hot, so for a present, a gift, I'd just like, like a pop—a cold, cold soda. Pop."

"What do you mean you can't go near the smoke-stack?" said Cal, interested in Fred's deviation in thought and look of grave concern about being within a certain proximity of the power plant of the institution, or at least specific to the tall smokestack emanating from its core, of which the Skunk seemed to fear deep in his own core. "It rises out the middle of the building and most of it is fenced right off. You can't get near it, but you're scared of that big stack for some reason, is that it?"

"That's where they burn, they burn us in there," said Fred, trembling in dread. "I can't get burned, not on my, on my birthday. Burn. Birthday. Never. Happy."

"Who burns you? Or who would burn you?" said Cal, a bit taken aback and trying to squeeze the more complete answer out of Fred. "You think if you go near there you'll get burned somehow?"

"Bad ones. No. Bad ones will," said Fred, shivering and rocking on his heels at a more rapid pace as he looked at the stack with Cal as if something like starving man-eating demons lived in the tall chimney. "If I'm bad. Bad burns. Fire. Burns. Keep clothes, keep clothes on. Don't go, go near it. Stay away from the, the creek. Bad ones go in, into the stack. Be good. Not bad. No bad. Good. Good."

Cal and Fred both looked towards the little creek on hole number three and the tall tan brick smokestack rising from behind it, towering out of the power plant at a height of two hundred feet. Cal inferred that Fred thought if he misbehaved in some manner or another—in this case, for example, burning his clothes or entering the creek—he would be punished by getting thrown right into the smokestack, or to be more realistic, he would be burned in the boiler where his essence in the form of smoke would see an ultimate venting through the stack. Thus, Fred must follow the rules of the institution or else the administrative powers that be within would make an inevitable move to set him ablaze, either as a complete roast or just for a little bit of a searing as punishment, in what would be dire consequences for the Skunk in any scenario, a first or final offense. Or maybe it was even worse for the patients, believing ghouls and monsters lurked in the smokestack of reprisals and any abnormal or frowned upon behaviour met a fateful end, a dance with the devil within. As Fred must have believed it all in his sorry mind, it meant he must ensure keeping his clothes on at all times, no taking a dip in the creek with or without soap, and no starting fires, even if that meant he must don all these heavy winter clothes during the summer months, the partial genesis of his awful smell. If rejecting the deal that Cal was offering meant it would ensure Fred's safety from the fire and smoke of the stack, the Skunk was out—he would forgo the soda pop, instead choosing the summer heat and the sweat over the inferno of helping to power the hospital. If he took the deal and went ahead with the burning of his apparel, Fred, too, would face an apparent burning of his own skin or soul as some ironic reciprocity.

"Oh, I get it now," said Cal, realizing with clarity and beyond inference that among patients there was a rumour morphing into a belief where egregious bad behaviour would lead one to be thrown into the boiler and vented out the gigantic smokestack coming out of the power plant that generated the juice for the asylum, or some similar version of that false speculation. "Fred, some nurse or someone is pulling your leg. They'd never cook you in there—that doesn't make any sense, not a lick of it. They're just scaring you to keep you in line, keep you away from your addiction to the soda and that sort of thing, that's all it is. Those aren't the real consequences. No way they'd do that to you or anyone. This isn't Germany, Fred."

"Burned. Birthday," said Fred, as if channeling his former track to return to those more pleasant birthday thoughts and away from the satanic stack of smoke. "It's my birthday today, and I, I'd like a pop. It so, so hot, hot out. Flames. Pop."

"You don't need no goddamn pop," said Cal, laying it on Fred with authority, growing frustrated at his utter lack of reason. "You need a bath in some vinegar and tomato juice, then rinsed off with a fire truck hose. Got it? That's what you need. How'd you let yourself go like that? Jesus. I mean, you should be passing out every time you breathe in your stink—your *own* stink. And what in the Sam Hill kind of a notion: Why, pray tell, are you wearing clothes for a flipping blizzard in this here heat? Where do you think you are, the Arctic? Jeez Louise. Where're your sled dogs parked at? Christ's sake, man. Come on, Frederick!"

Cal was trying to roil him up, get Fred going a bit further, and his success was becoming evident. Yet there was always a threshold, the fine line between a mere pout or a tear and an epic toddler-like meltdown. And Cal still felt bad after last week's episode, where he gave Fred some insignificant change, which afforded him that much-desired cola. After his round was complete a couple of holes hence, Cal saw him back in the parking lot not much later, where Fred must have chugged back the pop in the vicinity—as Cal had seen him do multiple times and without rest, in one giant gulp—and then pissed himself in an instant, soaking his same pants in a systemic fashion.

At the time, he was not sure if Fred drank the pop at such a rapid pace because of his own unstable mental condition or if it was because he had little to no choice but to down it quick enough to be able to consume it all before the butterfly police arrived, snatching him up and chucking his pop. And they would surely arrive, as always, netting their smelly walking lepidopteran dressed in dirty shades of pewter and walnut, dragging the filthy recidivist back inside the building to get washed up, and God knows what else he would be forced to consume in drugs, to endure in treatment, punishment, torture. *Burned?* Anything and everything, perhaps, but it was unmistakable that it was so worth it for Fred to obtain the sweet and divine nectar, filled with marvellous bubbles, in the clear and shiny, wavy bottle. Whatever happened, and whether he even remembered last week's events or not, Fred was back, longing for more soda, more sugar, as the one high, maybe the sole nostalgia, whether he knew it to be true or not, the singular inkling of freedom Fred could steal to enjoy something in that building: the Skunk's home, the institution. The hospital.

Cal felt that playing with him and ripping him would in fact help him better understand his condition—it would help Fred in a clinical sort of a way, whatever his specific and deep problem was, whether diagnosed as such in a certified capacity or not. Cal did believe in this altruistic effort, the conviction of his conviction. But he also knew in practical terms where the change (the coinage) would lead Fred, and it would not lead to a positive change (not the coinage) in his ways or in his daily life. *No, no it would not*, Cal thought. *Not one bit.* The monetary change would lead to: The pop and the piss, to Fred's pop, to the Skunk's piss, yet again—urine-soaked and stained slacks, for life. And outside of the cash injection, as gracious as Dr. Cal was in helping Fred with his profound and dark issues, the whole scenario was also just another great story for Cal—this much was clear. It gave him another brilliant gem of a yarn to tell all his customers, all his pals and patrons back in town at the shop, for the next week, month, and longer. It was golf tales ad infinitum, loony bin stories ad nauseum, read and recounted—in the first-hand, was ideal—by the trusted narrator, the primary source, Mr. Cal.

Cal pulled a shiny new coin right out from the back pocket of his trousers, presenting it with a flip of his thumb. It was fumbled by Fred on the attempted catch, bouncing off his grimy wears, onto and into the exposed shredded blades covering the still intact rooted grass, as Cal decided on a private recanting of the teasing while choosing to wish Fred a verbal and more authentic congratulations for the faux occasion, a true and sincere most happy birthday.

"You have a good one now, Fred," said Cal, concluding their visit. "Take care of yourself, you hear?"

In a desperate bid of stumbling around in trying to collect the small silver coin—this best gift, worth more now than real silver, even beyond the equivalent value of gold—Fred managed at last to pick it up off the ground. He blew the grass clippings out of his hand, taking the money and starting off, back towards the parking lot common to the golf course and the hospital—if one could even distinguish between those two things, or any other such boundary on the greater grounds. Fred had taken only a couple of steps when Cal saw that Fred could already see himself closing in on the shrine of the green fees hut, open by now, where therein lay the loot, the freedom, the... Pop.

Behold, the holder of cold, syrupy, fizzy beverages, and in such a neat cylindrical—even if almost serpentine—gleaming glass bottle: Ice-cold dreamland.

And then, as always, the guaranteed outcome: Piss-warm pants.

"Thanks, thanks sir, very much, very, thank you for, for the birthday... Pop."

Third hole:
In three on three with the three

Cal drove the green using an iron, as even he could overdrive with his driver or the three-wood. As unlikely as that possible scenario was, it was more likely to be driven one hundred and fifty yards ahead with a break of fifty to the hard right. The shot off the tee box with the three-iron had a flat and decent lift, so straight he knew it to be aberrant on impact and in the follow through. *Not as precise as the straightness of an arrow, but that's a damn fine shot in any event.* Cal took precaution in putting to within a foot of the cup, taking an extra moment to get the lay of the land on this green—with respect to topography—thus ensuring he could drain it on the next petite putt. With the most essential and gentle of slightest of taps, Cal was able to attain: The evasive and extraordinary par.

"Bloody brilliant," said Cal, aloud and more than audible in speaking to himself. He was beaming while longing for the cheering crowd of Augusta, the boisterous fans at St Andrews, all of whom were invisible and silent on this prairie course today, alas. However, he knew the multitudes of resident ghosts—from decades of digging around the local institution graveyards of close—had witnessed his brilliance. *That's good enough for me then, those throngs of great fans. Keep the serotonin flowin'.*

Fourth hole:
First you think, twice you blink;
you know you're going in the drink

The unseen *McElligot's Pool* of a water hazard ahead might as well have been the near-infinite Pacific Ocean staring at him, with whales and fish bigger than whales, and all the magical Suessian sea life. The magnetic brook—above ground, though, this brook—was a mere trickle, with nary a snail. This slightest of flows drained down through the tiniest of ravines—a one-foot-deep dip with a one-foot-wide crick in a three-feet-across gully. Even though it was not on the scale of the Amazon nor the Nile—more on the scale of a piss stream of pop dribbling out the bottom of the Skunk's filthy pants—Cal would hit it with a splash or a thud, every single time he managed to find the mini-coulee, in what seemed like was his destiny. Sometimes it was off the drive, sometimes from the wood—if the drive had been an initial shank, that is. Each time and at every attempt, he knew he was going to land there in the ooze of a stream in the spring, the leftover mud pit in the summer, or the dry bed of caked sediment in the fall. And so, Cal would smile after placing his tee, understanding the inevitable outcome on this ill-fated hole, at peace with his lot, therefore choosing the correct and simple path of rolling with it.

But then... Baffled and enraged to no end when he

drove the drink; or, pleased with the drive on the fairway or just into the rough, another smile before the wood; and then, the second shot would create the sad, hopeless, and infuriated non-Masters-winning golfer Cal.

One shot, two shot; the green you'll make... Not.

Cal could not even remember the last time he putted on that fourth green, as a recent and long-standing ritual was to avoid the curse of the creek, the drink of the damned, forlorn on four.

Unless he could land it on the green in one shot—so he told himself, his placebo with never any effect—it was easier at that stage of the hole to forget it altogether and move on. He watched as his drive almost made it past the hazard until it hooked hard and dipped fast at the last second, as if some magnetic or cosmic force was getting hold of the ball, sucking it down into some part of the minor fern green gully. Cal was not interested in whether it did hit the water, its muddy remnants, or even the thick weeds—he just forgot about it and carried on...

Fifth hole:
The Nanking cherry massacre

There was a second entrance onto the grounds of the institution, a road coming in from the other end of town which also passed by the tee box of the fifth hole. Cal walked across that road as he put the untold false splash on hole number four well and far behind him; the pseudo ripple of water or splatter of mud was in the past, even if his ball was only sitting in some dirt at the bottom of a jungle of quackgrass and burrs in the slight depression. Nevertheless, he set up his tee with a nice new dry ball, looking down the fairway with a heavy and serious stare of concentration. After a couple of perfect practice swings, he stepped forward to repeat the motion on the teed-up ball when a siren began blaring as a police car raced by, heading towards the main building—the hospital. Cal watched it speed off behind him until the local deputy's car was erased by the trail of dust it kicked up about halfway back to the institution. *I bet he's going to get pissy the Skunk and throw him in the boiler*, Cal thought, chuckling to himself. *I'll look for him and his pop bottle coming out of the smokestack, settling into some cirrus clouds later on.* Growing frustrated as his focus for the shot was rocked, he pivoted back around and drove it without much attention. He watched the ball sail a nice distance through to it landing an insignificant few inches into a tamer spot of the rough.

Adjacent to the green on the right side was another

hedgerow of caraganas and willows, planted in what may as well have been eons ago. Perhaps raised there for a wind break of some sort on the grounds, it was now serving as an aesthetic fairway border beyond its more utilitarian purpose, still managing to fulfill its function as cover there in the sometimes breezy valley. Behind the bushes, to the side and at a slight angle off the opposite road in, was a little orchard of cherries in two varieties.

The eponymous chokecherries made one choke, whether as a literal hack-inducing obstruction in the throat from the mini-pit within, or, more often, from the biting sour and bitter flavour that gave one's entire mouth a sensation of chewing little bits of chalk and then conjuring the strength to swallow the resulting paste past the palate. Sometimes an individual would be graced with a hybrid-cross version of a Franken-cherry, where the taste made one gag and the reflex would cause the small stone to be swallowed, which made one gag and heave that way, for a good and extra measure on the level of choking. These chokecherries were horrific, without anything other than the exception of a heavy-weighted ratio in favour of lots and tons of heaps and mounds of sugar as an added ingredient to whatever sort of innate and atrocious choke recipe the fine cook was endeavouring to make with it—jam or jelly, what have you. The other cherries, on the other hand... They, too, were not the sweet ones—they were not the luscious bright but dark red in pairs of succulent twos from the Okanagan or Oregon, rather these were the smaller, still somewhat sweet if a tarter version on an exceeding scale, with the slightest of marginal improvements to the chokes: Nanking cherries.

A few dozen of these sour dwarf Nanking cherry plants

were placed there along the row of much larger choke-cherry trees, a dozen or so of those, which came close to dwarfing the little Nanking bushes, but they were not of excessive size either. The Nankings had been planted here at a later date, but planted together they were, out on their own, a small autonomous garden away from the much larger and more structured rows of apple trees opposite the building on the other side of the grounds. On that back side of the hospital, there were also plums and maybe even some pears still growing around there with the rest of the more regal gardens and greenhouses at the institution, where many patients spent their days tending to the various botanical efforts as the seasons allowed.

The cherries seemed to be an odd and inefficient anomaly, but the tiny orchard in the rough was probably there for a specific purpose, like everything on the grounds. Antiquated or contemporary, it was for something—something that someone judged was important at the time, probably some medical authority or other of the given day, met with their own passion as a venerated gardener. It would have been reasoned to have its own purpose, providing a unique service or therapy—for special patients. *Glorious gardens and outstanding orchards—and a golf course. Treatment from God directly, therapy from the heavens—or so one must've believed.*

However, maintenance of the fairways and greens proved challenging for these folks—staff and patients alike. Gardening appeared easy enough, minus the general mess incurred from going outside and the requisite clean-up to follow. As far as orchards went, apples were more specialized, having their own ladders, boxes, and carts at the ready come harvest. A straightforward and marketable product, apples were more labour-intensive, where the management needed a system. Granting there was much less commercial demand for them, cherries did seem a simpler task, whether harvested the correct way or left to dry and die, falling into the dirt as rotting and decaying feral fruit of the desolate rough, where scavengers of various species and breeds, including wayward resident-patients joining in with the crows and magpies, could all have their filthy fill.

Being slightly hidden off this fifth fairway and behind the green, they remained visible to those who might be combing through the rough looking for a lost ball or even to those who were remotely sentient. And it was not a difficult task to be perceptive today, as one of the groundskeepers was present, this outside worker who also served as a de facto nurse, beyond his typical duties in the maintaining of the grounds—the mowing, planting, trimming, watering, and the managing thereof. With great enthusiasm, this groundskeeper was bitching out one of the cherry pickers, this hard-headed harvester, one of two assistant *Prunus* farmers out in the sweltering early morning heat of the day, whether this specific helper was there as a volunteer or not, and whether he was doing a good job or not.

Cal's initial reaction was that the picker was with certainty, in fact, *not* doing a good and proper job of the work at hand—not at all, not one iota. At a bit of a distance away, Cal was still able to make out that for some reason:

- the patient was not supposed to be out there picking by himself, as he seemed to be doing, notwithstanding the other patient present who was standing like a statue with his back to everyone as he stared into the abyss of the caraganas and beyond the rough (even though the patient appeared to be in control or at least in possession of some picking infrastructure with him, these buckets);

- the patient had picked more than half of the bushes clean, along with all but the highest unreachable branches in the tree, all by his lonesome self (efficient, to be sure, but well over the preset limits of his quota);

- the patient had been eating them while picking away, as if it was to also be his morning snack (who knows how much he overate, as he was covered, face to feet, in a Burgundian jammy mess of part-smushed-up fruit and part-acid-covered undigested berries he had vomited up on himself, along with what looked like might be a side dish of regurgitated grass and dandelions, or some such weedy greenery); and,

- the patient had mixed the crops by putting both products into the same communal buckets rather than in their individual designated pail for each specific commodity (a grievous error, this erroneous blend).

The tough and livid groundskeeper was swearing and screaming at this poor soul of a patient—a man who was beyond upset at his present state, looking even more worried and frightened at what might be the outcome of this forceful scolding, yet all the while managing to maintain his stupor zombie type of look, fed by whatever new drug, treatment, and punishment regime he might be on. *Is any of this yelling getting through to this crazed cherry picker?* Cal watched on in astonishment. *Is screaming at this uncertain facial façade of part-terror, part-lobotomy having any real effect on him? Or might the groundskeeper be doing just as well to go off and holler at the bark on the trunk of the lone blue spruce tree towering above and behind the cherries?*

What was a simple few seconds seemed like many minutes to Cal, standing there in view as he continued watching as a portion of the purple drool was dibbling off the harvester's chin. It was a constant but so slow stream, as if someone were pouring a fine molasses-like substance in a magenta hue, the trickle of slobber emanating from the patient's frothy mouth, where it began pooling at the base of his chin, with a drop every five or six seconds—the intervals seemed much longer to Cal, as if he were watching a Chinese water torture specialist dripping their violet drops. At the same time, the patient's claret forehead, cheeks, and ears all looked like the juices were crystallizing in place thereon, but the glistening amethyst crust was an illusion created by the sweat beading out from his skin, his secretions under the sappy and stained mushy mash of maroon.

At some point during the tirade, it dawned on Cal that he knew the groundskeeper—of course Cal knew him, but it took him a minute to focus on the howler, as he was transfixed by the trembling, if not quite numb purple puke monster, who was, strangely enough, not familiar to him, nor the now gradual rotation of the statue of a man posing behind the aggressive cherry picker. The keeper had been in to see Cal in the shop the odd time, although not on any regular sort of basis—maybe two or three times a year, at most. Whether a quick in-and-out trim of a client or just a brief pop-in visit on the way down Main Street,

Cal knew most of the folks in his town, many from the adjacent neighbouring towns, and still more folks in those towns and cities beyond. And folks knew Cal, him with his diverse and eclectic reputation, at home and afar.

Near the end of the dressing down, Walter realized someone was chipping out of the dirt. Cal hooked it right again, though he figured he might do that with the iron and so compensated for the lost angle to gain an extra precious and delightful twenty-five yards on this satisfactory shot. Walter then realized that *that* someone would have seen the drama meets tragicomedy unfold in front of him, out there in the little cherry orchard of the asylum—one as far removed from czarist provincial Russia as one could find, though one Chekhov would have surely appreciated; and Gogol for certain, even if this local madman did not keep a diary, assuming the purple puking fellow was indeed illiterate.

Walter finished the grilling on a softer note, calling him a nimrod, telling him he would be back with the wagon to help him collect all the buckets, but for now this patient must sit and wait for the groundskeeper to return. "Sit your ass down, right now, over there," said Walter, pointing towards the shady reprieve of the great white spruce and poplar rough in front of the thicker caraganas. And the imbecile was not to wander off anywhere. Further, Cal caught from the keeper that the patient was to, "Stop picking the goddamned cherries, dump them in piles, start sorting them into the proper separate pails they belong in, and for Christ's sake, don't eat any more."

Walter was a much older man, with the outward weathering exacerbating it even more: The wrinkles, liver spots, scars, burns, minimal greyish-whitish hair isolated above the back of his neck. Not to mention what one could not see, the non-explicit parts and those obscured, away from his face: The missing finger, missing toe (this could not be seen due to the heavy and pragmatic work boots, but Cal had heard the story, from Walter and from others, the infamous demonic stolen shears incident of many moons ago), a gnarl and systemic gash over the right thigh, limp in his gait, and so on. And this was of his visible stationary appearance—his mannerisms, physical and verbal, were all over the map. Walter was a chap from beyond the past. *Oh, the things he'd seen out here...* Cal's imagination was warming up and humming like a throttle.

Events and mishaps abound; on the old hospital ground

Walter had worked the grounds of the institution going back many decades, since he was a kid, right back to when it first opened its creepy doors. To Cal and other locals in the area, this was an ancient era, as if from a legend so far back that there was no single living person who could possibly ever remember day one when the hospital welcomed its inaugural guests of the so many, the so troubled. Viewing the building today was like looking at a long-abandoned European castle in ruins, from the 'much long ago before time,' in those now-historic bygone days. And yet Walter was there then, and he remained working in his role in the old and still-functional hospital, once beyond peak capacity in the hordes of thousands to the mere few hundreds of today. *Hell, he's still alive, which is incredible enough on its own.* However, today, it would not be difficult to mistake Walter for a primeval former soldier now residing in the geriatric veterans' wing. Walter could be, would be, and was still finding himself singled out as such by unwary golfers and new sanatorium staff—indeed, the hoary groundskeeper was often mistaken as a patient, Walter as mistakee, to the gross detriment of the mistakor.

The mistakes led to a classic incident every couple of years over the past decade or so, with other similar, if more minor, such errors occurring with more frequency. As he stood all the while watching the cherries of wrath unfold and conclude in front of him, Cal was racking his brain trying to recall some of these incidents, the blunders and bloopers, and their inexorable outcomes. He realized what he should have been doing all along was chronicling these occurrences over the years, doing so in a journalistic way with a detailed notebook or diary where they could be recounted with objectivity through time and well into the future with these also historical records. As he saw it, the problem was at this stage of the game so many other great stories had already vanished forever, becoming watered-down versions or were now simple legends, or they were fractions of legends and sub-legends from this place. The authoritative evidence of hilarity was fading with time and in haste, to be lost to history, which saddened Cal.

Cal did have a favourite story that he well remembered and with so much ease that it was as if it became clearer by the day. This tale was the one with the new French doctor at the time, but who had since left the patients of the prairies a few years earlier—the ostentatious wino doc: M. Grand Cru. Walter had gotten a lawn mower stuck near one of the central flower beds at the main entrance to the grounds, the tires spinning and caking in the mud, the underside knotted and interwoven with the undergrowth of some creeping shrubs. When he stepped back to try and free the blades from the tangled twines, Walter slipped while pushing and jerking the mowing machine, the cuffs of his pants catching and twisting by the wheelbase, seeming to tighten when he moved as if a python were wrapping around his legs to strangle him. Unable to free himself from the entwined jumble, Walter proceeded to melt down, furious at himself and the troubling situation he had brought on. The good monsieur, Doc Champagne, who had been out west in the interior for but less than a week, had only seen the culmination of the events leading to the present calamitous circumstance, having missed the genesis of this, the preface of the affair leading to the disaster. *And the French shrink surely hadn't yet had the pleasure of making groundskeeper Walter's acquaintance.* Cal knew it to be true. The doctor had not been out of his vehicle for three seconds before hearing the incoherent if solipsistic yelling, following his ears to see towards the muddy mess. And so, in an instant, he presumed this poor old geriatric patient of a man had gotten himself into this terrible and dirty, angry jam. *And whom, pray tell, would leave this most dangerous equipment out to facilitate such a happening?* Cal thought, assuming the French doctor was saying or thinking something along those lines at the time, in his baroque foreign accent. *Quelle horreur!*

As the French doctor lumbered towards the scene, without the groundskeeper even looking in the direction of the parking lot, Walter realized his one option to free himself was to somewhat tear and shred, then take down his trousers fully, peeling them off in proximity to his ankles. His mucky slacks removed—*Sacré bleu!*—Doc Champagne approached with some empathy, offering to help unfortunate old Walter back to his room inside the building where the nurses would settle him down, giving him a nice warm bath before a hearty dinner. *And no doubt some delicious torture for dessert, with a psychotropic pill of a non-chokecherry on top.* Cal was always thinking about what new drugs were being tried, learning about what new treatments were being administered, what tortures and punishments were being doled out to the various whackos—whether legitimate violent criminals or innocent guinea pig madmen—well inside the walls of the main building of the institution.

Walter's temper was already at peak boiling point when the new foreign doctor approached, so he could not do anything other than laugh in hysterics until... The thick, confusing accent tugged at his arm to lure him in. Walter pulled away from the physician, trying to move back towards the mower, when the doc grabbed the same arm of Walter again but with greater force, and, au contraire... The groundskeeper dropped his poor shoulder as a feint and used his good shoulder to throw a real punch to deliver a strange and unorthodox shot—as if some Bruce Lee-like slow-motion jab, married with a deceiving cross, morphing into this flying uppercut from the side, resulting in a most effective one-punch Superman-like KO.

One flash-like hook was all it took; one good sound pop, into the slop.

When this story was told—with or without Walter around, but often with, whenever he was back in the shop, as Cal quite enjoyed recounting it and liked hearing at least part of the first-hand narrative directly from Walter—the groundskeeper was always uncomfortable at the embarrassing front end of the tale, what with the muddy, torn trousers of his own unfortunate doing. However, Walter was most pleased with the conclusion (his conclusion!) of the affair, so he would often throw in his supposed final parting words he gave the French doctor, thus closing off the tale himself, with a rare and splendid smile: "How'd yeh like that there mud, froggy?" Sometimes that was it, while sometimes he threw in a 'Pthu!' for good measure—a full-on true spat if told outside, while a mere dramatic charade of the spitting finale of the event if the account was told inside or around any wholesome and respectable company, including in the barbershop, as rare as that might be.

As messy as that situation was, the pretentious disposition of one versus the uncouth demeanour of the other, Walter did apologize to the refined French doc some weeks later, inviting him out to one of his several groundskeeper shacks scattered here and there, storing this and that, within the greater perimeter and all about the hospital grounds. Walter wanted to make proper amends and welcome Doc Champagne here to town, and to the vast jewel of the Great Plains of North America. Walter set out a homemade foie gras, which he had prepared from a Canada goose of recent capture out by the slough between the sixth hole and one of the graveyards. Taking a short break from mowing the fairway grass and pruning some hedges, Walter ran up from behind and caught the large bird by the throat, almost ringing its long neck before remembering what he was going to be preparing. As this was where they sat down to enjoy the artisan, even if novice-made delicacy, the French doc had a look of shock while Walter apologized in that he did not have any corn to force-feed the goose—some plain local Marquis wheat was all he had for the gavage. Further, as he was not sure how long he should keep pouring grain down the funnel and into its throat, he gave it a couple of weeks before a final ringing of the neck and preparing the dish, which he hoped was savoury enough despite being nowhere near Paris or wherever in France. Doc Champagne obliged, trying not to cringe as he whiffed and tasted the crudely made pâté. His eyes lit up, and Walter's flashed in turn, although growing concerned he may have been a miserable failure in his virgin culinary endeavour. The French doc smiled and raved, asking for a second piece. Walter was thrilled—it was a success! It was not until Walter offered him a glass of his homemade plonk of a rhubarb, crab apple, and chokecherry so-called 'wine' that the French doc got sick.

With a genuine love for that story, in Cal's mind it was nothing less than a true classic. Walter was, in general, quite reserved and quiet. He even went out of his way trying his best to maintain it, a humble, introverted style. But he did not need to hold back there, not at Cal's shop in town. The barbershop: The place where they could talk, no matter the man or men, gentlemen or hooligans, elites or underclass, any shade of pigment. Cal reflected on his strong and diverse customer base while clarifying it in his mind. *However, no ladies, apologies, please and thank you. The shop wouldn't be the shop with the fairer sex present. And I wouldn't know how to provide those fancy curling and perming types of services even if they did let me try.* But he knew how to give Walter a trim, and Walter always opened up to the barber's own relentless prodding and to the unrefined, if appropriate, venue itself. On the surface and in polite company, the barrage of badgering was beyond annoying to many—on the street and in civil circles, men would wax loathing about Cal and his mannerisms—the crude, crass demeanour of such an oaf, that barber. But aside from the trim, style, and shave, they went there for the break, to get away—for the news, rumours, shit-talk, and stories (fiction and non-), including and especially those of debauchery.

They went there to be men, away from the gals, men as they are and were, now and always: Cavemen. Farmers, workers, merchants, doctors, soldiers, miners, bankers, bakers, peasants. Everyone opened up in there; whether they wanted to be there to hear the entertaining BS or not, they had to BS themselves as well, for the unwritten code said they must. The code of the sanctuary, the camaraderie of the barbershop.

Sunny day sanatorium

Whenever Walter was in—not of a regular frequency, perhaps for good reason—no matter who was in the shop, questions always came right to him as soon as they sat down, stood waiting, or took to the big chair for the business of the trim. The authority and the beeline for the townsfolk on the most important of questions. The grounds, these grounds right here. The institution. The asylum. The madhouse. The loony bin. The nuthouse. The sanatorium. The hospital. What was the latest, the latest and greatest, down the hill at our local yet world-class institution? What was the word, the news views reviews, around our finest of fine in town, our fair mental hospital?

The routine was to start out with basic and sincere informational questions:

- "Did you hear about that new doctor who came to town from overseas?"

- "What do you think about that new treatment, that therapy with the electricity—you know, the shocking one?"

- "I don't know if you've heard about this one yet,

but they get right in their heads—and apparently it helps many of them out real good—they poke at part of their brains, using a device sort of like an icepick?"

- "Have you seen that smoking hot new nurse, the one with the massive rack?"

Cal and others believed that some of these were indeed great questions, some of them leading to remarkable tales. However, before too long the questions tended to—they needed to—morph into the priority of what everyone wanted to hear about: Crazy patient antics. That is, the sad, the horrible, the hilarious: The antics of the crazy patients.

Crazy patient antics stories themselves then morphed into crazy doctor and nurse antics stories, most often as they related to the patients. Those mutated further into various sub-tales—almost always false—which were fictions as side-stories of the main tales, themselves fictions, or at least gross distortions of events that unfolded on some level, all making their way out to the barbershop a few miles away back up the hill in town. Walter was the bridge, the one sole living memory of it all, the primary source—maintaining some capacity, whatever he could still hold on to up top. Having been at the institution for the duration, the groundskeeper tended to the grand grounds on the outside from day one to the present, while also helping out as needed on the inside, assisting the plumbers, mechanics, painters, electricians, carpenters, engineers, nurses, orderlies, druggists, doctors of numerous kinds, and patients. Patients. Patients who still wandered around, shuffling about without aim on the grounds, including and especially on the golf course. And walking off the grounds afield, attempting to break through the artificial boundary of the property to roam even further yonder, into nature or town.

Fairway, green, water, sand; hazard, rough, soda stand.

Patients, right or wrong. Cal entered into a moment of a sort of lightning round of meandering reflection on some of the stories of the many others he was aware of who resided, past and present, within the massive brick and sandstone structure. *Those with mental illness, diagnosed in general terms; those with mental illness, micro-diagnosed and without consistency. Those with mental illness, diagnosed with a new condition, the discovery coined something clever, changing with the times and the theories, the fads. The quite different, but not having a recognized known mental illness; those with mental illness, but not different, seeming to be just normal and fine to most. Atheists, cultists, religious fanatics—of the wrong religions and the right ones. Enthusiastic agnostics. Veterans. Veterans from different wars—significant populations from the First and Second World Wars, fewer from the Korean. Perhaps a lone remnant or two still surviving in their final days as a last vestige from the Boer and maybe even the Spanish-American— not likely at this late stage for that ancient cohort, even if not impossible. Indian, Civil, 1812, Revolutionary, Armada... Peloponnesian? No. But yes: Veterans, young and old, physical disabilities and walking tall. Local veterans, heroes. Veterans of the nation. Veterans of the axis, accidentally. Non-veterans, young and old. Car crashes. Farm accidents. Psycho-geriatrics. Psychopaths. Petty criminals. The deaf, dumb, and blind—born and acquired. The criminally insane. Alcoholics. Addicts. Homosexuals. Heterosexual deviants—female adulterers. Unassimilated immigrants; assimilated immigrants who could not crack the English. Unassimilated locals; assimilated locals— much too intimately assimilated. Sundry deviants. Minor imbeciles. Innocent victims. Total off-their-rocker bananas, with a valid and official certificate of authenticity embossed with a gold seal. Neurotics. A bit of column A, a bit of column B; sometimes right through to some of column Z: multiple personality disorders. Sadists. Masochists. Sadomasochists. Madmen. General criminals—inmates. Patients. If they were here before or here now, they're all 'patients,' so-called. Poor, unfortunate souls, these patients.*

The number of patients at the hospital increased around wars, peaks and valleys, hitting full capacity near the end of the second war—more than exceeding any civil occupancy limits, if they were honest. The population bleed had become a slower trickle as of late, as the numbers had already been decreasing for some time, with a more rapid shrinkage in the recent past—the bright for ever so long 'no' light on the 'vacancy' sign was at long last fading to dark, a minor flicker, if not quite burnt right out. There were various and diverse reasons as to why the decrease in enrollment, each explanation holding different degrees of actual validity. One was natural attrition. Another was policies—policies that were changed because of changes in treatments and public perception of the field and sector, in the broadest sense. This also meant changes in the public perception of such facilities, now under the microscope, stemming from both the lies and the truth as told in the newspapers, books, and on the big screen. And those perceptions and changes included right here in this town, at this time, like anything else, there were strong and differing opinions on the problems (and non-problems) this would create. What would it mean for the local economy? Vast unemployment or new industries springing up from the creative destruction? What would it mean for criminal activity? Crime rates high and low, here and there. Petty crime sprees and rampant violence with fresh horrific murders or safe streets and business as usual? *And*

Jesus, who would pick all that fruit? Those delectable chokecherries aren't going to puke themselves up.

Bam! Back to the jam.

"What a hell of a mess you've got on your hands there, Walter," said Cal, grinning as he was still bemused concerning the disastrous situation with the cherry harvest. Cal did not want to wait any longer to speak with Walter and acknowledge his own presence playing on this hole, even though he knew that Walter now knew that he was right there. "You got these guys doing some gardening and picking fruit in there, or is this one baking a fucking pie in those thickets?"

"Morning there, Cal," said Walter, speaking at an unhurried, characteristic pace and in a bewildering tone of somewhere in the happy medium between embarrassment and not caring one smidgen about the great cherry quandary. "Sorry to disturb your game here. Honestly..."

In a nonchalant break, as he dabbed his dripping brow with his dusty forearm, Walter turned his head to spit some thick and tarry chewing tobacco at a safe enough distance into the dirt, landing his shot in the dust as if it were soot.

"After years and so many bloody years here, you think you've seen it all," said Walter, pausing as if in deep reminiscence on his time working at the mental institution. "Then one more nut does something you ain't never seen before. But it doesn't really matter, nothing surprises you out here. It just can't anymore, not after a guy's been doing this so damn long."

"Never truer words," said Cal, nodding with a positive response while slowing down the pace of his own speech to match that of the old groundskeeper's. "He's pretty funny in there though, you have to admit it. That said, I'm only half done with my round, and that's maybe not even the best one I've seen this morning already. Well, a tie anyways, photo finish. Soda pop snowman up on two—that stinky Fred chap. Freddie the fruitcake. Some call him the Skunk. Him versus your cherry zombie here. I feel like I could be waving the checkered flag right down on the line at the Kentucky Derby, but we might need to see the replays before we have our winner. Still, you got to tell the fellas this one next time you're in the shop. Patty cake in the mulberry bush. Jeez Louise."

"Yep. You know," said Walter, holding his hat in his left hand while running his right hand from his forehead, through his shaggy and greasy comb-over remnants of hair, to the back of his neck, "I'm overdue for a good trim anyways. And Greg, my boy, said he was heading your way today, in fact, later this morning. Needs to be cleaned up. His first shift working with his old man later on today. Or relieving me of my shift, today at least. But I'll have to train him to do it all right in the days and weeks ahead, for when he takes over here..."

"Oh yeah, I heard he was going to be back working with you again," said Cal, grinning with a laudatory nod, if not quite as phony as the earlier congratulations given to Fred. "Good for him. And good for you. But don't you work him too hard now, Walter. Starting right in the busy season, before winter hits. I guess leaving the elevator at a good time, too. Lots of farmers were in last week—some only starting harvest in the north and some already done around here. Incredible. Saying crops look not too bad, but if this parching heat, if she keeps blazing away like this here today and the past few weeks, some'll be dried right out and ruined, like in the worst days of the Dust Bowl."

Cal tried to keep it positive while segueing the conversation with a gentle if implicit acknowledgement of Walter's son's calamitous departure from the grain elevator, even though he well knew the whole situation around the exit was outright unpleasant, downright ugly.

"Those cocksucker grain hicks. My boy knows cleaning and grading better than any of them. And what they did with those hulls... Sickened me. I'd have killed them myself for that act alone," said Walter, trying to complete one train of thought while bridging right back to the cliché and safe haven topic of the weather. "But true, so true. Been more than two weeks now, over a hundred every day. Might be a whole month like that... Lord help us. And no rain. I think you might be right: Driest it's been since the Depression days, far as I can tell. Might even be drier, hotter—I was here way back then, too. Not even cooling down at night anymore. But that's why we got to get all these berries and fruits off before she rots. Hopeless moron—can't even pick berries right, simple as it seems. Might as well have done that brain procedure and stuck a couple fistfuls of blooming cherries in there when they were done. Then zap him up real good, juice him. Wouldn't be any dumber today if he had the purple jelly in his skull instead, that braindead head. Could've even helped him out. You never know. Jesus."

"You set 'em straight here, Walter," said Cal, preparing to take his leave. "And when they're done washing off simple Simon the cherry pie man in there, tell them to hose down the Skunk too, that old Fred character. The scruffy one with the winter garb on—smells like a filthy polecat. But hey, Walter, I got to keep on here if I'm going to go open the shop today, especially with Greg coming in and all—will have to give him a nice cut to start the new job out here right and whatnot. And I'll see you come by soon too, then, I hope?"

"True, I won't keep you, Cal. Carry on, then. Head into town before she gets too hot out. I got to get in myself—I think I'm getting too old for this here job in the brutal heat. Might have to train Greg up extra quick so he can have it. Put me in a hammock with a glass of lemonade, out in the pasture to boot, and I'll call her a fine day, finally done."

As they were about to part ways, the statue of a man pivoting at a snail's pace collapsed, fainting to the ground under the ironic shade of the chokecherry tree where he stood, hitting the dirt and kicking up a small circular dust cloud that formed over him like a halo as he passed out.

"You got another man down, Walter," said Cal, not having any particular concern with anything other than wanting to get this hole done and pick up the overall pace of his round. "Your soldier at attention couldn't take the heat."

"Isn't that the bloody truth of it," said Walter, even less concerned with anything other than the general disruption of his falling behind on the daily chores, which included this cherry harvest. "Soldier couldn't take the heat over there, couldn't take it after they nailed him, and still can't take the prairie heat back home. What the fuck's wrong with you, Corporal?" said Walter, yelling the final sentence as a question to the non-listening passed-out zombie statue man, kicking some additional dirt and dust towards him even as it landed a fair bit short of the mark.

"What's that you're saying, Walter?" said Cal, unfamiliar with the patient who Walter did seem to know. "What's this guy's story then? He's too young to be one of those old vets."

"Well, I guess he's a vet now, young one, but he was a soldier till a few weeks ago," said Walter, as he was looking between the two, realizing Cal was unaware of the identity of the woeful patient. "Calvin, this is Dwight. You know Dwight. Dwight, meet Calvin."

"Holy shit!" said Cal, stunned to learn he was staring at Dwight, the disgraced soldier whose name had graced countless above-the-fold headlines in newspapers over the past number of months around the town, county, country, and beyond. "I would've never guessed he'd be in here so soon after everything, with the recovery and courts and whatnot. I thought it'd take months. Unreal."

As Cal and Walter looked down to the fallen soldier as a collapsed statue, there was a proximate distraction with the purple puking chap, still sitting cross-legged next to Dwight, who began a second wave of vomiting up his cherries yet again, all over himself as if not even considering trying to somehow aim it away from his person.

"Oh, my Lord, these frigging imbeciles," said Walter, shaking his head, grinding his teeth, becoming enraged. "They gave me these two just last week. They're both beyond any sort of recovery, from before and after—they're minds are all gone, these beauties. I'm going to have to get them out of here, or I'm going to faint myself in the heat haze pretty soon. Would you mind giving me a quick free hand here, Cal?"

Cal followed Walter's lead and instructions, helping to get him and his workers (or 'dingbats,' as Walter kept calling them) out of the searing heat, and then get himself moving along to finish the round before the sunstroke or exhaustion hit Cal, which would lay him up and out of the trimming business for the rest of the day, an eventuality he longed to avoid. Walter took off Dwight's shirt, cutting it with his shears, ripping it in half, handing one piece to Cal, explaining how to use it to hoist the purple puke man into the wheelbarrow without getting any of the vomit on himself. After that moderate success, they moved down to the shirtless Dwight, seeing the exposed military insignia of his unit tattooed on his shoulder and a sword running a diagonal pattern across his chest. As Cal bent down to lift Dwight's heels, he was thinking about the grave and gruesome incident in the military he was involved with that Dwight instigated. The resulting arrest followed another specific incident precipitated by Dwight, the soldier, the expedited court case, and with that, he was now a resident of the institution forever more. As they dumped Dwight into the wheelbarrow on top of the cherry fiend, Cal was floored that this had occurred so recently and yet here Dwight was, already working under the not-so-gentle tutelage of old Walter, picking fruit in the rough of the golf course. *Amazing. Next spring they'll all be getting stuck together in the mud with a mower somewhere out here. Hopefully Doc Champagne returns right around that time.*

"Thanks, Cal," said Walter, as he grabbed the handles of the would-be ambulance of a wheelbarrow, about to set off, taking a moment to gather his breath and conjure up some strength to make the brief journey back to the main asylum building. "Appreciate the help with these clowns here. Don't stay out on the course too long now—this heat is way too much for anyone. And we'll see you in town real soon then."

"Never too early to call 'er a day, Walter," said Cal, waving him off as he started to gather up his golf bag, taking his first steps back down the fairway. "I might see if I can even get this round down before I start to look like your guys. Thanks, Walter—you take care now."

Sixth hole:
The great wall of caraganas

Failing to find the lost ball driven into the tall and thick hedge of prickles, Cal dropped a new one in a most favourable position on an irregular soft patch of grass, where he wooded it into the woods, dropped another one and duffed it into the dirt, did so yet again, then chipped out of the rough but shanked it over the road he drove in on.

Cal gave up after six on six, carrying on to hole number lucky seven...

Seventh hole:
Bogey boogie

Cal recovered his composure and bogeyed. There was nothing special about this one-over, with all slightly below-average shots for many, albeit well above-average for him. Thus, he could not help but be pleased with his effort. He felt plain old good, about to dance a little jig in exchange for his tap-in putt—he landed each shot well enough, believing par might even be achievable once he had hit the green—when he felt the stinger go in. There was a quick tickle followed by an acute pinch in the back of his neck. Cal slapped the mammoth mosquito, triggering an explosion of blood and what looked to him like some guts. Staring at the crimson liquid and assorted insect parts on his palm, he grew angry and flustered but wondered... It was his hubris, Cal assumed, which must have been what hit him fast like lightning, this resulting misfortune coming in the form of a mosquito bite. And so, Cal wiped the gory *Culex* shrapnel off his hand and onto his darker-than-his-pants back of his shirt, suppressed all thoughts of pride and excessive arrogance over the lucky below-average hole, and walked head-down, onward, like a peasant on a pilgrimage, over the silty pathway to the holy hole named eight, with a clear mind and fresh focus in tow.

Eighth hole:
No crazy eight

This was an important hole for some much-needed and deep self-reflection, repentance, fasting, prayer, peace—a reincarnated, without sin hole of blissful nirvana. A humble and modest pure double-bogey of salvific innocence was the resulting redemption. *Hallelujah and amen to that.* Cal was determined to enhance his levels of sincerity, hoping to regenerate some good vibes.

Ninth hole:
Nuthouse nein

The Sun had been rising ever higher over the past couple of hours on the course, now beaming its searing rays down in an uncomfortable heat via a laser-like direct path towards Cal. He longed to find even a brief reprieve of some shade, but on his last hole he also wanted to focus on completing the successful enough round and head back to town. As the intense heat of the yellow dwarf star was following the golfer like an inexhaustible parasite, all Cal could feel was a systemic burning through his clothes and on his skin, with the exception of the damp small of his back, where the expanding and regenerating wet diamond of sweat caused the shirt to stick in place, from as high as his neck to as low as his waist and armpit to armpit across, looking like a wet aquamarine plaid cloth kite.

Cal approached his ball for the final drive of the day, letting it go again but without a practice swing or giving much thought about the shot. His awakening on the eighth hole was humbling, bringing less pride and fewer expectations, as they were unimportant to attaining real and true happiness. However, he was also growing more confident by the hole, gaining precious yards and greater accuracy with each fresh swing of the new Wilson driver. And it appeared to be affecting his overall game as he watched the shots improve, becoming straighter minus the odd and natural errant anomaly, which he could work out well enough through the fall season. *Hell, maybe I should even hit a sand state for a few rounds this winter.* Cal was beaming to himself again, as if he had not just had his experience on eight, learning none of the key lessons on tempering his pride from only moments ago. *Maybe play a round with the greats, if Arnold Palmer or Jack Nicklaus are in the neighbourhood.* On some swings—like this last drive of the day and week, he knew it—he felt almost as if he was cheating. Cal felt great. But the sweating and burning from the scorching sunshine—and now the mild if increasing dizzying effects with a bit of heat stroke or exhaustion, or some such— was taking a toll on the requisite concentration. Cal knew he needed to find a final wind and regroup on this last effort to complete the weekly round—at the 'nutty nine,' he loved to say, claiming he coined it, trademarking the tag—and heading off to his other routine of work, hoping to find some semblance of greater sanity back in town.

After this last drive, Cal's tee was still sitting upright. It was unmoved in the grass, with the also remaining clump of earth beneath the tee—that grass and rootstock in the loose, chunky dirt had not moved one bit. Another first, this significant milestone. Reaching down to collect the tee in what was still mint condition, Cal was using a different motion than was his regular custom of placing the tee in the grass, as if showcasing his agility and flexibility, acting to himself as though this new movement was also a standard procedure. Realizing he needed to bend his knees a bit further down to compensate for his inability to fully stretch his back lower and forward to obtain the tee, he stumbled and nearly tumbled over in the process. Standing back up and straightening and stretching out as though his dexterity was indeed satisfactory, Cal grabbed his bag and was about to journey on down this fairway—a hole he now had a most reasonable chance of birdieing, an infrequent and magical occasion—when another screeching police car with accompanying screaming siren passed by, back towards the main road in, somewhere near the parking lot. Cal stood listening, trying to look beyond the course, but the foliage and flora walls rendered everything, with the exception of auditory senses, useless at this key moment of emergency and possible crisis. Frustrated with the blindness, thinking this incident had the potential to be another good story in the Book of Cal, he turned around while following the siren with his ears, still unable to view the cruiser—*Or cruisers, with an 's'*—surveying it with care as though he could glimpse right through the bushes, using acoustics and some fantastical x-ray vision to see it or them, if not at least visualizing the ruckus.

After ten or so seconds of letting the commotion pass his sentient senses, Cal carried on along the well-groomed green carpet, one of two fairways in such miraculous shape—a flawless look like some baseball outfield of a perfect rye and bluegrass blend, or whatever it was they were using here with such unexpected success. And this fairway was without rodent holes every few feet, as dozens of the pock marks could be found in an immediate proximity to golfers on the other holes on the course. *Maybe they've tasked some of those patients with catching gophers.* Cal imagined how such a hunt might play out. *No, if they can't even pick cherries, they sure's shit ain't getting gophers. They'd end up snaring, drowning, or poisoning themselves before killing any of the underground vermin. A suicide mission.*

Further ahead, somewhere near to where his shot must have landed, a new hubbub emerged: There was a feverish rustling in the lilacs, a couple of feet off the rough, which itself was a couple of feet off the fairway. The purple and white flowers of early summer had long vanished, but the leaves were an almost solid single shade of basil—the clean green hue was unclipped yet maintained a perfect and natural uniform height, with slight vertical deviations of out-of-place short and scraggly branches rising from the centre of the series.

Cal decided it prudent to slow his pace as he looked through the plants again, this time with no sirens to be heard and nothing else to distract him from this new immediate kerfuffle before him. The rustling became more violent, a more energetic fight within the lilac grove. Cal's mind was wandering. *Too much activity to be a small bird or a rodent. Perhaps it's a deer. Or some other animal, raccoons or something. Could be eating the lilacs. Porcupines eating the willow bark. Wait. Could be two animals. Fighting. Or mating. Deer sex, strange, with the antlers and all. Or, no. A patient. No! A madman fucking some other animal. A beast. Jesus. Or a person. Nutter relations? Disgusting. Or maybe jacking himself off, hidden out of sight, some quiet time away from the butterfly police. Gross. Oh, Christ.* There was no noise aside from the bushes shaking and rustling about with increasing vigour. *No loon-toon screaming—ugh, oh boy. Please and no thank you.* Having worked up his imagination, firing it up after having been in the heat for over two hours—which, as incidental as it was, still gave him a perverse charging up—Cal deemed the situation was now even more disturbing. He knew it, and so he was growing a bit concerned with respect to this unknown hullabaloo.

At about where his ball should have been, settling after the bounce and roll, Cal slowed to an inching pace on the edge of the rough, pulling the six-iron out of his bag with caution, choking up like the Bambino ready to hit one off Manhattan and all the way right back up the Charles River to extend the curse. Cal was about to poke the leaves to see who was poking whom, but there was a sudden squawk. A unique, specific shriek—a tangible terror. He stepped back, still flexing and choking up on the grip, but giving himself more room, as space and distance were his good friends here in this uncertain situation. It was clear it was a man, almost with certainty a bedlamite, tussling about inside the lilac fringe. *Was a deer in there, too?*

While thinking about venturing closer or right into the greenery to flush him out, from a part-backward and part-lateral position came a man flying out of the forest with ne'er a worry concerning scratching the hell out of his face, arms, and rest of his body on the blast through the branches. *The freak's going to put his own eye out.* The individual also had no concern with respect to taking off his shirt, raving around in one awkward motion out of the lilacs, stumbling, screaming, tripping, getting back up, continuing the frenzied dance now out on the tree-free and open fairway.

This person was an older man, or at least his appearance seemed to be that of an older man. However, on the institution grounds, that image could mean he was anywhere between forty and one hundred years old, or somewhere in the range of middle age crisis to centenarian. Thinking he understood somewhat more of what he was dealing with, Cal lessened the choking up on his grip and proceeded to lean on his club as if it were a cane, musing on helping this gent out. But in the chaos, Cal remained uncertain about who this person was, and he had yet to understand what this guy's precise problem was. As Cal watched the schizophrenic foxtrot, his mind wandered again. *Was this the natural condition of the yelping forest man, or an attempted creation of a new man through some recent treatment he'd received, perhaps a new acidic potion, an exotic snake-oil elixir of the day, brought in by some new sham of a French doctor? Or a German one! Germans treating madmen on this side of the pond— God, help us. Please save us from the irony, dear Lord, and save us from those Bavarians.*

The old man waved his shirt around with a serious intensity, while still twirling, leaping, bellowing.

"Wespe! Wespe! Nein! Nein!"

With those first two basic if confusing words, hollered two times a piece for good measure, it finally dawned on Cal just who this was, an obvious identification. It was John. As the all-pervading stench was to Fred, impassioned German was to John. Or Johann, as he was called before, his proper name, the first time. Cal had not seen him thus far this summer, wondering earlier if John was still around, if he was shipped back, or maybe dropped dead at long last. In recent weeks, Cal wondered, *Maybe he's tied down spread eagle inside the secret dungeon rooms down in the basement, being used as a guinea pig for testing some new treatments, or they're working on new methods of torture, modifying them with John so they'll know if they really work or not. Or maybe he's in the same position in a similar chamber, but in a Nuremberg cell, back in the homeland. Or maybe he's hiding out in the Peruvian mountains, taking part in the great Machu Picchu getaway, sleeping with alpacas in the elevated coca grove now—better there than with the deer here in the prairie lilacs. Or maybe he's relaxing in paradise, living life to the utmost and fullest on the beaches around Rio, the old man getting some year-round sunshine with those beautiful tanned titanic butts, riding out his now final years, or more like days.*

"Ich bin allergisch! Wespe! Insektenstich! Nein!"

Cal was not sure if he should laugh or roll his eyes at this event. It was hilarious, whatever John was doing and saying, without question. But he could not help continuing to think about it... *Germans. German farmers. German madmen. Goddamn Germans here, on this free, peaceful side of the pond.* Ancestrally, Cal himself was a proud mutt of a predominant English extraction and Scottish breed, with a healthy dash of Acadian and Blackfoot thrown into his personal mixing bowl. Who he was, here in his own lifetime in this era and in this town, meant Cal was a regular Joe with few and insignificant hardships, even with some of those otherwise racist assholes still about. However, Cal did believe with conviction that he understood both sides of the oppression coin—oppressor and oppressee, the oppressed. Because of his vast knowledge and personal lineage, Cal could not take any position other than that of his belief in freedom and equality for all individuals. *But there's just something about those dang dangerous Germans.* As harmless and comical as it appeared to others—notwithstanding the death and destruction from both world wars still fresh and simmering away in the minds of many—nothing but a bit of a humorous ruse in his routine as the great local comedian-barber, Cal's thoughts as jokes often gravitated to his punchline of: *I can't fucking stand them war-starters, not one little bit.*

"What's the problem, comrade? What are you doing with your shirt now, flinging it all about? And what the hell are you doing whirling around in them bushes there?" said Cal, wanting to appear somewhat sympathetic to the patient's situation, waving and pointing at the foliage in the rough. Positioning his club back down to the grass as though using it as a cane again to prop himself up, he lowered his voice, moving into a position of standing tall and leaning forward to ensure the disoriented old Kaiser knew who was boss. *John might have been able to breach the Maginot Line of the golf course lilacs, but he's going to get himself busted up real bad if he tries some sneaky panzer manoeuvre on me on this fine fairway of the ninth hole.*

At the same time, Cal wanted to try and settle him down, as John was sweating and turning red, huffing and puffing. John bent over, placing his hands on his knees, trying to regain his breath, remaining as focused as need be on his lungs and evening out the necessary airflow therein, yet still aware of the lurking and imminent threat that seemed to have dissipated, at least somewhat.

"Wespe!"

About to ask what 'wespe' was as Cal approached him with caution, the last wasp buzzed overhead, jittering John again before circling back off into the lilac jungle— no doubt to its fragrant nest of a home, where who knows what John might have done to it during his little visit, if by accident or otherwise.

"Wasps? Ooohhh," said Cal, understanding the peril John might have been in while believing he was most likely antagonizing the stinging insects somehow, as moronic as that would have been. "I see, you're scared of wasps? Fair enough then. You get stung in there, or just a bit startled?"

Cal was trying to offer him some sympathy while knowing full well that John knew some English, having some decent level of grasp on the language. Although no one knew for certain how much English old Johann could indeed understand.

"Allergic," said John, still wheezing and panting. "Bees."

"Well, those aren't bees in there. They're wasps. Vicious wespes? Yah?" said Cal, flashing John a patronizing smile.

"Insektenstich. Verletzt. Allergisch," said John, taking his time to enunciate the German words aloud, as if that would help Cal to better understand the dialect and his sorry situation. "Hurt. Doctor." John was pointing to his forearm, rubbing the small red mark to highlight it, if not exacerbate the extent of the problem. The mark of the injury was most red at the epicentre, which was to be expected. This little bump was fading out to a taffy hue, then becoming normal enough looking skin outwards from the limited radius around the focal point of the sting of the wasp. It looked like a dime the colour of a pale rose, the size of the whole thing no larger than a nickel.

"Yes, you better get yourself back inside there quick to go see the doctor now. Are you really allergic? You feeling sick?"

John attempted to put his shirt back on, fumbling as he tried to pull it over his head the correct way, then blundering about further as he reached down into his baggy pants, a hand in each pocket, searching for something, perhaps a remedy he carried with him for such similar scenarios, having seen analogous past precedents no doubt, bites and stings and reactions thereof.

"What were you doing in there anyways, poking at a nest?" said Cal, asking in disbelief while taking a step back, uncertain of what mystery item might emerge from John's pockets. "If you're doing something that stupid, you damn straight deserve those stings coming at you, allergic or not."

"Golf ball! Golf ball?" said John, his focus shifting from the imminent threat at hand to something else altogether. "You. You buy? Buy ball?"

Cal stared at the four golf balls John pulled out from the front pockets of his pants as if by magic—and having done so without any lingering concern for the visible sting wound in his arm (painful, but superficial), nor for the venom reacting within, the poisonous substance coursing through him (painful, and acute), all as if the chaos that just occurred had not happened at all. John's attention shifted in a dramatic fashion as the heavy breathing and swelling both worsened in a marked way. The enlargement of the bump itself could be seen growing on top of his metastasizing arm and up to his neck; the upper part of one whole side was expanding out in all directions like a pufferfish in slow motion, while the area of the sting was changing colour, encompassing all the shades of pinks, reds, violets, indigos, and blues the grand spectrum had to offer, exhibiting it on his once light peach skin, only moments ago.

None of the balls were new; they were of average brands, mediocre quality, one was an eccentric bright orange colour like a fluorescent tangerine, and each of them was scuffed up to one degree or another from the grass, dirt, and contact marks from golf clubs. One ball had a slight chunk missing, as part of the golf company logo on the ball was displaced with an extra, deeper divot.

"All balls. *Eins* dollar. One," said John, clarifying this figure by dropping two of the balls and holding up his one free index finger, placing it right between his nose and the sniffer of Cal. As he finished illuminating on the price for Cal, he dropped a third ball, took the last remaining one in his hand and proceeded to spit on it, going about polishing it with his shirt, continuing this practice in great haste until all four balls—as part of this deal, for one dollar—were as shiny and new looking as John could possibly make them.

"One dollar. Jesus, John. You think I'm a millionaire?

And these balls are a total disaster. They're a giant mess—you can see they are. I bet they wouldn't even soar right. Christ, they'd probably crack or break when I hit them with my brand-new driver here," said Cal, giving a gentle tap on the heads of the clubs in his golf bag with the protective six-iron still in hand, wondering if he should barter with John in any event, whether for the actual balls or perhaps for some extra ribbing to conclude the round on this final hole of the day and week.

"*Sechs*. Six balls, *eins*. One dollar," said John, pulling another two balls from what seemed at first glance to be out of nowhere, like an illusionist might, but it was evident they were obtained from his back pockets this time. One was more or less the same as the others, and the second one was a bizarre shade of an almost incandescent mint green hue, trying to show them all off while he was also attempting to retrieve the two balls on the ground he had dropped when the last two appeared out of some initial enigma.

"Where are you getting all these shitty balls from, and why are some of them not white, like normal? Orange and green?" said Cal, shaking his head while now realizing he was going to haggle with John in any event, a process he was already well into. "These aren't proper at all, not even close. It's like you're trying to make a damn fool of me or something. Is that what you're doing, John?"

"*Sieben*. Seven balls, one. One dollar," said John, pulling a final shiny new white ball out of some odd lower side pocket he had in his pants. John dropped all the golf balls at his feet and went to turning his front, back, and side pockets inside out, making it clear to Cal he had no more balls to offer, at least not from any obvious pockets in his pants. John had an impressive number of seven golf balls in total. Seven balls for one dollar is what appeared to be the final proposal, including this last top-quality item to seal the deal at a dollar.

As John was squatting down to collect the balls back up, Cal joined him to get hold of the shiny seventh ball, taking it out of John's hand to give it a more ceremonial and close-up inspection. Cal now had some level of legitimate interest in the lot of balls John had on offer, as well as wanting to keep up a little of the good-natured razzing to end the round. It was a new ball of a good quality, a premium brand name, hit perhaps a couple of times at the most, and had not been sitting in the dirt too long.

Cal watched on as John continued to swell up, a bit less of a pace than at first, but ground zero of the nasty sting kept expanding. John continued rubbing the mound, caressing his forearm in a strong yet tender way—from the bicep, past his elbow, down to the wrist, and slowly massaging back again, patting and stroking it over and over in repetition as if he were his own physiotherapist. It was as clear as anything to see his breathing was becoming constricted. Considering the offer price and the deteriorating situation with the severe reaction, Cal considered low-balling John for his balls, buying them at the spot price of a deep discount and moving on. Cal wanted to get out of there before John started an anaphylactic foaming, convulsing, and dropping dead in front of him, right there during their discussion concerning the transaction, the negotiation on purchasing these seven balls of John's, for just one dollar of Cal's, here on this overheating ninth and last hole of the nuthouse course weekly round.

Looking to the pleasant blue sky above and beautiful

green grass below, Cal considered the offer further: On the price and quality, and on wanting to land on this ninth green ahead, hit the flag in sight, and get the hell out of there. Then it happened… Cal's eyes grew huge, his pupils dilating like a cat's: An abrupt and extraordinary epiphany. There was nothing that John could do that would distract Cal from this greatest revelation of revelations.

"That's my ball, you cocksucker," said Cal, with genuine ire. "I hit that there ball right off the tee box, not but a couple of minutes ago. You ran right out and stole it. Then you ran back into the fucking lilacs to go and hide, you little pussy. And you got what was coming to you, you prick asshole. It's one thing if I lose a ball in the bush there—which I might do maybe once a year or so, at worst… But to come right out and steal a man's balls, right there on the fairway, way out in front of him. Dirty, sneaky little trick you got there. Ha! Bastard. I'm taking my ball here, Nazi. Blitzkrieg this!" said Cal as he stared John down, uncovering the mystery, flipping him off in a great victory.

Cal continued in this fashion for a few minutes, with authentic rage for the first bit, then ramping it back down to doing it in a more light-hearted and gentler way, without much real anger or hostility pouring out, as it was kind of funny. He knew about John, having had similar encounters in years past—it was all quite amusing, and it would make for yet another great story to share with the boys back in town, at the shop. It was plain that Cal was had this time, as he had not been paying full attention in following the trajectory of his ball off the drive, having been distracted by the tee, the resulting non-clump of dirt, and the racing police car hidden behind the hedges, its engine roaring with an accompanying siren shrieking away in the distance, the eclectic echoes.

Oh, John. John, Johnny boy, Jon-Jon. Johann. With little success, Cal tried to fight the oncoming daydream.

Johann: '*Ich bin ein verrückt Berliner*.'

The word in town was John had made his way here to the rural prairie mental hospital paradise with one sole word: John. There were numerous stories in the area and beyond as to how he came to be at the institution, the genesis thereof. The most common version, the tale told by Cal himself for as long as he could remember it, was that John—then known as Johann, born Mr. Herr Johann, or whatever it was—was some sort of mid-level officer in Germany. Legend grew this account to the point where he was a ranking member, and he was in fact a key strategist and secret senior leader in the military, which surely could not have been true if he was still way out here on the Great Plains of North America, but who really knew. John was in *das* Third Reich. And stories had him as a significant player in the Great War, too, which is how he ended up a key figure in the Second one. John, the holder of significant functions in the war effort, responsible for the execution of the executions—the summary killing of tens of thousands, at a minimum, from prisoners of war to bothersome civilians, to other despised enemies, internal and external, here and there—on both the eastern and western fronts, across the continent of Europe and further afield.

Johnny Johann had spent some time between Warsaw, Prague, and Budapest when outside of the mother Deutschland, but when the west hammered through the line, he was a bit west of east and wanting to be way back west. He needed to be as far away from the Soviets as thinkable and practical, where they otherwise would have capped him where he stood, with no hesitation. In the west, unlike the east, it was not a certainty that he would get knocked off and dumped in a random pit of masses of bodies, and he did not even have to surrender to the west, which is where the story, whether true or false, morphing into myth or not, became most interesting...

Johann, old Johnny German boy, found he had enough time to disrobe, with respect to giving up his heretofore proudly worn Nazi uniform adorned with the shiniest of full regalia and officialdom, the various badges, shields, and iron crosses, all festooned with the ancient religious Asian icon of the swastika for well-being, this great irony. Once stripped bare of the *feldgrau*, John made quick work of slaughtering a French farming family somewhere back over the line in the more western direction, shoving their corpses into the deepest recesses of the ancient wine cellar and torching the house, but not before obtaining—mending and cleaning after stealing, a cosmetic dirtying back up again, and the modeling of—his first disguise, as: *Le paysan Français.*

As the unmistakable French peasant farmer that he was, Jean went about coaxing two young non-French ally patrolmen to another nearby farmhouse, an explanation given to them under the guise of part-atrocity discovery and part-support by way of offering both a lovely Burgundian product for their assistance, some celebratory Champagne, on behalf of these most gracious hosts, the saviour of his family: Jean's fake French farming family, since departed of late.

After shooting those fine ally soldiers at point blank

on the top of said cellar steps right there in the soon-to-be abandoned farmhouse—with a Luger in each hand, pulled out from the magical peasant pockets (*just like the damn golf balls*, Cal thought) of the straw- and dirt-covered, shit-stained and -stenched farmer tunic, with concurrent shots in the back of their heads, respectively—John had no trouble being able to obtain the most critical disguise, which was disguise number two, as: Ally soldier. John was joining the other team, the good guys.

Dressed back up in the also now filthy soldier wear—albeit of a more patent and prim outfit—John of the west fled further south to a somewhat similar yet so distinct zone of the allies. The war was more or less over by this stage, wrapped right up with some light mop-up and basic security detail from here on out, or so it was hoped. At this location, in the remaining chaos of war, he went about attempting to rejoin his battered unit in what was a great fabrication during the disorder of the not quite post-war disarray. Determining the general location of where his phony fellow troops probably were—if they weren't already all dead in that certain locale—John headed as far from there as he could get while remaining within the sheltered confines of the now-impenetrable western front, the necessary shelter away from the Soviets. When John arrived there, he professed to be back with his mates, back in his decimated unit, which it was obvious he was not with, as he knew the real fake crew—also having taken more than considerable losses—were hundreds of miles away.

John began enhancing the charade on another plane, calling himself John in error—*If only one of the innocent allies he had killed was an actual John. It would have been even easier for him, maybe*—rambling on with incoherence in an eclectic stew of several languages. Chopping his sentences into solitary words of bizarre dialects—mixing it up with a little bit of fake booze thrown in, a few dashes of faux war-related mental illness—John had created the perfect recipe for the ideal concoction, his own personal final solution. With all this fumbling, mumbling, bumbling about—but stating his name 'John' in a most lucid way, as well as enunciating a few other well-spoken common English words, brief phrases and the like—well, this drama was all nothing but some excellent tactical and theatrical acting, a brilliant strategy. John—along with so many, but legitimate, others—was deemed shell-shocked, thus sent back 'home' across the Atlantic in as an expedited a manner as was possible for the time and in the circumstances where his diagnosis in the post-war bottleneck of hordes of patients was further hastened, along with the certain institutionalization, in one form or another.

Over here, on the much more civilized continent of North America, no one at the hospital would've second-guessed anything whatsoever at first. John was one fresh guest of over two thousand new souls at this sole location. The days and weeks passed by. And the months. Years disappeared. A decade and many years more... There were hundreds of soldiers who said nothing and hundreds more who mumbled nothingness. There were hundreds of veterans who spoke flawless this side of the Atlantic English, but they too were determined to be well off their rockers because of the war and its effects, caused by this or that during the brutal fighting. There were those great soldiers, now veterans, who were given their diagnoses as the result of heinous events in Europe, which Cal believed he could define better than the best head doc around. On a regular golf day, carrying on down the imperfect and often empty fairways while humming to himself in some alliterative reverie, the psychiatric handbook of diagnoses Cal wrote in his head included:

- Brutal bombing blasts + bad beatings = batty bedlam in the brain.

- Shots of slaughter + syphilis from the Sardinian sex = shell-shocked schizophrenia.

- Combat confusion + chaotic carnage = crackpot cuckoo crazy.

Lucky for John, or at least well planned out by John, he fell into each one of the key groups. The notable hyperbolic performances of this terrific actor ensured his place within each of the actual crucial categories, as laid out by the professional shrinks rather than the amateur Dr. Cal: John knew when to quiet down and knew when to offer up some muttering and spluttering for the show, keeping the production alive. And he knew when to throw a few of the rudimentary English words into the mix and when to pronounce them the correct way, those words spoken without accent. All of it was without accident, the speaking, silence, tone, and manner of John—a flash of brilliance here, an air of idiocy there, all well calculated in this quite flawless fashion.

And so, here he was today: John. He was still around, muttering to himself and others, speaking more German now than ever before, so many years later. Cal often wondered about John's reality every time he ran into him on the course, including today: *Is John still guarded? Is he still daffy? Or maybe he's still acting out this whole shtick? Was he even ever crazy? Or was he so fricking smart, a rare German genius who made his way over here to safety?*

The pace of John's arm-rubbing increased, as did the intensity of the action, the caressing. It was noticeable, his neck becoming thicker, face turning a deeper shade of red, approaching that of a dark currant or garnet, the colours morphing, breathing decelerating. Cal kept on with the charade, but he also knew that John needed to go inside and get treated, post haste. Cal decided he had to make the right move, so he gave up on berating John for stealing his new golf ball and took some small change out of his pocket—a few minor coins, not quite equal to the desired one dollar, offering it up to John for the six other balls that were not his own. *He might talk like a freaking turkey, so it's time to talk turkey.* While jingling them in his cupped hand as he went about an expeditious bartering for John's balls, a sunflower yellow water bomber flew overhead.

"*Flugzeug!* Coming!" said John, looking unnerved once again, as if he was about to start his frenzied lilac dance all over, up and down the ninth fairway, one more time.

Cal did not move as he stood staring at John, knowing another meltdown of some sort was about to occur if it was not already well underway. John was doing the *wespe* dance again, but the wasps were long gone. *Unless he believes this airplane heading north is the mothership of the wasps. Being the same shade of yellow, a not dissimilar buzzing sound.* John was right out in the open when he stopped to view the coins presented by Cal, but all he managed to do—right during their negotiation and imminent transaction, closing the big deal—was drop each of the balls, including the ludicrous green and orange ones. As if the music was turned back on, John quickly reverted to his agitation of a dance while also beginning an all-out senior's sprint back into the lilacs, the toxins flowing within him, probable asphyxiation be damned. The wasps meant nothing to John, and neither did his found balls nor Cal's money.

"Die Amerikaner! Die Russischen! Die Briten! Die Französisch? Nein. Americans, Russians! Sons of bitches," said John, as he was screaming and running, terrified to apoplectic proportions, shredding back through the bush, hiding, fighting back with an air gun, heading back to base, running an erratic pattern but in the general direction towards the main door of his home sweet long-term home, the mental institution.

Cal watched on in total disbelief, even to the point where he could no longer see John through the thick green wall. John worried about nothing more than getting bombed by some fresh water vapour—a most refreshing thought today, if the plane was full and spilled a bit, an aqua vitae rejuvenation extraordinaire in the penetrating heat. Yelling through his now quite constricted throat during his retreat, in several languages, John could be heard ordering his junior comrades around and telling them to fight back, forgetting all about his soon-to-be-fatal sting, not to mention his abandoned balls. John's real battle lay ahead and in front of him, right there at the hospital as home today rather than in the past on the beaches of Normandy or the streets of Stalingrad. It was the authentic wound— the true threat of the wasp sniper's bullet as a mere sting— that John could not process.

Cal dropped his—his!—ball about where it must have landed, in a perfect and convenient place, right on another nice soft and clean, green rye and Kentucky blue grassy spot, off the patchy dry dirt and away from the rodent hole pock marks of the near dusty rough.

Was John really enraged and terrified of the Soviet water bomber, the Spitfire watering can, the Fortress firefighter in the sky? Or is this just part of his epic ruse, continuing to hoax us all still so many years later? John was either so far gone or it was an accomplished façade to save himself from the rope or the lead. There remained ongoing trials back in Germany, with the victims (Gentile and non-) continuing to scour the nooks, crannies, and corners of Earth to bring Nuremberg or other forms of justice, better or worse, to any and all of the remaining xenophobic, genocidal killers lurking abroad. After all, the naughtiest of the naughty *Deútsche* and *Volksdeutsche* alike had now migrated far away from home rather than hang around *Heim ins Reich*. Slaughtering, murdering racist bastards who now hid in the lilacs, stealing and reselling golf balls of questionable quality, vending them as a silly scam back to the rightful owner who only happened to hook the ball but an inch or two into the rough.

Get in line. Cal considered the many Jews, Germans, and other noble current allies hunting the last lingering true Nazis around the globe. *Although the wasps might beat you to it. Here's hoping.*

One more down round;
no eagle (nor albatross) found

It was not easy for Cal to regain his composure and focus after the preceding Germanic gong show, but he thought, *I must try my best on this last hole; I must endure.* He wiped his squid-like hands on his pants to remove any sweat that might cause some slippage of the club during the shot. Gripping the wood, looking at the ball, staring at the pin, estimating the distance, thinking about where it would need to be cut clean, shuffling the feet, limbering up, loosey-goosey, practicing a swing, keeping his head down, viewing down the fairway to the flag, adjusting, preparing feet-knees-butt-back-shoulders-elbows-arms-hands-neck-head, the back swing, aiming, firing, contacting, following through, lifting sky high, thrusting in a brief zero gravity, returning, the trajectory of an arch to the heavens, down like a rainbow, bouncing, bounce, rolling, forward, pausing, rolling back slightly, stopping.

"Bam, on the good old green in two! Did I ever get hold of it there with that three wood," said Cal aloud, soon realizing he was alone again as he finished his exciting thought, the resulting sentence. "Beautiful!" Cal knew he must watch and suppress the instinctive and inherent hubris lurking within him. *Like a Dachau camp prison guard now tending to llamas in the Andes, hide it and hide out. I best move on...*

Cal heard the emergency sirens screaming yet again while putting on nine. It was typical for him to spend some time exploring the grounds a bit further, visiting some old clients and pals who still worked here. His buds—Willy the carpenter, Ronny the plumber, and Terry the electrician—would all be having a coffee about now in their shop behind the main building. Doctor Oxenham would be working on some interesting new treatments, creating some neat new drugs in his lab with a fresh crop of young assistant researchers from the university. But Cal knew he was already running far behind of where he had hoped to be at this stage of the day, as early in the morning as it still was. In direct relation to that, Cal was well aware he had committed to an earlier than usual and infrequent appointment on this golf morning, which he would already be late for by the time he had made it back. Even though it was an informal enough appointment with the physician, it was scheduled nonetheless, with a demanding and paying client who had a specific desire for that prime-time slot, requesting that Cal write him into his non-existent appointment book.

Picking up the pace, needing to return to town and open his barbershop, Cal made it back to his car and proceeded to head out of the parking lot, turning onto the main road on the grounds leading towards the last hill he drove up on, sending him on his return journey, again parallel to the river and the ascending big hill. The mason man was returning home from his morning work of fixing up his stone wall. Cal reflected on the man's incredible project, having started working on building a stone wall from scratch at the time of his institutionalization when Cal himself was a young child. The builder had such a diligent focus set on this personal project, no matter the change in staff or methods over the years, they believed him harmless enough to go about and collect large rocks on the periphery of the hospital grounds and as far as the top slopes of the dale, and then to go build a short but three-mile-long wall along the river road from the hospital all the way out to the bridge. It was a wall he was now maintaining and keeping in good repair till he keeled over one day soon enough, perhaps right while patching up the wall, dying doing what he loved. It was a project of tangible success, a veritable monument here, something to stand for many years and decades ahead. In comparison, the architectural effort was so different from Fred's project of begging for his daily birthday change, and it was so unlike the cherry-picking job of the purple puke man... It was so polar opposite of the task of the Nazi golf ball collector.

The mud man walked in front of him and to safety across the road, so Cal turned the corner. He was not a hundred feet from the parking lot when a doe jumped out in front of the car right by the three-way stop sign at the main entrance. With a micro-hesitation and a glance at Cal, she carried on towards the bed of marigolds before the deer jumped clear over the little stone wall, heading out into the deeper parts of the river valley. *Wasps, Nazis, and whatever else, it looks like she's had enough time in the lilacs as well.*

Inconvenient emergencies

George could not sleep. He was unsure if it was his recurring stomach troubles or the obstinate heat, both persistent over the last several weeks. *Perhaps it's a bit of column A and a bit of column B,* George thought, trying to rationalize it and reassure himself. He felt fine otherwise. And so, he was sure and hopeful it was not another one-off illness of sorts, a miscellany of maladies, whether of a gastrointestinal nature or not; it mattered not to old George. He was never the type to feel stress or even understand what it was all about, what it meant when others said something like, "I'm so stressed out." However, as of late, he had carried an odd anxiousness with him at times, exuding as much anxiety as one might feel without an explosion of a full-on panic attack, shaking and vomiting until they passed out. It could well have been this, again, and he had a good enough idea of where it was stemming from—what the cause of it was, if his elementary self-diagnosis was correct or even in the same ballpark. George mused from time to time about what options there might be for a possible cure, considering it much more often of late. The cure was not evident in its entirety, but the problem seemed clear enough. George wondered why he kept on denying it. To determine a course of treatment for a patient, the patient must first be diagnosed in the correct manner, a methodical and thorough check-up. Next came the 'do no harm' principle and some such, Hippocrates this and that, etc. The real problem was the diagnosis for

George was as clear as clean glass.

On this night, George was in bed, having hit the comforting pillow, when the final thin layer of evening light on the edge of the horizon disappeared into an opaque mulberry. He continued to lay there with his eyes wide open, sweating, right through to the first hint of morning light appearing on the other side of his house a few hours later, mere moments ago. The sky at dawn looked like a dark crocus blooming overhead in the early summer morning, expanding into a brighter pink rose within minutes.

Deciding it futile to waste any further time continuing to lay there awake in bed, George drove down the main street and parked at an angle, nosing in to face the front door of the police station. Flicking on the single light switch to set off the full fluorescent brightness in the large room as he entered the building, George walked to the back of the office, putting on a pot of coffee while looking back towards the front desk where his secretary was supposed to be. *Or is she supposed to be here at this hour?* George was unsure of himself. Disoriented, looking up at the clock and realizing it was indeed that early, he grumbled and sat down at the kitchen table, grabbing the newspaper—the big city daily he read each and every day, albeit one day late, unreliable delivery schedules from the metropolis to the town to his mailbox being what they were. He flipped through straight to the sports section to read the box scores and stats from Major League Baseball, the one part of the paper these days that did not cause him any trouble, notwithstanding the recent rough skid the White Sox were on. As enjoyable and relaxing as it was worrying more about which players were hitting above three hundred, who were the leaders in strikeouts, and which team was atop the American League, his brain was forcing deviations back to immediate matters concerning his job as the sheriff in this small town right here and now, as the cities were far away, their own concerns mattering not. However, reading the paper in the profound morning heat was inviting and allowed a bushed George a lone moment of solitude and to doze off in his chair...

In the brief span of his deep sleep, George went about dreaming where he found himself in the stands in New York, watching Sandy Koufax pitch against Babe Ruth. It was the most pleasant experience, sitting in the bleachers eating greasy, buttery popcorn and gritty, salty peanuts on a beautiful not so hot summer afternoon... Until he realized this fantasy match-up was not at all possible, at least not down here in these more recent and contemporary baseball years on planet Earth. As he was trying to process this unreal real game being played right in front of him, the fellow fan next to him was speaking away in an indecipherable language. George gave a slight swivel to take a look, seeing the man had a large platter of food on his lap, as he was pigging out on this personal buffet of crispy chicken and buttery perogies, along with a bowl of coagulated tomato soup in the middle of his tray. *Odd and quite uncharacteristic snacks for the ballpark. Chicken, perogies, and soup?* The man looked to George, seeming to offer him some of his ballpark food while yammering on in this angry eastern European dialect. Then this man seated next to George was starting to melt off like an ice cube placed on a warm sidewalk, continuing to talk gibberish and eat the entire time, while he released a gradual emission of a foul and gassy stench, steaming as he was continuing to disappear on his seat, from and to the Sun.

George snapped out of his dream state, still seated at the kitchen table in the back of the office, the coffee pot continuing to drip. *Jesus, a power nap nightmare to last a lifetime in less than a few minutes.* George was trying to clear the cobwebs. *What in the hell was that about?* He picked up the paper and headed towards the washroom. In hoping to try and relieve one end of his indigestion, George considered his unease. It was not a complex problem. Of late, the station had been getting many more calls from the institution to deal with incidents the folks at the hospital used to handle themselves, but they were handling no more. There had been changes to policy with the new administration and new doctors, which was not the first time for another incarnation down the hill, just out of town. There were new theories from the ivory tower of afar, and there were new practices by diktat from the bureaucracy of the near. Both of which were coming down from on high, these new treatments. These were the obvious facts concerning the situation: The hospital and society, specific and general. It was all changing.

However, and well beyond all of that, there seemed to be a new type of patient at the asylum nowadays, even as the total numbers of the poor and damned souls dropped down ever lower, year by year, if not by the month or even week. Many of the long-time customers—the veterans and sundry ancient geriatric patients of questionable origin and arrival—were dying off. All the while, some of the other veterans and geriatrics were being sent to live in different, more open types of housing, in the community and communities further afield, trying other outside methods for the milder cases, newer medicines for lightweights.

And yet there continued to be new clients always showing up at the hospital, from all over the place, claiming that new bed as if at a hotel, as per the decades of similar past practices. *Maybe these new institutionalized folks are not new types of patients at all,* George kept on brooding to himself. *Maybe it's the other changes, to therapy and the drugs and other treatments that might have made them seem like new ones— they have a fresh new look but with a mask, a façade, appearing duller yet crazier, the processes and system scarier, all in turn.*

George straightaway thought through many of the cases where that was it, these files racing through his head—the person went in for whatever reason or purpose, and today it had to be much worse than anything in the past. *Yes, that has to be it. They're worse coming in off the street, the cases of a more extreme nature, then it doesn't matter at that point once they've entered through the main door and the latch closed behind them.* And whenever it went haywire—again, for whatever reason, but this time the mischief occurring on the inside— George and his deputies were called in. They either had to come to the rescue in saving the day, or to the mop-up operation afterwards—the scene of the crime, and not always with the foregone conclusion that it was perpetrated by the patient, no longer a requisite certainty.

Seated on his throne in an oxymoronically uncomfortable yet comfortable firm position, also located at the back of his sad police station office, George flipped open the broadsheet to the second page, where his eyes deviated to the right, to the photo at the top of page three. Seeing the smaller photo of the decorated soldier in his austere dress, in the inset of the larger military photo, George's mind turned to wanting to crumple the whole newspaper up and wipe his ass with it—wipe it right over the face of this celebrated soldier from his more innocent and happier times, and wipe it even harder over the face of this soldier today, this veteran who was no longer a soldier, only some other random guest for the institution, this new nondescript patient for the hospital. But George was not going to throw the paper away without reading the important and relevant story, and he was nowhere near ready to use any such news or any other paper for the other immediate business at this stage, alas.

A right sad thing, the poor, unlucky kid. A terrible, tragic break. George stared at the picture, recounting the events as best as he could remember them...

The book of Dwight

The story of Dwight began in a place not fifty miles north of town and ended in a courthouse not fifty miles south: The former, a couple of decades ago; the latter, a couple of weeks ago. Dwight was with an elite infantry unit in the popular/unpopular contemporary conflict abroad. As with all stories that touch the institution in some way, Dwight's did not come with a happy ending. However, it's the middle parts that are perhaps even less cheerful.

After the completion of some level of high school, Dwight fulfilled his dream of becoming a soldier, achieving success in his goals in the army from his first painful exercises in basic training right through to his first tour abroad—from running for first place in a collegial competition on the grassland base to running for his life in the thick of a far-flung Delphic conflict in some foreign jungle. On his second and final tour overseas, Dwight was in a special forces unit that was sent in advance to a key location well ahead of the front line. They jumped from the chopper near the head of a ravine, parachuting in at night and spying to get the lay of the land for the larger advance. Strict orders from their commanding officer at the forward operating base were barked that there was to be no engagement with anyone unknown in the area, no matter the circumstance. But they got lost coming in and out of the coulee where they ended up meeting some local farmers and what looked like a small group of contractors who were purported to be engaged in some sort of minor humanitarian infrastructure project in the region, said to be present before the skirmish and now wanting to get back to their work as soon as the peace had been found and kept. The close-to-subsistence or at least peasant farmers invited them all in for a delicious lamb dinner, the contractors able to speak the extraterrestrial-like language of the locals. The soldiers figured they could then get their bearings and go at trying to skirt back through the area the next night, until they got trapped in the gaping gorge. Trying to fight their way out, they were outmanned and outgunned, with most getting killed while a few of them ended up captured and tortured. When Dwight's army mates advanced the front line forward a couple of weeks later, the enemies abandoned their posts in a hurry, allowing for the rescue of the mistreated and abused Dwight and fellow few remaining soldiers—they were a bloody and broken mess, with heinous and savage acts having been inflicted upon them.

With a modicum of rest and feeling something inside him beckoning his return to the field, Dwight was sent back out into the lingering chaos mere months later. The battle more intense, the public mood waning. *He should've been forced back home here right at that time, could've talked with the nuthouse quacks, and none of this shit would've ever happened.* George went on reading through the news article about Dwight's recent formal legal proceedings while cross-referencing it with his own remembrance of the original events as he knew them, before confirming some of it by reading his newspaper of today with yesterday's date. *It wasn't neither of the monstrous German wars, but war it was nonetheless. Poor Dwight.*

What happened was—the nearly identical (and unthinkable) series of events on the front end, with a much different (and unthinkable) outcome resulting on the back end—Dwight was somehow cut-off from his unit again, and when he met some local folks this time, he razed their peaceful village: He beat as he had been beaten, burned as he had been burned, raped as he had been raped, all by his lonesome one-man army self. He murdered as his fellow soldiers (his brothers in arms) had been murdered. When his colleagues arrived, they knew poor Dwight was well melted down, long fallen off his rocker, laying on the ground as he worked away at salting the earth throughout this village. After his arrest and return home, he was up for an expedited dishonourable discharge, a court martial, and the military trial of the decade—the charges he was facing included all that he had done, notwithstanding that he had a hopeless and irreconcilable case of mental illness, one of nurture over nature, as imposed on him on the front.

In the pre-stages of the trial, it was believed that reasonable Dwight's sense of responsibility and owning up to his actions were married with an unreasonable, hefty and stressful dose of a chemical imbalance sloshing around in his head like a pot of frothing cocoa at full boil on the stovetop, even if some basic sentience might have remained.

And so, one evening during this grim process, Dwight hung himself in his cell, using an innovative creation of a modified and reinforced piece of torn cloth. Not found until the next morning, he was still alive if struggling to hang on, as the supply of oxygen to his brain had been cut off overnight, his circulation shutting down. Dwight was in a deep sleep of another variety, alive and breathing in an ethereal state, no longer with the good folks down here on the real and physical ground of Earth but rather suspended just above it, somewhere else, in some indeterminate purgatory.

Although I guess he's out on the actual grounds now, and so soon. George shuffled the newspaper around to fold it and frame the article, staring at the photo of Dwight with a group of his fellow zombies being led by a nurse in front and on each side of the unsteady column, walking single file past a flower bed that George knew to be of light pink petunias and bright aureolin marigolds, near the parking lot in the front of the hospital. *The blasted reporter didn't even need to get out of the car for that picture, lazy prick.*

The sheriff longed for a significant quieting down in his town. George could not say it aloud in public, but he dreamed of the peace it would bring to these parts. People in the area also talked about it, but the slow bleed of the de-population through de-institutionalization... It was much too slow for him, the dribble of molasses in January. *Shut the fucker right down, and right now. No more frequent visits, no more saving their asses, no more one-way trips out there—this cowboy's done with it all.* Right in front of him, if things played out to his wishes, George could feel it with precision, in the wonderful wistfulness of his thoughts, of what it could be and would be: It would be nothing more than some minor disturbances, routine traffic and parking violations, rare and petty victimless crimes, bums in the drunk tank. But there would be no more vagrants in number than those of the missing cats having run off, gone feral and up into the trees. This romantic ideal made him well up, tearing and bringing even more pleasant sensations elsewhere. *Fill that loony bin up with all the screwballs and nut jobs around here and afar, and burn her down, torch it.* George chuckled to himself while wondering if he was only half-joking. *All the cats in town too and throw in the deranged cat ladies for good measure.* In more serious deliberations, the sheriff often fantasized about how this true local utopia might play out for him and his town, his nerves and his citizens. *Even if we don't follow through with the part about the cats and their old maids, it'll be good enough to start it and end it with the nuthouse.*

As he tossed the newspaper on the floor so he could concentrate on his current and pressing mission sitting on his other office throne in the back, the sheriff thought nothing of the looming and somewhat eerie coincidence when he heard the phone ringing out at the front desk. George's first consideration was how the evening deputy had gone home late last night, and it was still before regular office hours at this point; the secretary was not yet in—the sheriff was living in a no man's (nor woman's) land. His second thought was on the lack of any tangible progress he was making on the gastrointestinal struggle at most immediate hand. George would not be answering that call; no way, no how. It was also clear he was not going to be answering anything in the can at this moment, so he decided to move on for now—it was time for an attempt at getting back to some real and more productive work...

Having acknowledged his uncomfortable reality, with his pants almost pulled back up—his zipper unzipped, his belt unbuckled—the phone that had ceased ringing began ringing once again. *No doubt a lost bicycle or another stupid cat up a tree. Albeit even a bit early for either of those otherwise antsy types. One of the many spinster cat bitches had her pussy run away and up into the treetops above, again? Perhaps. It's nothing more urgent than that. Nah.* George tried his best at this game, but his rationalization did not settle his physical stomach, nor relax his mental mind nor nerves, those key connectors, bringing the two together in unison and harmony, an equilibrium like the zipper and belt he secured to fasten his pants.

As the phone was continuing to ring off the hook and doing so ad nauseum, as George washed his hands and got tidied up, organizing himself, he heard the front door open. Popping his head out of the washroom door at the back and looking towards the front, George watched his secretary, Mary, close the main door behind her in a feverish struggle, pulling her tangled purse back around and trying it again, flustered but still rushing and making it to the desk to take the critical cat call, the one that would not stop with the phoning until the moment when someone picked up the police station receiver...

"Yes, hello, police station here, and how may I help you?" said Mary, maintaining her pleasant and sunny composure even in her scatterbrained disposition on her apparent late arrival.

George finished drying his hands in the washroom and, with everything under control, he took his time in making his way back out front, not wanting to startle Mary or throw her off any further from where she already was, seeming a bit wobbled.

"No, no, I'm sorry," said Mary, keeping up with the cheerful banter and demeanour, even if she gave off a vibe suggesting she felt that the timing of the call was a bit of a bugbear for her. "He's not in quite yet, but he will be in short order. Can I take a message at all from you for the sheriff?"

George cleared his throat as he was now standing outside of his office door, not too far from her desk in the front. He wanted to alert her of his close presence, although he was not sure if he even wanted to take this specific call at this early hour in the morning, however trivial it might be in an ideal scenario. George, the sheriff, was categoric in not feeling like taking any call at this time, which was not of an actual non-trivial nature, only if a true and real emergency.

"Oh, oh, I'm sorry, he is in, OK, I see now. Can I tell him what it might be with respect to?" said Mary, as she was still trying to manage the call while maintaining her pureness and sense of honesty. "I'm sorry, what was that now? Please, calm down, please, calm... What? Oh, oh my... OK, yes, yes, please, one second please..."

"Sheriff, it's the mental hospital calling. They say it's, it's most urgent..."

The trailer park beyond the tracks

Laying there in his slipshod bed with eyes wide open, longing for any semblance of true peace, whatever that might look and sound like, he was listening to the baby (*Or babies?*) crying in the other room, listening to his wife stomping her way through the trailer over to Gregory's quasi-quiet spot. She was already up, although it was beginning to dawn on him that the Sun was shining through the curtain, beaming straight onto the pile of dirty clothes on the frayed carpet floor by the broken closet door. In her wrinkled nightie and disheveled hair, Deb glared at him, asking with contempt: "Why, if you, you lazy piece of shit, don't have anything to do, are you laying there wide awake? Why don't you get your ass in there and go and feed and change them? And clean up your shit while you're at it!" His tangential but somewhat unrelated rage and solipsism rendered her movement and voice noticeable only on the margins, nor did her tone nor content fully filter through his faux shorting out. However, he absorbed the gist of her fiery onslaught of a message—her mood was an unmistakable, and of late, common resentment, which was obvious even if he was still in his morning trance-like near coma. No translation was necessary.

Him or his aul' wan; someone's come undone.

That was all Greg had felt from all quarters as of late:

Pure hostility. No matter where he turned, he saw direct and unfiltered scorn, mockery, ridicule—he was plagued with torture, as verbal as it mostly was, words over the sticks and stones. Inadvertent and seemingly implicit though it was, his co-workers and wife had joined forces in nibbling away at his nerves. On recent occasions he began suspecting they also joined physical forces, of the intimate kind—he was certain of this; there was no need to suspect it when they went on explicitly behind his back, as though he did not know, believing him too stupid to catch on. On his emotional and mental levels, Greg was gone. The final caustic straw, that last laugh, was his firing last week—the grain sack joke was on him, and yet he was the one who got sacked for it. The shitheads of the silo had succeeded—hurrah to them.

He had been off and on, and on and off, since he was a toddler. Terrible two was a gross understatement—for Walter, first and foremost, but the ripple effect of the terror touched anyone and everyone in its path. The original settlers here were used to dealing with twisters, those dancing spouts of dust. But they would not have been able to handle the true tornado, which was young Greg.

By the time Walter was well into his middle age years—well into it, advanced right through and beyond—and far up and over his still virgin-green hill, he was accosted by a beautiful, lone, young recent immigrant of eastern European origin. She approached Walter right as he was mowing the grass on the grounds by the little stone wall on the road in, as he did so often in the summer—past, present, and whatever future he had left in front of him. She came out of nowhere—in fact, as if an angelic miracle, she came right out of the hedge-as-a-fence off a lilac and willow grove behind and down said stone wall. In traditional garb of some sort, albeit a tad scant, she approached him in a part-scared, part-flustered, part-desperate bid to win him and make him—solo ole local blue-collar and eminently available bachelor Walter—her unwitting hero, her western saviour.

Walter had seen this blonde beauty in braids before, more than once, with all occurrences occurring in the near recent past, and they seemed to be in random passing each time: In town at the grocer (both entering from off of the street and exiting back onto it at the same moment), walking in front of his house (of all coincidental things), here on these grounds (aimless wanderings around, not unlike some of the patients, but she carried a purpose about her, and without wearing the official bracelet or other hospital gear). He remembered each of these times as they flashed before him. And now she was standing before him, in his real and present time, alone.

As soon as she had popped out of the bushes, she pulled him back into the scrub, popping his cherry not too far from the Nankings and chokes. Not five minutes later, they popped back out again, together, ruffled. Pop!

The long story short was: She (Anna was her name) had been in the New World but a year when her fellow new New Worlder husband upped and keeled over while working on the heavy plough. Anna grieved for some time, a marginal period more than others would have, perhaps. However, the grieving over the corpse mutated into a deep anxiety over many other things: Soon she would have no money, no home, no anything, and she was already in the awful position of having no other family or friends, out and over here, in this supposed promised new land. And she had next to no English, the pioneer dear.

She went into town, thinking it the natural place for where she could turn, seeking help and sanctuary at the church. The one with the light-yellow steeple stood out, the one she had seen on her visits to town, the church framing the town from a distance out. It was not the eastern Orthodox one, which might have been a better fit, but she understood that church to be a few towns over, further down the road somewhere else, alas. The kind ladies of the town church in the town of her immediate vicinity did help, at first. But poor Anna! Her level of agitation, her profound stresses. The local English church ladies of old could only take her inane Slavic babblings for so long, which was not long. The trembling disposition of Anna, in this accent, caused a separate stir amongst them, disrupting some quaint routine of unimportance. That, plus a general indifference, led them to believe the best course was for her to obtain some serious help, and there was nowhere better to get such assistance than at the great institution, the hospital a couple miles outside town.

At first, the purported intention was for a short meeting—they assured her of this, as it was nothing at all untoward. However, having set foot in the building, she knew what was coming—it was omnipresent in her view, what her late husband had heard, relaying it to her, setting her imagination afire: Butterfly nets, canvas straps, electric shocks, colourful drugs, insulin coma drips, freezing cold / boiling hot / steam baths, needle-based torture, general assault, specific ice-picky lobotomies, loss of being, possible to probable fortuitous death.

Anna thought of her once young and now dead husband, and the memories of her family whom she had left back in Europe—way out in the eastern parts of Europe, to boot, out on the great big steppe. *How can I get back home?* Anna wondered if it was even possible, running uncertain scenarios over and over in her whirring mind. *Or is it safe to go back there now, if it's even an option?* After all, that was sort of the point, or at least a key part of the reason they left; there was no more Kiev for the kulaks, not at this Moscow-induced terrible Terror-Famine time.

Enter: Walter.

Anna saw Walter as she left her first 'meeting' at the hospital. She conceived of the conception idea in that arbitrary moment, right out of the bleak shades of the various alternatives she might have, all of which were a dark and horrifying hue of blackish blue. In a moment of reflective reason, innocent Anna chose to stalk Walter for a few days and then threw it all out the window to pull his dirty, shirtless lawn-mowing ass into the bushes for a good ole romp in the spirit of rolling the dice, throwing the Hail Mary.

Enter: Gregory. Grigorij. Grischa. Greg.

She made it clear after the brief lay that she had nowhere to go, and she wanted to go home with Walter. With the irrevocable popping of his own cherry out of the way at long last—albeit outside the periphery of his own orchard of chokes and Nankings, Walter often mused—Walter obliged without hesitation, then did right by marrying her up weeks later, no shotgun needed. The problem for Greg was his mama had already gone through so much heavy stress and mental trauma at the point of his conception—from the frenzied gestation period through to the harsh labour—that he was born with a wicked mixture of the chemical imbalances bestowed on him from both of his biological and off-kilter creators, respectively. As was nature's wont, this led to a lopsidedness for him of the highest proportions, living in a centrifugal spin. For Greg, the cerebral variance was nature, not nurture. Then again, it was also about the nurture...

Greg was three months old, one year to the day—maybe the hour, maybe the minute—after the lilac screw, when his mama got hit by the train. She could take it no more— no more English, no more poverty, no more loser husband Walter, no more sight of the brick and stone façade of the asylum, no more longing for being back home with her real family, no more part-bastard son Greg. Anna had made the decision to take a long, epic, Greek tragedy-like walk one night. She left their dumpy house in town, strolling down the hill and along the river path with a final saunter of painful nostalgia through the hospital grounds. About three miles down the main railway line from the elevator was where she sat down in the centre of the rough aggregate and laid herself out parallel to the ties. She stretched herself out to gently allow for the support of the back of her neck on one of the cool-to-the-touch tracks while pushing her legs straight out across and perpendicular to rest her calves on the other track, awaiting her permanent and dismembered sleep, away from it all this final evening on the railway bed, out past the hospital, itself beyond the town. "Grigorij," Anna said, whispering her sad last words to herself on the vibrating tracks as the light grew brighter. "Grischa."

This was part of the full and total weight carried by Greg from his earliest sentience until today. He was unstable. He was made fun of, for sure, but he also made fun—he pulled pranks, managing his fair share of joking around. As deliverer and recipient, he got in fights—lots of scraps.

Classmates liked him or hated him; teachers could not stand him in unanimity. It seemed he took it more than he gave it—it was close, but not certain. And right about the time he would drop out of school once and for all—as he had started working at the local elevator, taking on the tasks of the most menial, dangerous, and dirty jobs they had on offer—he found Deb. Deb loved him and he loved her. A silly, baseless young romantic bliss.

Greg should have reflected more on the early courting of Deb, but he could not, would not, should not—well, he should have, yet he did not. Whenever he was enraged, he remembered his mom and all the stories he had heard from others, including from his old man, Walter. The tales were largely fictions, but he did know the truth, mostly—or at least he figured he did. The mad turned to sad; then he would try to move on. But after yesterday, right there at the elevator...

He could no longer focus on channeling his thoughts, not here at home, not any longer. And their trailer stunk.

Food and mould; garbage of old.

It was with disgust he inhaled the must—and the dust.

He loved his babies, but the comprehensive colicky crying drove him to the edge; the bottling up of his emotions were bottlenecking, ready to explode. Greg was going to work with his old man back at the hospital—where he had both played and stayed in his formative years. This was the answer, but it seemed many things may have already spiraled too far down by this point. And that was the case if he did not stop thinking about the elevator and those grain handlers, and got himself the hell out of this place, his home, right this moment.

Greg grabbed his keys and smokes and headed to the other side of the tracks in town. *To the better side.*

The barn of the blackberry booze

Standing all alone with its giant lanky but sturdy legs, it rose as if growing straight out of the thick green floor. Like a giraffe in the tall quackgrass and sundry weeds, legs spread equidistant without any knees, hoisting the body from under the cylindrical torso—all four rising up from the ground at angles like a trapezoid, the crusty, oxidized steel stabilizing the unit. Resting in solitude and with no head, the body looked like a giant rusted over soup can, unopened and without a label, tipped on its side in a position to roll from the sky. It would come crashing down if the legs buckled, tumbling along, flattening the verdant shag rug below. Bill's ancient statue, his real living relic. It was his artefact, one of historic and current critical production to him and his enterprise, his mobility—essential on this most specific of days, today on the old family farm.

Bill looked up from the light green on the ground and the dark green in the bushes, up to the early morning dawn of the late summer sky, where from behind the tank a cerulean background with ripe peach-orange and lavender-pink strokes were brushed there by the Sun—a similar portrait would be painted again tonight, on the other side of the yard, another beautiful picture to be sketched out in fifteen or so hours and change, another masterpiece from the cosmos. Taking his time in continuing with the fill, he was viewing the abandonments around the grounds of his farm—his own personal and wonderful rural ruins.

His pleasant early peace of scanning the landscape was shattered, again, disrupted by the incessant cawing of the black bird. It appeared massive. He never saw it fly in or land, but there it was now perched on the top rung of wood of the ancient corral. Tweety songbirds were struggling to compete with their cheery, chirpy melodies in the vicinity. Behind the tank, on the low wood-weaved barbed wire-tipped fence, the black bird sat cawing, gawking. Bill was unsure of what the dark scavenger wanted, but he was sure it was too early—and he much too busy this morning, and today, and this week—to go and get the Cooey.

Bill placed the nozzle back, slamming it onto the hook within the rusty compartment, a careless move in chipping off some of the flaky ochre bits in the process. He opened the door, stepped up and got in, firing it up: The timeworn yet trusty Ford. A grumble in the back choked out a thick charcoal plume with the combustion sending the crow or raven on its way, fitting even if rude. Giving the machine a minute to decongest before leaving the decay, it then went idling forward in a rattling first gear, heading back towards the silo, blowing smoke which was becoming less opaque than on the initial start-up.

Parked at the corrugated tower filled with grain—which he had topped up with his new crop of wheat over the past few days, using his auger to create the teeming inside mass of the current harvest, now in the near home stretch phase for him—Bill stepped down and walked around from the back of the barn towards the door at the front. The crisp, hard white glow of the door and frame from years ago had weathered and was now a dirty eggshell off-white, rippled and peeling away, exposing a dirtier and former white coat from decades earlier.

The barn went up when Bill was quite young, but he always remembered his dad, dad's brothers, and neighbours, all working to put it up, a new textbook and iconic red barn for the family farm. His grandfather watched on as they replaced the original homestead barn that he had built at the time of the original settlement, his barn which was so sadly scorched in a lightning storm mere weeks before the new build—an electrical nightmare of charring from the heavens, the summer night seared into Bill's memory till his last day, that eventual and ultimate final breath. He always figured the end was right around the corner. *Not too far off now—must be coming pretty soon...*

The jarring memories abound—Bill himself a granddad now, or gammpa or Grandpa Bill, as the little one and the older one called him, respectively and respectfully—were forcing up those memories of the past, of the farm and all this rich, personal, family, sentimental history. It was ordinary for this to happen near the end of the annual harvest, and much more often in recent years, the older he became. It was as if he wanted and needed to lock the memories down, as futile as he knew that was in his brain rather than on paper, where this history could live on for the family when he soon bit the driest of dry farm dust, in a natural manner or otherwise, the lamenting of the inevitable end of Bill and his recollections, his account.

As he slid the barn door open and stepped in, Bill always remembered his folks, and his dad's folks with their stories before—the master Old MacDonalds, a generation he believed would never be replicated again. The homesteaders who were only a couple or three generations past at most, at least for old-timers like Bill. The jacks-of-all-trades, independent individuals—individuals creating these little local micro-communities in the country, then as communities bigger and further apart, by distance and relationship. These pioneers, each on their own and on such a small scale, arrived in the void, showing up on a train from the east, or via the east straight from Europe, dumped off out here in the far west at the time, which meant the middle west today.

It seemed it was a harsh and barren land—dusty and snowy, with nothing much else. Countless stories were recounted through the years—exhaustive clichés, generic family histories, interesting anecdotes, the most fantastical fictions, surely. However, with one truth, from his family and his neighbours—it was a hard and brutal reality, having next to nothing, if not quite sweet nil, naught, zero, zilch, on arrival. *What the hell were they thinking? How'd they make it here? How'd they get here and manage to stay? They had a resilient drive and some rudimentary skills. And some luck, that was it. But still: How irrational and eccentric they must've been. And yet, they were so rational and cautious, in their time, in their own way.*

As Bill looked at the present topsoil dust blowing before him in the heat, he considered... *The pitiless and cruel cold, the harsh and fierce winter for months. So unforgiving in every respect, white walls of blowing snow rising all around them, the enveloping squalls. Blowing dust, tornadoes. Labouring away in the snow and in the dust, gusts and downpours, extremes of way below zero, working out in the elements, explicit frostbite, frigid feelings outside, shrouding the home and cloaking the body with a profound intensity—inside the sod or clapboard house. Inside your clothes. Well above one hundred degrees, with your skin burning and frying away, sweating all hours—not unlike today, without certain contemporary conveniences to mitigate against the severity of the conditions. Hauling, digging, hammering, planing, sawing, chopping, pulling, lifting, plowing, churning, cleaning. Three stories up, dangling between the roof and the ground, in a trench, in a well, trampling through the snow, through the dust, in the mud. Filth. Sowing, reaping, sheafing. Milking, plucking, calving. For many others: Sowing, reaping, sheafing the grain of someone else, making someone else money, cutting away the straw. Trying to heal up from your real efforts—your blood, blisters, bruises. Having far-out dreamy hopes of your own sickle, hoe, real modern equipment, seeds, horses, surplus labour—your own plot of land. Then you would do it for you, your exact same heroic effort, but labouring away for you, for your family.*

Not too long ago, back when the settlement dust had settled, most farms had one of these cookie-cutter barns dotting the fields—stereotypical red boxy rectangles, section by section. Each man and each family—an Old MacDonald yard. His labour for his family, production for their consumption at home on the farm and all of the surplus products sold at market—in town at market, at the butcher's, at one of the grain company elevators that would in turn sell it elsewhere. It was not that different now, except the young guys were farming bigger: More cattle, pigs, more corn, wheat, more specialized knowledge, more new equipment, sophistication—more land on each farm, as consolidation had well set in with 'economies of scale,' he had once heard, ever since the days of the Dust Bowl and Great Depression, and now since the end of World War Two and the economic growth thereafter as well.

This majestic barn had lost its sharp cardinal red glow of the past, fresh hues fading through the seasons. The former brilliance was decaying towards ruin, but still purposeful and essential, still beautiful. The barn was the centrepiece of the farmyard, positioned between the house and the road, surrounded by old crude equipment weathering away off to the side. It was further surrounded by the pens of certain livestock, everything more random as the radius expanded outwards from this barn at the core of the farm, the nucleus of the yard.

Each adjacent quarter section fanned out and was more organized than the rest of the yard: Corn, oats, and wheat, all for sale; pasture with a few head of cattle—meat for sale, a couple of bovines saved and fattened up to be butchered for the house, plus dairy for the family. Bill farmed three adjacent quarter sections of grain. Nestled between the wheat and oats was a much shorter and single solitary row of rye, while between the oats and corn was the remaining one lonely patch of barley, which seemed to be a most inefficient and peculiar way to farm. However, these key rows were for Bill and for market. This barley was not for the black kind of market, as with some other items of value-add processed production, but rather it was for the neighbours and friends in the local barter type of a market they still had in these parts, offering good quality barley in small batches. The rye was for Bill only, and only for Bill.

At the end of the yard, he looked at the side of the new house—the current house they lived in, which was next to the old, abandoned house he grew up in, now but a pest nest of a mouse house. Bill looked at the new old barn as the three structures formed a triangle in the yard, and there within the garden grew. The back and sides of the garden plot were protected by thick bush, then spruce, then elm and poplar, then caraganas and willows, then hemp—the latter serving as a last line of defense windbreak for the garden in the summer, screening the house from dust and snow in the summer and winter, each serving its important purpose in the key stormy season. There was a fourth row as part of the garden, where fruit bushes created an inner wall of the oblong: Raspberries and blackberries. The latter thickets were Bill's proud contribution of a few years back, which for beyond regular consumption functions, served as critical ingredients in exciting unique recipes of both those of his and those of his wife, Rose. Fruit trees formed the side border, apples and plums. Vegetables filled in the large rectangle, where within it were planted and grew: Potatoes, yellow and red; tomatoes, red and redder; squashes, winter and summer, but only grown in summer; carrots and parsnips, orange and white. *And yellow if they ever mated, conceiving some new root vegetable down below the topsoil.* There were peas; beans, green and dry; cucumbers, green and wet, cool; onions, green and yellow; turnips; and red cabbage with a purple look like a big leafy boysenberry. And when rabbits came along, plump in their late summer season of toffee fur, they made a welcome meaty addition to an otherwise superb growing vegetable stew.

Rose kept up the garden and tended to most of the produce. Via their kitchen table assembly line, a majority of the produce ended up in jars—for them, for family and friends, and for selling any fortunate small surpluses at market in town, which she did during select seasonal market weekends, setting up a little table amongst those larger ones of the efficient if competitive farming co-ops and colonies. The garden was not its original self, being much smaller now and with decreasing production, yet remaining productive enough, even if more due to organics than design. It did not have to be what it once was, so it wasn't. And it was largely her now, with him only as he felt like it, sometimes, on rare occasions. The kids, siblings, cousins were all long gone—some to town, many further afield, out to the city, and living in cities beyond. The location, structure, and shape of the garden was all the same, but it had shrunk in both the total number of species and the production figures of gross yield by weight—in years past when it might have almost been measured out in tonnage, today it was weighed out in mere pounds.

Bill heard a faint wailing sound coming from the direction of the highway, moving closer towards his yard. It was a distant, subtle horn sound, whining in and out with a certain consistency. Within a few seconds, it was clearer, and he realized it was a siren, although he had already had a feeling that that was what it was, a feeling of some confidence. He could hear it approaching the farmyard road and could see the dust trail forming behind it, looking like a comet rolling on the ground and rising on an angle above the caraganas right where the wall grew and ended by the entrance to his home yard. The police car sped past the gate, continuing towards the river. Bill knew they were not headed to the river. In the past the occurrence used to be much more frequent, a minimum of daily while dissipating even further every few months. Within a few years he only heard the police car siren maybe once a week or so at most, while sometimes but once a month. At present, the past number of days and weeks, and again here today, they seemed to be returning to a daily frequency, even as the huge number of psychiatric patients from the past were but a current fraction of what it used to be. And when the police made their return trips back up the road and out to town again, the comet was slower, the gravel rose with less dust, the lights were turned off, and the siren was silenced.

Bill carried on, looking ahead to the back of the barn, to the piles of hay stacked aslant, resembling the beginning of a triangle; it was sloping down to the dirt floor as if an asymmetrical pyramid with steps, with the base about two thirds of the way forward and straight in from the door. The half of the left side was to mix with forage and grain to feed the livestock—for the cattle, as a secure and essential supply for his few dairy cows during the winter. The pile on the left half was much larger. The right half was reserve stock, if needed, but served its own unique secondary purpose, which was as a practical wall of sorts, as it looked like it might in fact be. On walking up to the right side—and climbing the ladder to the loft—there was another shorter wall of hay bales creating a similar effect. By removing one key bale wedged in a unique position between the large ground wall on the right and the mini-loft wall, there was an opening and a ladder leading down to whatever was behind it all. In what revealed itself in this zone of mystery in the back was a small solitary wooden tool shed surrounded by straw on each side where the ladder led right up (and back down) to its door. There was nothing but dead space between its holey roof and the cobwebbed rafters of the porous barn ceiling.

Taking one step inside and pausing as if bracing himself for an inevitable outcome of the floor collapsing, Bill wandered in when he believed it safe to continue, heading through the concussive blast of heat and without any reflex, not even a wary blink. His ears focused on the sounds of bubbling, steaming, clanking. Bill's auditory senses were overwhelmed by the olfactory overload of intense aromas of grain—of corn, barley, and rye, albeit for the most part indistinguishable in the general process—of grain cooking, of bread baking, of hunger-inducing fresh bread, of yeast. *The stench of, the oh so pleasant stench of, the impressive fermentation.*

He pulled up the stool and sat down to view the labyrinth of equipment housed on the base of galvanized sheet metal, the custom and ad hoc flooring shaped like an irregular polygon. The apparatus was an intricate tangle of his bespoke operations, looking like some static octopus. Rickety shelving hung in rows on all three of the non-door sides of the little hut of chemistry, the shelves old pieces of fence rigged onto the clapboard shack with rusty old gate hinges. One shelf held an assortment of various clay and ceramic vats; another was stacked with empty glass containers. Bending in the middle like the curve of a hockey stick, a third shelf housed full containers of Mason jars of different capacities and antique miscellaneous bottles of different volumes, shapes, colours. Piping of a decent width was constructed through both the ceiling and the back side by the bottom shelf, basic holes which were once used to vent it when the shed was newer and when it was stationed outside of the barn, as an independent facility in the main yard minus all the thick insulation and security provided by the current layers of straw and hay.

Not too long ago, this stand-alone factory of a shack was indeed outside in the open, where it remained for some time until the move inside, when Bill could accept, live, and grow with the change. For when there used to be many swine on his farm, the tiny manufacturing facility attracted the pigs much too much; with the muggy-yeasty-fresh bread aroma, they would take a whiff and then eat through a cinderblock wall reinforced with rebar to get at that smell and whatever the taste, had they ever been given such an opportunity.

And so, Bill tried his best to deter the pigs by transplanting a dense and thick bush covered in prickles and thistles; one dug out from the river valley nearby when he was looking for some saplings of obscure and wild apple trees and native berry plants that he could transplant into their eclectic and diverse garden on the farm. This bush was raised, grown and nurtured from nature. This plant that looked like it could have been a shrub designed by demons and used as greenery with practical applications at a Nazi POW or death camp of concentration. This shrubbery and barbed-wire growth and destruction, this type of New Man for plants. It was a plant from the depths of Hell. Bill cut the shit of his hands, arms, and neck moving it—when it was a foot and a half tall, a fresh and soft virgin spring plant. He had been wearing overalls, gloves, and anything he could think of except armour in that heroic effort of transplantation. When Bill began a new batch of product and started venting it out of the little shack wall where the replanted plant was situated, the bush began growing in an instant and at a rapid pace, feeding off of the enduring feast of carbon dioxide, wrapping itself around the entire side of the structure and another two feet straight up, towards the heavens like Jack's beanstalk on some wild new fertilizer, from this minuscule spot of Hell on Earth, on Bill's farm. Within but a few short weeks, it reached up and out in a beautiful and masterful harmony and unison of leafy razor blade growth. For the security of the shack: A great success, a brilliant move. But then...

The pigs moseyed away from the scrumptious and generous buffet of the trough one fateful morning, out for a nonchalant light stroll around the yard while Bill was working in his shop—the shop of a mechanical nature over that of his more immediate chemical one—when they found the mouth-watering plant. *Mighty tasty only to a pig, to be sure.* His swine ate through the plant like it was soft butter drizzled with warm liquid chocolate, if it was anything at all, devouring it in no time flat, seconds. No cuts, scrapes, or scratches on the pigskin for them sows, just delicious Tyrian purple flowers and forest green sappy, juicy leaves and sticks, all on this yummy foe-of-man torture bush. *A cactus of our own,* Bill thought. *For our open plains and prairies.*

Bill was cautious and no dummy. It was always justifiable to be nervous about snoops, be they family, friends, foes—it was an objective nervousness. Or rather a foe snooping, or family or friends being a bit too nosey for their own good, then a bit mouthy when they left the farm. Even if he was being ever so gracious as he was—in sharing the bounty, offering samples of his fine craft product, these hard-laboured artisanal gifts of his from the local farm—it could still happen. *Regardless, it isn't none of their bloody business anyway. Nosey fucking honking geese.* Not that those allies would do anything untoward, but even the most harmless of people could still slip up and hurt you, which tended to be that way if they were too goosey—honking away down on coffee row, at the bar, in their own home sweet home. *Then the wife gets goosey and honking downtown, on Main Street, at the salon.* The sewing circle of rumours, the gossip of horrors. News spreads like an airborne virus in a small town, a tornado of talk, a cyclone of chatter. With these clear realities of the presence of both geese and pigs, Bill made the prudent move of relocating his operation of beverage production a couple hundred feet over and into the safer confines of the barn itself, which is when he built the nifty and cunning lair of bales around it. *A golden castle wall of fortress-like security. It's obviously venting itself well enough, that pongy carbon, as the distilling parts have never exploded, no fires, not even a hint of a spark, not yet...* And he had no intention of seeing another great barn go up in the yard. No flames meant no further construction, no more rebuilding.

In the middle of the tiny room sat the mostly shiny copper contraption, even if with a bit of corroded green tinge: A polished, almost raw sienna glow, with a dull emerald meets fading olive mineral look of weathering on the seams and joints, an intricate series of pipes leading to and from one main cylindrical unit. The still had a look of great complexity, but after years of experience—a lifetime of experience, learning from the generations down the paternal line before him—it was all quite simple enough. He removed one old bottle—a large glass jug, which was filling up with liquid under the system—capping it and replacing it with another empty from off the shelf. This was a special corn and rye blend of a batch that his dad used to make, and his dad's dad's recipe before that—a favourite mix of theirs during prohibition, the one under which Bill apprenticed and learned to drink like a man.

Dry or wet; Bill didn't fret.

He could now leave this new bottle in place to take its turn in receiving the continual slow flow of marvelous drips and drops of the drink...

Bill's moonshine, his hooch, his crafty product, from his own farm-grown grains, a fine liquor he made, this spirit, whether whisky or whiskey. Bill's distillery.

The back of the room had various unique set-ups in the two corners and in the middle, processes appearing independent of the copper still and unique to each other. In the corner to the back and right side sat an old beer keg of battered aluminum. In the opposite back corner on the left side was a similar sized and well-aged vessel, some sort of old water-barrel of now tattered plastic. The slot at the back and centre of the room was something like the back-left device. In the right, it was yeast and barley; in the left, yeast and honey, plus a new addition of a pail of his lovely, mashed blackberries; in the centre, yeast and pulverized apples. Bill took a simple glance in each of the containers, taking a quick dip with an old tin can for a tiny taste test of each solution. It was all well and good with these samples, the vessels bubbling about with precision as they should be, the *Saccharomyces* eating away at the sugar from starch in one, the sugar from honey in the other, the sugar from apple juices in the middle.

Bill's brew, this mash and slurry, bread interrupted, from his barley, this beer, reed straws not included. Bill's brewery.

Bill's honey wine, his fruit melomel, from his garden berries, along with some honey from a kind neighbour—via his even more courteous bees and their hard-laboured product from their own great shops of industry, these magnificent hives and honeycombs of a perfect hexagonal form, supplying this critical nectar of the *Apis* gods. Bill's meadery.

Bill's scrumpy, the triumphant apples, picked fresh from his trees around the garden as transplanted from the bush around near prairie sloughs and river valley of nature, allowing for an extra ripening in the yard, sitting in the cellar, then a mashing and a thrashing, straining and containing, now this soon to be enhanced apple juice. Bill's cidery.

For methodological reasons and for extra good measure, he took another dip from each vessel, this time in a greater quantity but still managing to drink each of them in one giant swallow. With the basic chemistry set in a flawless enough motion within his hidden shack of fermentation, Bill made the reverse climb out from the fortress of hay, up to the loft and back down to the front of the barn. As he exited the main doors, he looked back to the truck and silo, then to the field off the concession, the main county grid road. He had a wave of dizziness, even if mild and subtle, wondering if it was the proof level of the product or the escalating temperature of the hot morning in this ongoing and ostensible never-ending heat wave. *A bit of both, probably. No doubt about it.*

Bill was scheduled to make two deliveries to the elevator today: One this afternoon with the truck that was already full; the second one would be a fresh load from the bins, with a quick shoveling and augering out, and back into the same old grain truck. Then all he had to do was take off that last few dozen acres of corn, take that and another couple of loads from the bins, and harvest was fully complete. Bill figured if he could survive the heat until Thursday or Friday, that would be it. And his grain truck would have to survive it as well, even as it was on the terminal fritz, with acute and chronic symptoms needing to be dealt with before the truck ended up in the palliative care section of his farmyard, the hospice of a parking lot, joining the ruins with the other forms of antiquated junk. That was all Bill needed now, survival of his truck and of his person for a meager few more days.

After a wrap on harvest and until the snow fell, Bill would focus on some work in the yard and shop. He had chores that never ended: Tending to the gears and brakes of the trucks (his grain one and his everyday one both needed some tender, stern love), fencing in the small pasture, electrical in the shop, mechanical on the farm equipment (tractor, bailer, swather, combine, etc.), shingling on the house. Picking in the garden. *Christ, harvest isn't going to be the end of it after all.* This theme was a recurring one, presenting itself again in late summer and early autumn each year. *And painting this bloody door.* He exited the barn at last and headed back towards the house.

It was still too early to head to town, so Bill went back inside. Rose was awake and up now. She had the coffee and oatmeal starting on the stove, but she was not present in the kitchen. She had had a pounding headache for several straight days now, maybe longer. "It feels like a constant and forceful vise on my ears," Rose said to him yesterday, as it was in the recent past few days Bill had realized her true discomfort. She would never complain in an overt way. *Not even during her absolute worst times, she always holds her peace.* However, it was clear to him now as she could not conceal the pain from him any longer. When confronted by Bill, she confessed that nothing seemed to alleviate it—nothing worked. Stemming from a pinched nerve maybe, hammering away at her drums, concussing through the skull and brain, temporal and frontal, on a systemic shotgun blast-like path up top. Blacking-out twice in the past two weeks, she assumed it was a tumour, and whether malignant or benign, the end was near for her, not unlike Bill's thoughts on his own grim if more general health status. Stoic Bill still figured it was nothing serious, nothing dire for either of them. The same thing had happened to Rose at least a couple of times before, although less than once a decade during the many years they had been together. Then there would be an eventual dissipation, and often in short order. Maybe this time it was different; becoming a more advanced age was making the woes harder to cope with.

Bill poured himself a cup of coffee, breaking the steady rhythm of the percolator. He preferred some grinds resting in the bottom of the ivory mug, imparting the real flavour, chomping the sediment down on the last sip. *It's the only way to drink it*, he thought, sipping away at the unpolluted dark black coffee, looking for the thick, chewy finish.

Bill walked back outside to the porch, surveying the yard while lighting a smoke, hand-rolled the night before—a few hours earlier, in fact. *Where in the hell is that dopey dog?* The dog being the one he yelled at, he could not stand, and yet he loved with a total and unconditional affection. The beautiful heeler-collie cross—white and black, black and blue—was a neighbour's mutt pup he took on nine years ago. Today, teaming up to wrestle away at the pup's body and soul—as well as Bill's heart—was the sad and sadder dysplasia and dementia setting in with an obvious pain for the dingo doggie. Bill had not seen him once this morning, wondering where he was and thinking of him multiple times already while fueling up the truck and checking on the assortments in the beverage factory. He assumed the dog was still sleeping in somewhere, hopefully in peace.

"Where in the hell is that goddamned dog?" said Bill, asking aloud this time, although still to himself, assuming that would do the trick. At long last and sure enough, as if channeling the dog with his thoughts before his words, Max came ambling down the grid path behind the Quonset.

The large hut was full of Bill's farm equipment, even if as the years passed by it was becoming more of a glorified garden shed of corrugated steel than anything. The structure was much sturdier than the wooden shack of the elixir-making, and it would make a great potential site if he ever needed to ramp up production of his hooch or swill to serious levels, if the tiny wood hut one day ceased to cut it. Bill fantasized about how quickly he could move from his niche production (as if his current operation was a pilot project), scaling it up to demonstration and then a major expansion into a commercial plant (if whatever phony stars aligned for him), this grand daydream.

Why is Max coming all the way back from the main road? Bill looked towards the grid. *What in the hell is he doing way out there?* The dog was running or at least jogging well enough, but he appeared exhausted from both the heat and the numerous health conditions hamstringing him.

Bill gave his mutt a welcome pat on the head, a rub and scratch behind the ears, and a pet down the back before the dog could dash off again, this time towards the barn. Standing on the veranda, Bill took another sip of his coffee, realizing again that he had yet to even see Rose this morning. It was clear she had started making the coffee and porridge, thus was not keeled over somewhere or had not awoken. She was bagged, remaining a bit off from the piercing headache, so he decided it best to check on her before heading to town. Back inside, he pulled the pot of oatmeal off the active burner, walked upstairs, and peered into their room. Sure enough, she was back in bed, sleeping sound on her side, no doubt induced by some heavy painkillers to bomb the migraine—if that was what it was going to take, so be it. Bill saw that Rose was breathing fine and looked as comfortable as a bundled-up baby in a crib, all safe and sound, so he made the cautious choice to take his leave.

Returning downstairs, with slow steps, taking care to be silent, he sat back down to have a bowl of the now cooked oatmeal. Bill enjoyed the steel cut variety, which came in a handsome tin as purchased from the local grocery store in town, which in turn purchased that brand right from the processing plant two towns over. And so, for all he knew, they could have been his own oats he was eating for breakfast—after having grown, harvested, and delivered them. This was something Bill thought about every single time he ate them, each day, for years and now decades on end. Bill's oatmeal. *I should start making a stout, too.*

He finished his coffee by downing the grounds, got back in the half-ton, and headed to town. There were a few key errands to run before becoming overwhelmed with the tail-end and conclusion of harvest in the days and, at most, one week ahead. The harvest finale would start this afternoon with hauling out that first load to the elevator and taking off the last of the overripe acres of crop still out in the desiccated field. Bill knew it was going to be a busy and most eventful one today—he could sense it in his mind and heart, in his core.

Book II

Bedlam and the Helix

Bloodletting and blueberries

Doctor Putnam was already there, as prompt as the esteemed small-town physician could be expected to be, sitting and waiting in his onyx black Cadillac Sixty Special parked at the curb plumb alongside the barbershop store front. He recognized Cal's car driving by and turning around the corner, heading towards his private owner's parking spot behind the shop. However, as the doctor knew there was no back door at said parking spot, he got out to meet Cal in the front, standing in the shade under the awning next to the signature helix pole, spinning its dizzying ribbons of red, white, and blue. With the morning heat haze emanating off the concrete sidewalk, the whorl gave the illusion as if the colours within the pole were melting. The doctor imagined the red ribbon alone, as if it were the mercury rising, so fast and to infinite and torturous degrees of heat—like he was on the actual planet Mercury, solar flares erupting in the immediate neighbourhood—bursting the thermometer.

"Morning, Doc," said Cal, greeting Doctor Putnam, this first customer of the morning and week, penciled in as he was. "Sorry I'm late, Doc. Today's my golf day. And that round took a lot longer than it should've, I should say. Almost every single hole you face delays as you run into the craziest loony bastards out there... But no excuses; let's not keep an important man waiting any longer though. Come on in then."

"Not a problem at all, Calvin," said Doctor Putnam, smiling and not bothering to respond to, nor even acknowledge, the specifics of Cal's excuses, whether the length of his round of golf or of the patients of the institution who were the purported cause of the delay. "I am not in any real hurry this morning, I am thankful to say. And as a matter of fact, it is only a couple of short minutes in any event." Doctor Putnam wanted to put Cal at ease, lest he take issue with something else and fire any friendly comic shots right back to himself for the brief duration of his Monday morning haircut.

Cal nodded as if in thanks, jingled the keys and opened the door for the physician to enter first, directing Doctor Putnam towards the oxblood leather chair: The trimming throne. Beyond the keys, the door had its own jingle from a small chime on opening, then closing slowly in an automatic way without force, letting out a long creak from the wood, a piercing screech from the bone-dry hinge in need of lubrication, a loud clatter on banging back onto the door frame, with a final little jingle of the bell as it reversed itself into its final closed position.

Having cleaned up the shop well enough at the end of every day—nice and thorough on Saturday nights, even more so on those which were the day before the golf eves—Cal could start working on the first gent to walk through the door; or, at least right after he had started his essential percolator to begin its bubbling and brewing away on the side table, the necessary morning coffee for his customers and himself—but for him, first and foremost. Thus, Cal put the coffee on.

"Well, what'll you have today, Doc? Will it be the blood-letting, the tooth extraction, or the trim?" said Cal, describing his professed core services as he began his phony negotiation, already well knowing what the physician would want, that being his usual trim, the same style, just a little off the top. "Or you can pick any two of those that you'd like, those that you wish for, and I'll take half price off the third one for you. That's just for you though, Doc. Don't you tell any of those other pricks down at the hospital, you hear? Not your good and proper hospital, nor the other mad one down by the river. It's a special deal, for fine and select customers only."

Doctor Putnam did a little shuffle, a bit uncomfortable settling into the big barber's chair. He smiled, trying to match the faux if not asinine grin of Cal's, then the physician chuckled and blushed a tad as well.

"What's so funny, Doc?" said Cal, as he tried to hide his own grin and suppress his laughter. "Those are the offerings—that's what that there pole says out front. You're an educated man, a man of the world, no?"

"Yes, yes, true, I guess I am," said Doctor Putnam, still with the slight smile. "But I am afraid I need my teeth for some while yet, as I do enjoy a good steak from time to time. And if I lost a single drop of blood in this heat today, even a mere pinprick worth, I would be sure to faint in a quick second. And so, I guess that leaves the trim for me, something I do for sure require, and your excellent services thereof, Calvin."

"OK, fair enough. Alrighty then," said Cal, as he parachuted the giant beige bib over the physician's front, tying the back string in a large bow at the back of his neck, about to commence the clipping—the grand trim for Doctor Putnam. "I got some new tools the other day, and a brand-new washbasin, so that's a good goddamn shame that is. But I'm happy to oblige you on just the trim, Doc. So let's get at 'er here then, my services thereof. Heh. And I'll try to avoid any bloodletting for you today. Don't want you passing out in this chair, or I'll have to drag your ass out to the sidewalk. I'd have to keep the business running, you understand. The operations must continue on."

"Ha," said Doctor Putnam with a nervous chuckle. "I will sit here right and proper still then, like a statue in Pompeii, to avoid any errant nicks."

On the first snip from the barber's scissors, the orchestra of the door repeated itself in unison, minus the initial notes of the keys jingling. In walked George, wearing his full and proper uniform, breathing heavily and sweating as he was lumbering forward with effort.

"Morning, officer," said Cal, piping up, acting as though at military attention. "Hot enough for you yet, George?"

The sheriff sauntered towards the coffee, where the pot was still in its early brewing process. George took off his ivory cowboy hat, wiping his brow with his sleeve. He was not quite dripping, but the beads could be seen forming on his forehead under the brim nonetheless, his shirt highlighted by damp spots in the key glandular areas of the chest and arm pits.

"So hot, and so damn early," said George, speaking to Cal even slower than Walter had earlier in the morning on the golf course. Notwithstanding that in the heat the sheriff probably did not need a hot coffee—not to mention what it would do to further facilitate his gastro issues, those acute troubles of the tract—George grabbed a luminous jade mug from the counter and viewed the brewing apparatus in process as he continued dabbing at and wiping down different parts of his sweaty head and neck. He looked back at Cal, who was now more engaged in viewing the trim before him, his immediate job at hand, using his awkward claw-like hands as if the scissors were an extension of his fingers, growing out from or off his wrists like knotty aspen branches. "No break, neither. What's it been now, five, six weeks? Maybe even longer?"

Looking beyond the barber's chair out towards the street, the sheriff's train of thought was meandering, his focus shifting in a new direction every few minutes, from the heat to the coffee to Cal's scissor-hands to this brand-new event he discovered and was viewing out the front window. "Well, now, what in the hell is this out here again?" said George, flummoxed and disturbed. He set his empty cup back down next to the percolating pot, set his western hat back atop his sweaty head while adjusting it in a formal manner, upped his reverse pace to brisk as he walked back outside into the morning heat, onto the side-walk and continuing across the street.

"Anabaptists, Doc," said Cal, sneering, as both he and the physician looked on with interest at where the sheriff was heading and wondering what he would do about this inauspicious circumstance. "You know anything about them?"

"Yes, for sure, I know of them. I have seen a few as patients over time, quite regular check-ups and such, but on rare occasions," said Doctor Putnam, responding in as general terms as he could muster, knowing Cal would be trying to bait him in some strange Socratic game he often liked to play, leading his barbershop customers down cryptic verbal paths laced with landmines. "I suppose I see the ones from town more often than those from the colonies, as they are quite different, at least in their lifestyles."

"You treat them?" said Cal, with a look of confusion and sounding disappointed, as though the doctor had committed some grave sin. "You speak German?"

"No. I mean a bit, but no, not really. Their broken English is not too bad, the country ones. One can surmise the gist of the problem, and so can treat them in a rather effective enough manner—at least that is most often the case. And many of the ones from town, they have been so assimilated that they do speak perfect English, many without any accent whatsoever."

"But they're not even from town," said Cal, as if he were now more confused as to the physician's response. "They're from out across the county line, a different jurisdiction altogether."

"Well, no. The town ones are in town. You are speaking of these specific folks across the street with the sheriff, I presume. With those folks, and any others, mind you, if someone shows up to be looked over, or needs to be treated for an emergency or something rather serious, I am not going to turn away a patient in need. Or even for a smaller fix, which can often be completed in an expedient fashion. Rejecting them would not be the right thing to do, Calvin."

Cal continued with the trim of Doctor Putnam, giving a brief pause to consider the wise remarks of his patron, the physician, albeit with a look of some ongoing mystification.

"Very noble, Doc, indeed," said Cal, nodding as if in approval. "The Hippocratic Oath still stands, which is good to know—it's not just some relic from bygone times, like so many other things. It's real, even today." Cal spoke with a tone of mild condescension and some sarcasm, although Doctor Putnam could not quite read him.

"You do not see them in here, Calvin, only outside and around town the odd time?" said Doctor Putnam, treading with caution so as to avoid any unforeseen traps. "Maybe they come in here to get a quick trim from you once in a while?"

"Yeah, I see them around town sometimes, like out there now. But they don't come in here, not for cuts. I mean, look at them. They don't shave, that wild hair under those hats: Sweat, grease, dirt. I wouldn't doubt if they had bugs and spiders and their eggs and such. Lord knows what else. They'd have lice, the way they all live together—it's like a poor man's barracks on those colonies, from what I've seen. I don't know if I'd want them in here, to be honest with you. Lots of extra clean-up work afterwards, to keep my shop as pristine as it is. I'm not sure it would even be worth it for me, my time and effort for what? A few paltry bucks. And maybe the biggest problem of all is I don't speak any German," said Cal, as if the physician's point on broken English was not said nor understood by the barber.

"Oh, you have been out to one of the colonies before?" said Doctor Putnam, with a genuine curiosity about the supposed communal sect, while prodding to see if Cal was pulling his leg yet again. "I think it would be fascinating to see the past way of life, how they still farm and such—no modern equipment or machinery, no electricity, chores all done in the old-fashioned ways."

"Yes, I've been out there, watching them ploughing the fields with horse and ox. And I was helping them plough their other fields, in a sense. Heh. I saw their women doing the milking and churning butter by hand, their men out threshing the grain by hand and cutting wood to keep those shared home fires burning all winter. Imagine the smoke in those cramped buildings like that," said Cal, as he was speaking to the physician via the mirror in front of both of them, giving a mock gag at his thought of a smouldering cloud hovering throughout a large colony home. "Real romantic, if that's your idea of idyllic, Doc. That's a terrible lifestyle; everything about it is."

"What business did you have out there, if not to cut their hair?" said Doctor Putnam, questioning why Cal would be in their community at all if he felt the whole concept grotesque. "You were not really helping them in the field, I cannot imagine... Oh, I know. You have been out there to buy their produce, get some fresh garden vegetables and such, maybe some baking, sure thing."

"Sure thing, nothing," said Cal, moving with a deft swiftness to shoot down the doctor's hypothesis. "I wasn't out there to get; I was out there to give. I'm a man of great charity, Doc, you know me. I'm a philanthropist. Although, you could say I did get some, too—yes, yes, you could say that. Heh. I guess it wasn't all about the altruistic giving part of it, a smidgen. They hired me for my services thereof. Ha ha. But I wasn't taking their hair as I'm taking yours here, Doc. I left a little something behind; hair of a kind..."

"OK, and what was that, your services thereof?" said the physician, perplexed by what he assumed was another nonsensical riddle that Cal had cooked up, and he was hoping for Cal to stop beating around the bush. "I assume it has something to do with your barbershop pole there, the helix. You did a tooth extraction? A bloodletting? The corkscrew licensure. Maybe both, but I hope and am sure you did not give them the same special deal as you have offered to me? Come on now, Calvin."

"Doc, I cannot believe such a brilliant man as yourself is having such a dilly of a struggle with a simple, little puzzle like this. Let me tell you. What I left behind was: I left behind my glorious hair. Some call it ecru, others say burlywood. Close enough, but it's not blonde. And I should say, I do know my hair colours, Doc. I also left behind my beautiful eyes. Some call it ebbtide, others say reflecting pool. Close, but they're not blue. I'll give you sapphire, maybe. Anyway, I left them right there for those old-school Germans to take and to have. I did it because I'm helping them, trying to make them less backwards, so they diversify that stagnant genetic swamp they're living in. And I've done it a few times at some different colonies across the land. Twenty bucks a shot, let me tell you..."

"Oh, Calvin," said Doctor Putnam, interrupting Cal and rolling his eyes at him through the immense mirror in front of them, and then a direct eye-to-eye eyeroll minus the glass. "That old story is nothing but a puerile myth, an asinine old legend. They do not do that, not for those purposes. No way do they do that. Not still, if ever. No, never."

Cal and Doctor Putnam looked outside to where the sheriff was berating the vendors, yelling something and waving his arms about as if he were a large bird of prey about to take flight. The rickety produce wagon of the Anabaptists looked now like it was about to be packed up before they could even unpack and set up shop for the morning on the Main Street in town. George took out his pen and notepad in a feverish display and began writing away in a huff.

"I'm telling you they do it. They sure's shit do so. You're just jealous," said Cal, taking pauses to brush the loose stuff off Doctor Putnam's neck as he trimmed the remaining bits of hair, snipping away at them with great attention as if he were a surgeon. "My penis doesn't lie, Doc. Otherwise, they stay all inbred like they are, and they get more and more inbred over time. Dear Doctor, don't you remember your basic biology training? If I don't do it, to bring in some variety to that tired old German gene pool, they'll start growing tails and third eyes and such. They'll get sicker and sicker..."

"Calvin, Calvin, Calvin," said the physician, unable to stop smiling but not willing to entertain him with the full-on laugh Cal was angling for.

"And sicker and sicker," said Cal, continuing to talk while wrapping up the trim. "But say, listen, Doc. Speaking of treatments, you have antibiotics in your office there, right?"

"Um, yes, of course," said Doctor Putnam. "I do have some penicillin in my office, for emergencies. But the pharmacy is the proper channel for that, after I give a patient a prescription, should they require the medicine, after an examination, diagnosis..."

"Right, right, sure," said Cal, taking his own turn to interrupt the doctor. "But if I needed some, in a pinch, you could get me some? Maybe bring me some in here, say, next time you come back around for a trim in a couple of weeks?"

"Well, no—no, not really. You see, you need to come to my office and I could examine you, and give you a prescription if warranted. Do you have a need for a check-up now? I can certainly see you tomorrow, or even later today perhaps, Calvin. You saw me in here today, so I am quite happy to see you at my office today as well, in return," said Doctor Putnam, pleased with his generous offering of reciprocity for the barber, as uncertain as he was on where Cal was going with all this oblique talk of prescriptions for antibiotics.

"No, no, I'm fine, thanks Doc. I'm just fine right now," said Cal, not sure how to bridge to the heart of the subject. "It's just... I'm taking a little trip, you see. Down south, to the city there in a few weeks or so, and, uh, I, uh, I'd like some drugs, some of that medicine, you know, in case something should happen, as things can sometimes happen, in the south, and in the city."

"Well, Cal," said Doctor Putnam. "Whatever for—why would you need such a thing for travel to the city? It is not that dirty there, and nothing to be really concerned with. It is not as if you are travelling through the jungles in the Amazon or up the Nile, or somewhere with all those dangerous fevers and poisonous plants and bugs and such. Although, if you were going there, you would want long pants and need a gin and tonic more than anything. Ha ha. For the city, you will want to ensure you have your directions and are in the right neighbourhoods, the correct parts of town when you are down there, do not touch..."

"Listen, Doc," said Cal, cutting off the good doctor's counsel on reasonable travel tips. "I just want some fricking penicillin in case something goes wrong. If you could go ahead and bring me some in here, I'll pay you, and we're all square, OK? I'm not asking you for an organ transplant, or even some stitches or nothing."

Jingle, creak, screech, clatter, jingle.

"They think they can up and stroll into our decent town here, pull up their seedy old wagon, park it and start selling their veg on the road there, taking our money away and leaving their horse shit behind, not chipping in their fair share for the town services," said George, incredulous and with a feeling of insult as the sheriff made his return into the barbershop, searching for where he placed his essential coffee mug as he rambled on. "And right next to our own good greengrocer, of all the damned places to do it."

"So, I guess I'll see you a little bit later on then," said Cal, hastening the physician off, all the while trying to nail down his enterprising arrangement as he removed the barber's bib and brushed the last remnant bits of hair off the back of his patron's neck. "Thanks a lot, Doc. You look great, as always. I do say you'll be helping your patients in style this week."

"Pleasant enough folks, I do say. It's just you can't even tell them apart anymore. There're so many different kinds now, as similar as they might seem on the surface, with those clothes and the European accents and all," said George, pondering away aloud as he was trying to understand the different denominations. "Some of the men have those hats and beards, Asaph and Philander there with the plaid shirts and otherwise all in black. Not quite Johnny Cash, mind you. Great at farming, they are, no question about that. The women are always smiling, wearing those floral dresses and those doily bonnet thingamajigs in their hair..."

"Calvin, thanks a lot for the trim, and do please let me know if I can make an appointment for you—we will get you all set up, right and proper so," said Doctor Putnam, responding with appropriate graciousness but not taking the open-ended bait, which he believed Cal would have viewed as a concrete promise to return with said drugs in a time-sensitive manner and in due course.

"Some drive trucks and use fancy tractors and the newest combines now; some still use the horse and buggy like these folks here," said George, continuing his prattling on to himself with his examination on the lives and practices of the Anabaptists, as he saw it. Cal and Doctor Putnam were not paying him any attention on that topic, set as they were in their own unproductive dialogue on the practices of physicians, the processes of pharmacists, and the prescriptions of penicillin. "Some speak flawless English without any noticeable accent; others don't speak a lick of a word that's not a choppy German sound..."

"Sure, sure. Thanks, Doc," said Cal, with a clear agitation and wanting to hit back at the physician, as he knew he was not going to get his way on this one. "Say, Sheriff. Did you know our Doc also treats those Germans there? That's no doubt why they keep coming back to town: For Doc's tender loving care—and to run the grocer out of business. And we all know Jim catches them stealing from his hardware store, pocketing items, and what have you. But it turns out they get their noses wiped and their warts burned off by our good old Doc here. I was saying to him just now, you shouldn't keep letting them in like that, Doc. You should be turning them away, like I do. Jesus."

Before Doctor Putnam even had a chance to defend himself, the sheriff's mood was placated by the coffee he was now pouring for himself, taking in deep whiffs of the aroma emanating from the steam as he tipped the pot with a firm focus. "Nah, at the end of the day, they're harmless. And citizens just like us," said George, his anthropological diatribe and philosophical trance broken by the coffee. "Some people need the Riot Act read to 'em the odd time, maybe a little roughing up, write them up and make them pay the fines if they've no proper permits, a possible broken taillight on the wagon—have to keep them and everyone else in line around here. These folks today, well, they just needed to move down a few stalls is all—about half a block. Plus, the wife loves their sweet corn. And their wild blueberries, Saskatoons, huckleberries, what have you... They're key to her delicious pies, so I can't really force them out, not quite now, not during the important upcoming baking season, anyways."

Doctor Putnam smiled, set his payment down on the front counter, and gave a final look to Cal through the cutting mirror. "Thank you very much, Cal. It does look quite nice, indeed—great work, once again, sir."

"Hey, no problem at all, Doc, happy to help. Thanks [*jingle*] for coming in [*creak*], and you do something about those [*screech*] hillbilly dandelions in your front yard, looks like [*clatter*] a fucking [*jingle*] jungle," said Cal, speaking louder on each step of the doctor's, as he took his exit back out to the street. "George, you should write him up for that—it makes the whole neighbourhood look bad. Like we're in a ghetto in the wrong city, or out in a redneck's pasture or something."

"Jesus, Cal, you got a big ole bumblebee up your ass again?" said George, generally disinterested. "Relax. It's too hot for all that BS, especially with all that's going on of late. Including today, even this morning."

"Ah, nothing. Sorry to spoil your mood there, with your nice, fresh commie produce and all. Whatever. Now tell me about the commotion this morning out at the madhouse. I saw you racing around a couple of times, including as I was teeing off with my new driver. You made me slice right into those tall cypress trees off the road," said Cal, his mood and thoughts were also changing on a dime, and not wanting to pass up the opportunity on being the first one to hear the latest and greatest police story from the hospital. Cal would be the first to hear a new gem from the sheriff, again, which he could recount with great verve for his customers, over and over again and again, starting today and for months and years to come.

"Where's the sugar, Cal?" said George. "You know I take a tad of the sweet in your coffee here. It's so potent, this abysmal black sludge, as appreciative as I am and as fine as it is. I need you to sweeten the deal a little."

Extra! Extra!
Read all about [the horse]!

Jingle, creak, screech, clatter, jingle.

The paperboy walked through the door with this sense of duty and a look of purpose in his youthful and vibrant demeanour. Andrew had the coveted Main Street route in town, taking Monday morning off school to be able to deliver the 'hot off the press' local weekly newspaper to the business district in town. He also held several other routes in the afternoons and evenings, delivering the big city daily (albeit late in the day) and various flyers, as he was working hard to earn some money for himself and for his education, his future. He was also now helping his family, his younger siblings, hoping for and looking towards better days ahead for the household, the paper routes being part of the route out.

Andrew learned all kinds of indispensable lessons when passing through each and every single door he entered on his route. What he learned were practical lessons, essential ones for a young man to help advance himself along in this tough life. He learned a great deal about business, trades, and services. He was taught about history and culture. He watched the manners of folks, even if the social behaviours at this one specific stop might not be the most desirable type of manner worth emulating. These were the things he really needed to know but would never learn about while sitting at his school desk or reading his academic books of the curriculum, as many of the clients and proprietors explained to him. Andrew loved school, loved reading and learning, but the teachings he absorbed while delivering the news were real-world, clear, and now—invaluable lessons for life, authentic and no-nonsense.

On the various lessons of life and experiences with real people, nothing compared to what Andrew was often subjected to listening to once he walked through Cal's door. During his journey to the barbershop once a week, after that final jingle on the way in and before the first jingle on his exit, Andrew heard... Unimaginable, fantastical stories. Blunt truths. Obvious fictions. Hilarious, biting anecdotes. Unthinkable horrors. Jokes, clean and perverse. Oh, what Andrew was hearing in there! He never dared tell his parents nor siblings—he would not have dreamed of such a thing. He never dared tell anyone any of what he heard in the barbershop; save for maybe some of his schoolmates and, even then, he only told some of the tamest of the tales to his best of best friends on a sworn blood oath of secrecy.

But today he arrived, bringing the newspaper to folks downtown, along with his little brother in tow—one of his several little brothers, and this one a good six or seven or so odd years younger. While out for the fun adventure of a walk with his oldest brother, who was no doubt pulling double duty in babysitting him as well, this little brother also looked as if he was apprenticing to take over the paper route when Andrew would move on to some shifts at the café, or make an expansion play with his burgeoning grass-cutting and snow-shoveling business units, or somewhere as such, climbing up the labour force ladder within the next couple of years. The workload and the climb was the exit strategy to get out of his full house, taking leave of his home.

"Morning, Mr. M," said Andrew, flashing a cautious smile as he was holding the door open for his little brother, guiding him on in and directing him where to head to as he entered the barbershop. "Morning, Sheriff."

"Well, hi there, Andrew," said Cal, beaming as he leaned forward, showing his uncharacteristic non-crooked off-pearly front teeth in what seemed like a state of genuine happiness. "What's the good news today? And who do you have with you here on this fine morning—a little news helper?"

The younger brother stuck close to Andrew's side, trying to hide behind him as shy as he was, but also smiling as he peaked out to look around the curious shop. From his entry and with a quick scan of the room, Luke was becoming transfixed, looking beyond the barber, checking out the large canvas painting of a horse on the wall next to the barber's mirror, and another but different horse painting on the wall above the chairs in the cramped waiting area. The little brother then locked his focus towards Cal's porcelain horse figurine, which was standing on the counter next to the brushes and tools, right against the base of the mirror.

"Yes, sir," said Andrew, seeming concerned about his sibling's present awakening in the barbershop. "My little brother Luke here, he's been begging to come out on the route for months now, and he didn't have any school this morning, of course, what with late summer holidays, so here he is."

"Lazy teachers," said Cal, shaking his head. "Well, yes, you should show him around our fine downtown. Show him your route on Main Street and teach him all about the news business. He's liable to take over your route one day soon, I would imagine, as you're getting pretty old now to deliver the news, aren't you?" In this encouraging manner—towards Luke, even if with some subtle and light condescension towards Andrew—Cal swayed on his heels as he straightened out his back in a stretch, lessening the lustrous grin somewhat, wondering what little Luke's inquisitive smile was all about.

"Horsey!" said Luke, with a loud enough oomph, as much as the cheeky tyke could muster. Luke stood looking at the horse in a euphoric delight, with all his fears or discomforts on entering the unfamiliar shop (with these alien characters) having been rendered harmless and blown away by the concussive force of his equine-based jubilation, and maybe softened from a hint of Cal's warm grin.

"What's that, son?" said Cal, not quite comprehending him and so looking at Luke, who now pointed over Cal. George was also smiling, but as routine he was trying to conceal his own less white enamel that were more of a cornsilk hue. Andrew was a bit concerned about where all of this could lead, even as innocent as it appeared on the surface, while Cal turned himself around and looked behind and towards where Luke was pointing and now jamming his index finger forward like he was poking at something. "Oh, oh yes, my horses. My horsey! You like horseys? Yeah, that one on the end is a beaut. It's an Appaloosa, with that gorgeous coat. And spots! Great colours on him, what with that chestnut blanket. His name's Seabiscuit. You want to see him? Here he is," said Cal, as he reached out to pick up the select horse with some delicacy and finesse with his wonky fingers that looked like dull blades of a blender. He turned back towards the boys, hesitating for a second before bringing the figurine closer to Luke's eyes, giving him a good thorough four or five second viewing and leaning forward again, flashing a fresh grin and handing the horse over to an ecstatic Luke as if it were some rare gemstone or a nugget of gold.

"Careful with that, Luke. That's Mr. M's horse," said Andrew, shuffling in unease, trying to get one hand on it or at least in a position to cup and cradle it should Luke drop it with his slippery fingers. After standing still and staring at the horse in his hands for another few seconds, Luke went about playing with it, waving the horse around in a clucking manner, through the sky in giant leaps, a horse like a dolphin, galloping and jumping through the sub-orbital barbershop air; gravity be damned.

"Jesus, Andrew. Relax," said Cal, giving the paperboy a look implying that he should leave his little brother alone and stop babying him. "You can see he's fine. He's just playing with my horse. Luke, you like my horsey? I'll tell you what. You go ahead and you can keep that fine horse for yourself. You'll have lots of fun with him—he's a good one. He doesn't need to be in this stuffy old barbershop anymore—he needs some fresh air and nice grass in greener pastures. And you take real good care of him, you hear me?" Cal gave an affable wink to Luke, who was now beyond thrilled with the new toy that was not really a toy.

"Oh, thanks, Mr. M, but Luke doesn't need to take your horse. And he's already got a little toy horse at home, a soft plastic one, don't you, Luke?" said Andrew, as he was trying to fish the horse turned dolphin or fighter plane out of the sky, adjusting and rotating the paper bag over his shoulder in the opposite diagonal way to maintain his balance. "Yours is a Clydesdale, right Luke? With the big furry feet." Luke was oblivious to Andrew's attempted receptions, now jumping up and down across the room with the horse figurine in one hand, taking gigantic up-and-down motions, bringing the horse's hooves from the depths of the dusty and dark oak hardwood floor up to well over his own head, into the ether. Luke jumped up and the horsey jumped up even higher; Luke dropped down with a hard landing and the horsey thudded down even harder.

"Andrew, leave him alone. It's Luke's horse now, not mine. And it's not yours neither," said Cal, becoming irritated at Andrew for not letting his little brother have some fun. Andrew was also old enough, and Cal knew him well enough now, that he was rising in the great chain of people open to be ribbed at will by Cal in his barbershop, one more part of the key lessons Andrew would need to succeed in life, and lessons which only Cal could so impart with his unique wisdom, as a budding self-selected father figure. "Luke's having a grand old time here, ain't he? Or are you pouting because you're jealous I never gave the horse to you after all these years?" said Cal, snarky and satisfied with how pleased the kid was. Cal was smiling to himself while also directing his grin as public good to George, Luke, and Andrew, and back and forth, and over and over, with his ridiculous iridescent grin.

George remained content on his stool, enjoying his coffee in an ethereal solipsism as he was already reading the newspaper delivered by Andrew, the current version unlike the one he was reading earlier in the morning after his baseball dream, that paper dated and leftover from late last week. As he sipped his fresh coffee, it was as if George had just discovered this brilliant smelling and addictive beverage in some faraway foreign land and brought the exotic drink back home to the wild applause of his townsfolk. Or maybe it was because of his thorough reflection on the absolute perfection of the sugar-to-coffee ratio he had obtained, all in this peaceful moment. He looked up on occasion with his own grin when his self-reality was punctured by the commotion produced by the boisterous others around him. George would adjust the tempo of his smile to the volume and tone of those yammering on back and forth, as being amid their hullabaloo caused an inherent irritation—but the sheriff kept out of it, instead keeping up his blissful grin to maintain the serene plane of his personal satisfaction from some other world.

Andrew could do nothing but relent, letting Luke carry on as he fixed his paper bag's position yet again and made for the door. He was signaling to Luke that they had to move on with the job at hand and finish up with the route, this paper route that Luke felt some desperation of wanting to tag along on today with his sage older sibling, the big brother, out and about the town.

Luke looked back towards Cal, smiling a thank-you sort of a smile and turning his head as he proceeded to gallop the horse on the air road to the door. On the grand finale of a crosswise jump for both Luke and his new horse, Luke caught the toe of his left shoe in a chipped-out chunk of an original burnt umber-shaded piece of the oak floor, falling to both of his knees in a concurrent unison. The horse jumped and flew one final and magnificent vertical hurdle, towering through the air...

A total silence enveloped the room as everyone positioned themselves to witness the horse jump, now seeming to take place in slow motion. The event, the room, the barber, the sheriff, the paper boy, the paper boy's kid brother—all were in their own stationary pose, locked into their respective spots without even a blink from any single one of the eyeballs entranced by this uncertain scene, watching the strange Appaloosa show jumping horse trip on the obstacle with a brutal fumble, blowing its first off-the-shelf attempt at equestrian. Luke was already down and out, and now it was the horse's turn, tumbling back down from the rarefied firmament, back down to the hard reality of the ground—the hard as rock oak, this solid ground floor of Cal's barbershop.

The Hummel of a horse exploded on impact, hitting the floor between Andrew, who was standing at the door, and Luke, who was swiveling up and onto his side from his now-scraped knees, in his present place by the base of the main trimming throne. The horse busted into four or five decent chunks, including one being a more or less clean break of the head. And there were at least a dozen smaller shattered pieces, plus some powdery residue sprinkled amongst all the solid bits and pieces for good and unrepairable measure, landing as if to provide a coating of ceramic dust over the cocoa-coloured floor.

Luke cried in an as instantaneous and hysterical manner as imaginable. It was a great tragedy, this fatality for the little toy horsey, and this casualty for his own two tiny knees, with delicate scrapes but in the end repairable, unlike the Hummel. Andrew stood blushing, mortified, with a sad look but also one of knowing this or something similar was the inevitable outcome in such a circumstance. Cal, the older childless bachelor, was in shock, with an authentic expression of being stunned beyond belief that such a terrible thing as that could possibly happen. George let out a loud 'heh,' smiling wider as he was finding great humour in the tragedy and went right back to reading the newspaper, taking another sip of his divine coffee.

"You broke my beautiful horse," said Cal, in a true rage, steaming. "You little... Rascal!"

Luke carried on with his bawling, brought on by his accidental destruction of the horse, his bloodied knees, and the anger of Cal and Andrew, although in no particular order. Andrew gathered himself up, collected the substantive horse pieces in his hands with care and offered a speedy and profuse apology to Cal while berating his inconsolable brother. Andrew set the collectible ceramic litter in the soiled garbage can under the closer counter by the coffee pot, returning to collect Luke, pulling him up off the floor, doing so in a part-angry punishment, part-mother hen, part-protective brother mode while offering a final apology and salutation to Mr. M.

"Sheriff, you need to arrest this boy," said Cal, using a tentative if strong tone, somewhere in the grey zone between dead serious and a mere joke. "He broke my horse; you saw it for yourself. Caught red-handed, right here."

George was struggling to read Cal, as normal Cal would have his crooked smile on with a glint so you knew where he was going with it, and it was fine. Because it was such a small child this time, even if he was in fact filled with genuine anger, George did not even need to bother looking up from behind the newspaper. *Just deadpan Cal. My condolences on your loss. Heh.*

"I didn't see nothing happen, no sir," said George, without deviation from his near trance-like state as he continued sitting on his stool at the side counter. "Nope, but I did hear that loud bang. Calvin, was that you dropping another mug of your fine coffee again?" George peaked out from the side of his paper, catching Luke's teary eye as Andrew was dusting him off, giving Luke a wide smile and an amicable wink. "No problem, son. Minor accidents like that are bound to happen from time to time. That's just the way she goes."

Already recovering somewhat, this gesture by George was helping to soothe the boy and placate Andrew, and Andrew knew all was fine and dandy in any event, knowing Mr. M well enough as he did. However, Andrew was still embarrassed by his kid brother's clumsy antics and disastrous actions. Luke then looked back up to Cal, with a glance of terror and sorrow and apology, when Cal reverted to the original warm smile of his welcoming first greeting only moments earlier.

"Of course, of course. I joke, I kid," said Cal, grinning and empathizing with little Luke. "Sheriff's right. It's no problem at all on the horsey there, kiddo. Time to put him down anyways—he had a good long life in here as it was. But he didn't do nothing but sit up on that ledge all day, getting tired and old... Just like our good sheriff sitting right there. You have a good older brother here, Luke. So you go finish the paper route with him today, and next time I see you in here I bet you'll be the one bringing me that paper. We all need to read the news, keep up to speed on the events in this here crazy town of ours."

An introductory meeting

Bill headed into town, driving down the main drag on the side of the street across from the barbershop, pulling his half-ton truck in behind the re-parked Anabaptist wagon of fresh produce, giving the local German farmers an empty space of enough room in front of his truck so they could still unload to vend their garden goods without touching his front bumper. When it was determined he had left enough room for that, Bill opened his door and noticed someone had pulled in right behind him within seconds, an individual who was also now getting out of his own vehicle, some beaten to hell compact wretch of a car.

Bill got out of his truck first, having the slight lead, proceeding to cross the street, heading towards the hypnotic spin of Cal's corkscrew helix. He was halfway across the street when he realized the man in the little car on the tail of his truck was now on the tail of Bill's person. Bill did not think much of it, as the street was now vibrant with shoppers moseying from storefront to storefront, and to and from the large park off the town library, which sat kitty-corner. Reaching the sidewalk and the base of the steps leading up and into the barbershop, Greg was right there, following his bumper, his heels, culminating with this meeting at the door. Looking at each other, parallel and bottlenecked at this place, Bill nodded as pleasantry and looked towards the door while Greg did as well, both now pondering on who would try to take that one cordial step up and open Cal's creaky door for the other fellow also in need of a trim.

Bill remembered Greg from the elevator. At last year's harvest, Greg showed an inability to give a proper visual grade of the grain as he went about in his awkward mannerisms, including this apparent depth perception problem of invading the personal space of another. Greg's recollection of that specific encounter with Bill was there, if vague, but he did know of Bill with a greater certainty, the town being as small as it was, the farming sector even smaller, and the elevator's customer base smaller yet. And he knew of Bill all the more so with Bill being the preeminent maker of craft beverage products in the area, those coveted by all and enjoyed to the utmost by residents lucky enough to obtain some of his special goods.

Each of them went ahead with a slight movement at the door handle, in concurrence as if they were dueling feints. With an overload of these simultaneous events and in too close a proximity, both then backed off and deferred to the other one, seeming to continue this silly dance on the sidewalk. Greg looked down to the step and Bill looked up to the barber's 'open' sign. Bill grumbled without subtlety and moved at the door with force, where he opened it up and stepped aside for Greg, making the decision clear. "Go on in then, pal," said Bill, almost shooing Greg inside at this stage.

Greg extended Bill's invitation by way of walking straight into the shop and hopping right up into the empty haircutting chair, not slowing his stride even an iota, while signaling to Cal on the way in that that was indeed where he was heading. The barber had no choice but to 'OK' the move in turn with a thumbs up, knowing from Walter that Greg was on his way in and Cal knowing he needed to get busy now with two paying clients in his shop: One seated and ready to go; one about to sit down in a waiting chair.

"Well, hey there, Gregory. Go ahead and sit on down now, would you," said Cal, offering a pleasant greeting to Greg, all the while approving of his action to the more cognizant guests and patrons, even if in his patented blunt and sarcastic tone.

"And hello there, Bill. Good to see you, too, sir," said Cal. Bill sat in the regular waiting chair next to the same area where the sheriff continued sitting on his stool while leaning on the counter, continuing to sip his sweet and miraculous coffee, setting his mug down next to the newspaper now laid flat out on the shelf beside his elbow.

"How are you two fine gents doing this splendid Monday morn?" said George, rotating his position to acknowledge and greet both Bill and Greg.

"It's a hot son of a bitch out there. That last bit of crop has got to come off, the wife and dog are sick, and both my trucks need some sweet, tender love," said Bill, as he gave a slow nod to Cal and pivoted his head even slower to acknowledge George, who nodded back in full agreement. "That'd make a good country and western song, wouldn't it?"

"I saw your old man early this morning out on the course, Greg," said Cal, beaming again with his vaudevillian smile. "He was giving right hell to some nutter picking berries in the rough on five, making a hell of a mess, puking all over the place. I'd have beat the purple monster myself—and I don't mean my own," said Cal, unconventional in his way of beginning a story and trying to glean further information or at least an opinion from others, all the while looking for a solid laugh from his crude jokes and style of humour, if not unpopular. "Well, I kind of mean that too, actually... Anyways, your pa's a forgiving man, though—he's a good man, Greg." Cal wrapped the bib over Greg and began the trim. He knew Greg's style—he knew the style of everyone, whether they knew it themselves or not. Cal would take care of it with his strange fingers and hands, and his unique and odd method of going about providing a dangerous, if necessary, haircut.

"That sounds about like pa," said Greg, with a blush and a smirk. "A new story every day out there with those lunatics. I don't know how he's done it for so damn long. Not sure how long I'll last myself on those grounds."

"Yes, I understand you're going to be working with him now, which is great to hear. They need more good men at that place. Wild place gets crazier and crazier by the day. 'Every new moon; brings scores of fresh loons.' Doesn't she go something like that? Heh," said Cal, as if a poet trying to recount some ancient rhyme he had either heard at one point or maybe one he had just made up himself off-the-cuff at some past stage. "It's called the lunar cycle, get it?"

This flurry of activity since opening the shop had, for some time now, diverted what was still bubbling away in Cal's mind throughout the entire morning. Cal could not let it go, but he needed the perfect moment as a gentle segue to broach this most important question now well beyond the top of his mind—and sure to be on the front burner of the minds of these others in the room, or at least the sentient others present. Cal knew there was an event of some consequence, the goings-on he had heard on the course, and he could see it and read it all over George—his demeanour, disposition, mannerisms, and his tone even suggested he wanted to shout out the explanation for the early morning commotion. Cal could tell the sheriff wanted to tell them the story, and he wanted Cal to bring it up to allow him to recount it, which would occur any minute now... There were many stories and great tales, but today was not the same—this seemed bigger for some reason. To get George to talk, Cal created what he assumed was that perfect bridge he was looking for, by citing crazy Greg going to work back at the institution with his also nutty father Walter, and with all those resident-patients at the even madder loony bin. However, it appeared to Cal he would need to be a bit more explicit...

"So, our fair sheriff, George: What, pray tell, was all that racket about going on down at the hospital at the break of dawn?" said Cal, throwing the question right out there for him and the others, lobbing this softball Sheriff's way. "You or your boys threw off a couple of my shots with my new driver—first round with that beauty new club I got Jim to order in for me. You should see the distance I can get with that fine new Wilson product. It's brilliant. Persimmon wood, steel shaft, they worked in some graphite for this alloy admixture perfection."

"Well, Calvin, I was about to go and ask you the exact same thing," said Sheriff, obliged now to answer, but not before he got Cal worked up a bit first. "Figured you'd know more than anyone else since you were present and could even help with the investigation, perhaps."

"The only thing I know that should be investigated for certain is that Nazi maniac," said Cal, with a sureness in his voice. "Christ, you should've seen him this morning. No real need for an investigation though, as we all know. They need to put that homicidal maniac down before he hurts someone else here on this side of the pond, the right side. After that's done, we'll get back to investigating whatever early morning games you were up to down the hill. If I file a noise complaint, disturbing the peace or something like that from during my round, you'll investigate that, Sheriff? And sure thing, I'll help you out on that and anything else, George."

"Yes, sir, Calvin. Let me get my notepad out here..." said Sheriff, moving the slightest bit to leverage himself up on his stool while pulling out of his back pocket an air notepad on which to write nothing down with his non-existent pen. "Fancy new club not working as advertised... Misdemeanour for sure, at least."

"Oh, charades then? Hilarious!" said Cal, with a light laugh. "I'll come by the station later, make it real formal and official for you. But in the meantime, I'll tell you what I saw: I presume there was lots of dust coming behind those caraganas, after looking up from hearing that first siren on nine, but I couldn't see anything. I assumed it was you and your crew, hearing you ripping by so fast, looking around my little obstruction, and you were long gone. And that was after almost getting hit by your trusty deputy on the other road off five. Where in the hell did Corb learn to drive like that? You know, come to think of it, it wasn't moving, but I even saw a car parked across the road on the island, just over this side of the bridge on my drive down real early, and it was still there on my drive back. That's a bare minimum of at least three cars I encountered. How many police colleagues did you have to have out there this morning—a few of you at least, unless it was you were practicing some silly drills or something else?"

"There were a few of us, yep. Sure was," said George, about to unload with the full story, but he figured he should still rib Cal first, since Cal was so concerned enough to do some ribbing of his own stemming from the noisy and purported disruption of his precious weekly round of golf. "The deputy was, in fact, in the area when you were still in bed—might've been him on the island by that point. That was something else, though, nothing to worry about there, the first one you're talking about at sunrise or so—not related to him almost finishing you off by the fifth hole, where you must have been jaywalking, which is illegal. Anyways, that one was some kid from out of town, jerking off while driving his car at night—not a smart idea, even if it might have seemed so at the time, horny and bored as he must've been. He was whacking a little too hard and pulled his wheel over, I guess, hitting a huge poplar tree by the road coming right off the bridge. He went straight through the windshield like a missile, landing in a patch of juniper before a little black bear came along, gorging away at his torso when we arrived before dawn, pants still down around the poor kid's ankles. Case closed on that one."

The haircut was paused as three faces with dropped jaws and wide eyes stared at the sheriff in horror as he continued on with his surreal police summary of the first of the chilling events of the morning.

"It could've been anyone on your return trip, though, for the main incident of the morning. It might have been Corb on five as well, since you say it was him who you saw, so it must've been. But on nine, hmm... No idea. That might've been one of the several—and I do say, *several*—cars from a few of the towns over, came to help us out, the purported good folks they claim they are. We'd help them, too, but, you know... None of them have much going on in those towns, pretty tedious stuff, so not much we could do in any event, and they like a little action with us once in a while—it keeps them on their toes, good training for them, every now and then. But on nine, Cal... We were pretty much wrapped up by then, so I'm not too sure which one or from where though, the one that was affecting you, to the detriment of your important game, Cal. Or should I call you Sam, Mr. Sam Snead? But either way, let me tell you, on behalf of the fine men in blue everywhere, we do, with sincerity, apologize for any inconvenience it may have caused you and your exquisite new Wilson driver; this club of some alchemy and those unfortunate sirens bunging up your pivotal yardage."

Everyone had a good chuckle while listening to the sheriff's disturbing monologue, taking a few extra seconds to process that new information from their pal, the sheriff, George: Police cars from neighbouring towns, seeming to be quite a few of them, or at least might have been a bunch. It was something not insignificant that had happened down and out at the mental hospital. Yet Sheriff was back here now, lazing away in the shop with a wide, coffee-sipping smile, seeming more concerned with unlicensed produce vendors than anything else. And so, it must have been put well under control earlier, and by this hour it must have been long over and done with, whatever it was, as George had just confirmed.

"Yep, one car flew down the concession by my place first thing, too. Going to beat hell on that road, towards the river behind the hospital," said Bill, figuring he should chime in before the conversation got going too far along. "Then I was working in the shop and the barn, and in the house and whatnot, but I'm sure I heard more than one or two during the course of it all, whatever major ruckus you and your boys were attending to."

"Right, and we know what you were working on there, in your modest shack, Bill," said Cal, wanting so much to know what the mêlée was all about, yet in an odd move he was changing the direction himself, trying to triage so many important conversations, which would impart so many critical answers, all at once. "So, how about some more of those amazing samples? We'll do a taste test for you, for quality control purposes, to help you out. Those would go over real well right now, hot as hell as it is out there. And by the way, Bill: Where's my last order? Yeesh, man—you need to ramp up your production, scale it up a bit."

"Well, it's your lucky day, I guess, as your order is in the truck, behind your German friends with their beets and rhubarb and onions and such, whatever they're selling," said Bill, pleased with the fresh creation he had bottled last week and brought along this morning, knowing Cal at minimum would be interested, and George and Greg would be sure to welcome a taste as well. "And since we're still in the a.m., today's sample is a sweet, fruity little number, most unique. I hope and trust you all enjoy blackberries and honey loaded up with some serious kick. But before we have a wee snort, I'd also like to hear George on the hospital or river activity this morning. My curiosity is piqued."

"Yeah, way out on the river," said Sheriff, offering confirmation as he teased the assembled barber and patrons. "Or everyone ended up down there, at least. That's where he went when they saw him take off from the grounds. And Bill, don't you worry about me writing you up for all that unofficial product—I only want you to see here that my cup's almost empty, coffee as it is. I'm getting mighty thirsty myself in this heat, if you get my drift. I'll need a little splash of something if we're to get into the weeds of this here story. Need to wet my beak to loosen my tongue a tad."

"Sheriff, for Christ's sake, cut to the chase with your chase story," said Cal, an excited, agitated, antsy Cal, who could not handle the flirting around this drama any longer. Cal was of the strong opinion the emergency foreplay had gone on for far too long, the preface well complete, and it was time for the main action.

"Jesus, ants in your goddamn pants," said Sheriff, trying to settle Cal down. "Hold onto your horses, Cal. Well, your horse is gone, I guess, shattered poor old thing. Rest in peace. But hold on to something, will you? Your horse paintings up there, maybe. The story is this: There was an escape this morning. A serious one, from someone you don't want escaping. But—*but*—he's back inside, strapped to the cold concrete floor and pumped back up, all full of drugs again. They're pumping him full, even into his broken arms and legs. Probably even zapping him up a bit by now, too—what are we here, about eleven or so?" said George, looking down at his watch, then up to the clock above the big mirror next to one of the horse paintings, confirming the correct time, or averaging out the close enough results. "Not quite eleven, but yes, we're getting there, indeed."

"Christ, who got out?" said Cal, the suspense peaking, along with his energy. "One of the batshit crazy vets, or one of those new loony folks from the east? No, you guys wouldn't give two shits about them. No harm, no foul. Ha—I got it! The Colonel. The man in all white, am I right?"

It's thumb suckin' great

They referred to him as Mr. Sanders, one alias among several other made-up names. He was about forty years of age at the time of the original events, which precipitated his final and absolute institutionalization—there was no getting out for him again, stuck as he was in this different sort of a coop, where he would be housed for all time. Also called the Colonel—this synonymous moniker, or the Dirty Bird, as a more eponymous one—he indeed lived on a farm himself, but one from a few towns over, around forty or so miles north and east of the hospital, and well within the catchment radius to the point of almost being considered a local lad, at least by the big city newspapers. He had been in and out since his earliest days, over and over—a repeat offender, even if for sundry and minor violations, this recurring patient. He did not open his mouth until he was a four-year-old; he screamed for the next four, then babbled in incoherence thereafter, for all his wicked days outside of the pen. Between his folks—the poor bastards, having a literal lack of wealth, as well as being hard done by in a more general sense, and with this calamitous spawn of an offspring—and the doctors, they had him drugged up in a twenty-four seven zombie stupor after he kept killing the family pigs, trying to make such flavoursome bacon in the yard with not much more than a knife and his teeth, using a blood-soaked and -dripping clothes-line to cure the pork belly and flesh over a fire and out in the sunlight, something he did even if it was cloudy or rainy, a soggy take, and in the frigid winter months, a frozen cut. This occurred multiple times. Drugs were administered: Downers, lots and lots of them. But one morning, when his ma was laying down with a headache and an earache, and his pa was in town running errands, including buying Aspirin for his wife and refilling downer prescriptions for the son, what happened was the incident to end all incidents...

Mr. Sanders had a coffee (not a mere mug but a full pot) and some soda (not one lonely bottle but a six-pack)—rinse, lather, repeat. He walked out onto the porch, leaning on the rustic veranda, viewing the neighbour's home quarter across the concession line, looking at their big red barn, squinting next to the barn, past the horses and to: The little white chicken coop. The Colonel ran as if not needing to pace himself nor catch his breath, sprinting a robotic full out for five minutes—an incredible, if unorthodox, under four-minute mile, this new Olympic champion in his tight dirty jeans and filthy tattered classic blue Cubs cap.

The pleasant neighbour wife was washing the family dishes at the time, humming a wholesome hymn to herself, glancing a nonchalant gaze through the lemon-yellow curtains of the filmy kitchen window. When the plate she was scrubbing slid back through the soapy suds onto the serviceable stainless-steel bottom, she grabbed the edge where the counter met the sink, which cushioned the collapse, but slick, wet hands could not hold on as she slipped onto her behind on the hard floor. Her young daughter did not move from her steaming bowl of oatmeal—she could only stare on, as she was also stunned, if for a different reason than her mom. Her older son ran over without hesitation to help his fallen mama. *Did I really just see what I saw?* She was sitting on the kitchen floor in total shock. *Should I scream? Should I cry?* While she was about to yell at the kids to ensure they did not look outside that same window, the deafening blast they all heard beat her to it and drowned her out. Their pa, who had been in the vicinity during the episode, fired a round straight up—birds scattered and other livestock sounds could be heard throughout the now zoo-like yard and beyond. At present, the barrel, double, in fact—twenty inches of pure twelve-gauge power; buck or bird chambered, it mattered not—was pointed at Mr. Sanders, where if fired, the pattern would have been a complete head-to-toe pulverizing kill shot. In an absurd concurrence, the shotgun was also pointed at the chicken, who would have been but a poor fowl of collateral damage and death in this potential scene of a macabre and compounded tenderization.

"Sophia," said the father and husband, screaming back towards the house as loud as he had ever yelled. "Don't you look outside, Sophia. Call the sheriff. You call him right now, you hear?"

"I'm calling him, Pa," said his son, the obedient and responsive boy, moving with hustle while still attending to and speaking for his mama, a fallen Sophia. He was intuitive enough to understand the urgency of his father's voice, regardless of what ghastly scene was playing out in the yard through that kitchen window of horrors. "Deputy is on his way, Pa—he's coming."

RIP, Dear Chickens.

"No. No, Mr. Sanders, the tender chicken-lover... He passed on a few months back now," said George, explaining the situation while not sure how the gossipy Cal had not already heard about this most existential of news through the local grapevine. "The Sanders family were as disgusted as anyone else, so they said to put him in a numbered one—disowned him then and there, as if somehow they weren't already quite yet at that phase. Yep, chicken-lover is in the great numbered field now, way down the road, and way down below. 'Where no one goes; where no one knows,' I like to say. Well, Ming helped me out with that one, a bit of a riddle it is, kind of. Anyways, the Colonel is buried, tucked in all safe and sound at the bottom of the greasy bucket. He was still wearing that juvenile ratty Cubs cap he always wore, his one possession in this world, that old blue rag of a dirty hat—a funny kind of sentimental value there, but it didn't work to cage in whatever was going on under that lid, or it sent it way down into his filthy drawers, alas. And so, he's probably getting raped by demonic roosters as he now burns in Hell, forever. Getting cocked by the big red cock's cock today, and for always. A Prometheus for our prairies—the eternal torment part, not the creation part, that is. And he won't have no Hercules to rescue him from that terrifying ole devil of a rooster—not down there, no way, Jose. If there's any true and divine justice in the afterlife, I should say."

"Died! What? How come I wasn't told the chicken-fucker died? I've told the Colonel's story a dozen times in the past few months alone, and here Mr. Sanders is not even with us any longer," said Cal, baffled. He was stunned, but when George had finished his long and steady monologue, Cal had to let up and present a damper version of the fake rage. There was legitimacy in his disappointment in that he was unaware of the event of the demise of this beast, hoping for just enough anger to show George his displeasure at not being notified of this important news of the departed, but not enough to further deviate from the key new story at hand, being the escape of some pugnacious and depraved patient earlier in the day.

An embarrassed and flabbergasted Cal ripped the bib from Greg, shook the loose hair to the floor beneath, signaled Greg to go sit back down at the waiting chair—he knew Greg would want to stay and hear this story out to the end—motioned Bill forward onto the trimming throne, and stood waiting to bib him up. All the while, Cal was still flummoxed by the untimely (timely) demise of the poor old (evil monster) man of the coop.

"Cal, you didn't get our news release on it?" said George, pretending to be perplexed. "Nor the one from the hospital? And you'd have sensed the paper and radio station would have come right on by the shop here to get your reaction to the breaking story, if not to even write the obit. I'm stumped. Well, I'll tell my secretary there, Mary, to ensure she has your correct coordinates so there won't be any similar miscommunication errors in the future."

"Sheriff, speaking of secretaries, you should have seen the one I saw the other day, this incredible blonde lady with rosy lips, wearing this ruby lipstick, and sporting a colossal rack, er, I mean, ears," said Cal, showing his deft ability to change subjects on a dime, even when he knew he wanted to maintain his focus on a different trajectory. "Well, this one, she walked by here, right in front of the window late last week—good lord. It was right after lunch, I got back from Ming's, and I'm sitting here reading the paper and looking out to the park there... Ah no, that pathetic drunk bum on that bench—you've got to do something about him, George... Anyways, the Sun's out high and bright, and she turns into the window to adjust herself, looking into the sheen so she can find the right angle of the reflection—you know, to fix her make-up or hair or something. Come to think of it, I should've invited her in to use my proper barber mirror here... But I was pretty stunned myself as she leaned forward, and those tits—my goodness gracious. Massive! To protect and serve, am I right? I almost went and wet myself, sitting right there where you're sitting now, Greg."

"Jesus, Calvin," said George, putting his hands over his face in mock disgust. "Please don't talk about Mary like that, not around me nor anyone else. Please. Please and thank you, Cal."

"Jeez, it felt a bit damp here, Cal. That's gross," said Greg, smiling, as he felt great being brought into the conversation, socializing with the group even if sometimes at his own considerable personal expense, though not uncommon territory for Greg, pathetic and pitiable as he was, even if through no real fault of his own, those being the breaks as they are.

"Christ, Greg," said Cal, hitting back. "That's you getting yourself wet from hearing that story. Whoa, clean yourself up, man. Anyways, so if not the chicken-banger, who got out today? The ghost of the Colonel, the spirit of Mr. Sanders, risen up from the unknown numbered stone to tenderize and spice up the bird yet again? Who got out then? On my round, I saw Fred the Skunk, some vomiting purple sleepwalker, Dwight... Yes, by the way, another side-note: I saw Dwight, Sheriff. He was standing around on the fifth hole with Greg's dad until this newest zombie collapsed in the heat, and I sure's shit didn't get your memo on that one neither, Dwight's arrival in town, checking into his new and forever abode. I had to pause my game and help Walter out with that ghoul, tossing him in a wheelbarrow. And I saw Johnny Nazi, so I can rule out all those nutter folks myself. What about that giant perogy-eating mess? He slaughtered that family. Wouldn't want Yuri out, now, would we? Eating our perogies and killing our kin. But if anyone is chained up in rusty old iron shackles in the basement dungeon, it's got to be that guy—come to think of it, it begs the question on why they let him out for the annual perogy-eating contest, to be sure. But if it wasn't him, who the hell was it?"

"Yuri's not in shackles in the dungeon, not even close," said Greg, thinking he might have some other new and valuable insider information for Cal, even if unsure of its relevance. "I was shocked as shit myself yesterday when I went to see pa about the job stuff, and there's Yuri going by pushing two wheelbarrows like, one in each hand, and they were full to the top with ripe apples, some rolling right out and under as he wheeled them along. Unsupervised even. I couldn't believe it—I was a bit scared to get out my car. I rolled up my windows in case he smelled my beef jerky in the car and came running over thinking it was bacon perogies or something, the size of a freighter as that bastard is, he could probably flip my car right over for a snack. We all know his appetite. Jeez Louise."

"Greg, what in the hell are you talking about?" said Cal, enunciating each syllable in the question. "George, what in the hell is Greg talking about?"

"Yes, I'm afraid Greg's correct, Cal, as that sounds about right," said George, in a matter-of-fact sort of way, as slow as his words came out. "I've been concerned for some time now, and I've requested that he should be chained up, er, restrained. Done it numerous times, in fact. But one of those new doctors assures us they've got him so drugged up enough that he's harmless, giving him something like sleeping pills for an elephant, a real one. Although he can walk and function under the influence of the medication, but his brain is in some transformed state that he can no longer think his murderous thoughts. The doctor's adamant on that point, which that feeble judge in the city seems to concur with. And they seem to need all the help they can get with their apple harvest going on now, so…"

"Oh, right. How could I have ever forgotten about that critical endeavour?" said Cal, rolling his eyes. "What a joke. Like Bill here, he's got lots of harvest going on, several different crops to take off—which, Bill, we're most certainly grateful to you for, remember. And so, Bill, when he needs a hand at harvest the odd time, he brings in unshackled mass murderers to help him pick his crops, you know, wheelbarrow the barley and oats around and the like? No! Bill doesn't do that because Bill doesn't want to get shot or carved up and slaughtered. And Bill wants to keep Rose good and safe. But at the hospital… Oh, la-dee-da, they need some extra hands in the garden to get them McIntoshes off in time. Jesus Murphy."

"You're right, Cal. It would never happen, but can you imagine…" said Bill, thinking of the worst outcome. "Imagine that lone little girl, her new family, her aunt and uncle or whoever she's living with now… Imagine they bring her out to see the flowers, get her a new toy or little chair from the industrial shop, take a photo with the river as a nice backdrop, or whatever. And they're up there, sniffing the pretty pink petunias right as big old Yuri strolls on by with his wheelbarrow, whistling away to himself, perogy dreaming. I couldn't imagine the poor thing. That would trigger the worst nightmares for all time for anyone, and especially the sweet little girl. The lone survivor, hiding under her bed that day, watching the blood drip down from the quilt above, her dead siblings on top. It'd be an instant nightmare right then and there in the day, wide awake, triggering God knows what kind of sickly flashbacks. Unreal. And so, so sad."

"Well, good point, Bill," said Cal, in full agreement on the problem of Yuri. "Bang on the money. She sees Yuri shoot and stab up her entire family, and then she sees him in the line-up at the cop shop to put him away, where that bastard is supposed to be drugged up beyond comprehension and chained up to the foundation stones in the basement, those massive homesteaders they used. If we're being true, he should have been done away with on-site when they nailed him, a quick bit of copper and lead. But yeah, innocent thing should never have to see him again, like Greg did there. And now George is telling us he's the one who got away. Revolting, indeed.

"Oh, shit, my man—he's really struggling out there today," said Cal, distracted by the scene outside his front shop window. "What's Corb going to do to Lester?"

As the group kept thinking about the wandering Yuri and his escape, they approached the window so each of them was able to look out at the angle that Cal was able to see from his haircutting position, where they watched the tragicomedy of the deputy and Les unfold in the park, across the street and kitty-corner to the barbershop. Les was laying on a park bench a couple of feet off the street and sidewalk proper, shaded by the old green elm trees, out of the direct sunlight and the heat. George's key deputy, Corb, walked slowly up to Les, giving the local Irish tippler a nudge with his boot to wake him up from his morning slumber.

The works of Lester

The age of Les was unknown. He might have been in his thirties, although could have been as young as to be in his late twenties; or, he might be as old as to be in his forties... Or fifties, maybe. He was a fine-looking chap, like a mythical Celtic warrior, as if he were from some other life in some distant barbarian human past—not really so long ago. Les enjoyed painting pictures. He was also known to enjoy a nice drink at least once in a while. In both vocations of painting and drinking, he was outstanding in the select capacities. He painted scenery of the local and regional variety, adding in precise patches of a specific shade of green without fail, as if to channel his forefathers on the ancestral Emerald Isle. Les painted the geography of the area: Farmyards in the nearby country-side, canoes on the river, shinny on the pond, cattle in the pasture, harvest in action. And he painted town streets-capes, including neighbouring towns and their own town main drag right where he now slept in the park on the opposite side of the street from the barbershop. His favou-rite subjects to paint were horses, going so far as to try and squeeze a horse or two into each painting, somehow—this was not always met with great success, but they were valiant efforts nonetheless. Les was such a good artist that a bank commissioned him to paint murals on the sides of some of their branches in the region, as well as paint por-traits of the retail storefronts on the main street blocks of many of the towns along the highway and further out, each where their bank centred the painting. And Les made sure there was a gorgeous horse somewhere on the road in all those chronicling portraits and murals.

The only thing to throw Les off his art game was the poison—and no doubt some deeper and darker demons that led him to the bottle in the first place. He got back on the wagon to paint long enough to allow for a reserve of sufficient funds in the piggybank, then he fell right back off the wagon again, a harder fall each time, it seemed, gravitating back towards the Gaelic glass. Les would soon go AWOL, losing sentience, leaving the task of painting for weeks at a time. Eventually he would come to, needing to get back up and at it, back on the wagon, resurfacing at the area rodeos he so enjoyed, ending up back at his work in the park, and back on Main Street to sell his undeniably great works to the proud art collectors of town.

Cal was a huge fan of the art of Les, believing the more prominent the horse, the better the painting. If he could only get a little bit of help for his artist, Cal believed Les would end up gracing the walls of the finest galleries around the world, hung in rococo mahogany frames in the rooms of Queens and Kings, Presidents and Prime Ministers—any sound and proper leader, just not some bastard maniac criminal Führer. *It makes darn good and eminent sense that Les will one day have his own dedicated gallery here in his hometown, too. I just hope it won't be of a sad and posthumous nature, but who knows. At the end of the day, who cares, I guess. But he deserves it. I know it to be true.*

Cal was a tireless champion for Les, as he figured such a unique art gallery would drive tourists to their town from all over the region, country, and well beyond. The hordes of tourists and their ready dollars from further afield could see the world-class art, splash in the aquamarine lake, fish for the record trout, hunt the biggest buck, and play a round of golf at the halcyon nuthouse nine. *They could eat some zhu sun at Ming's for lunch and have some of Sheriff's wife's berry pie for dessert.* Cal was daydreaming away again as he was looking back at George. *Or his secretary's pie.* Cal considered that maybe if they continued emptying out the institution (or even if not), an individual could spend a pretend few hours or a day as a mental patient, a practical experience with some novel verisimilitude. *It could be a new kind of tourism, where you could get pretend lobotomies, along with some real treatment methods in small doses, such as receiving a minor shock, taking a micro-dose of a pleasant drug with no known side effects, a brief psychedelic high or that new thing Doc Ox was talking about, with no risk and no strings, that sort of thing. You could even get a steam in the sauna of a box, but that will have to cost extra.* Cal was already imagining the new money flowing in, while seeing himself being nominated for all sorts of marketing awards, the genius already walking up to the stage to give his acceptance speech, determining which of the select few he would thank. *You could even try out certain specific treatments in full, like the tourist-patient taking their morning cold or hot bath, with a nurse who will tie you down, cover and lock you right up. Maybe they could have contests set up to see who could take the longest bath and the like...*

The barber was trying to distract himself from the kerfuffle outside by explaining his favourite painting, which was the main horse piece of art hanging nearest to the barber's mirror. Cal was talking about this one painting by Les, then spoke of the others he had at home in several rooms: One painting of some kids having a snowball fight, one of the ancient days of harvest with an old threshing crew, one of rounding up cattle in a pasture. All the works in the portfolio of Les were tied together by horses—both

Cal and Les dearly loved their horses, respectively. Cal brought his private fantasy out into the open of the barbershop, telling his pals and patrons how one day all this original art will be highly desired by the most discerning of global collectors, fetching enormous sums at auction, with many of the works owned by Cal being housed in a museum. Bill gave a hearty chuckle, Greg giggled like a schoolgirl, and George laughed so hard he welled up and began a self-forced coughing fit to regain his breath.

"Laugh all you want, you dummies," said Cal, knowing their inevitable reaction was coming. "He's the best we have around here, with his unique art, and he's got no competition. So, you're bloody well rights he should one day have his own museum. And tell me, why in the hell not?"

They all laughed aloud again and laughed even harder as they continued to watch the incident unfold in the park, looking out the window and starting to question the sanity of Cal, thinking him possibly delusional, perhaps resulting from all the time he spent on the grounds of the mental institution, diagnosing a clinical osmosis of sorts.

"I know a banker who bought some a few years back, seemed to be collecting them like you, Cal," said Bill, acknowledging the barber might not be so far off with his fantastical daydreaming, even if with a tone of some doubt. "But he moved to the city a while ago when he got promoted, so I'm not too sure if he took them along with him or maybe chucked them out in the move. The thing is, Calvin, you can't have a museum if there aren't any paintings unless you go and buy them all from now on, creating your own monopoly. Find a way to miniaturize the murals. You'd still have to promote your friend there to the big city artists and scholars at the colleges, and then you'll be the wealthy benefactor art-dealer type of elite guy. You could call it *Lester's Modern Art Gallery*, *Cal's Private Collection*, or something fancy, something cultured like that. Big city folks might eat that right up. You might make a mint."

The clients of Cal continued staring out the window, looking towards the park. Startled from the jolt of Corb, Les shifted as he woke, elbowing his brown paper bag onto the ground by accident, it seeming to land between the small dirt walking path and the tuft of grass leading onto the grounds of the park encircling the library. The dutiful deputy, Corb, began giving Les a tough time, while the barbershop observers were unsure if the poorly concealed bottle had been broken on its fall, considering what the contents might have been and what might have been remaining of whatever it was. Continuing to give him shit, Corb took the bag away as he was pointing and yelling at Les, telling him something along the lines of that he should get his ass moving out of the park and get his shit together, or some other such similar counsel.

"That bag might've been a sandwich, a nice roast beef on rye from Ming, from his new western menu," said Cal, in a half-hearted tone and lacking any sincerity, as it was plain he was disappointed in the scene, his conviction and dream beginning to fade, his fantasy losing the luster of Lester.

"Now, why in the hell would Corb steal such a thing, Calvin," said George, defending his deputy even though he understood the level of disappointment Cal was feeling. "That's a lot of beef juice and condiments coming out of that bag. Look at that thing dripping away."

"That's disgusting," said Greg, wanting to chime in with something, anything.

"I know, I know," said Cal, conceding that his great artist had some difficult issues, perhaps ones that were irredeemable.

Les was slumbering further down to a position of sitting on the ground with his back against the bench, putting his hands over his face, about to run his hands through his long, greasy hair before Corb returned to the scene. Having taken not ten steps forward, Corb came back to shoo Les off and out of the park, back to somewhere such as his art studio, or more likely, to the liquor store parking lot or alley behind the building.

"Calvin, you're telling us that drunk sod of a bum out there, Paddy O'McFitzPatrick, painted your picture here, this celebrated horse?" said George, knowing it was true. George looked back towards the equine art to reflect for a moment on the painting, the colour and depth of the strokes from the brush. His focus shifted to the mirror below the frame, staring through it to view the always empty extra cutting chair across from where the painting hung—with all the frequent bullshitting and one customer in the main trimming chair, Cal did not even bother trying to juggle two active trimming chairs, so he used the spare one for setting out his supplies, draping the coats of his guests, and such. "And Bill, how about those new samples? And all our many orders—have anything with you today? Thought you said you did."

"Sheriff, you know I love my horses, no question. And that's a hell of a portrait there, am I right?" said Cal, jumping in first to ask George in a decided tone, but scanning the other patrons for their concurrent endorsement of said picture he so loved. Cal continued to look back at the grand work of art, viewing the painting of the darker-than-darkest chocolate-coloured horse—with a lighter shade of a heavy blanket draped over its back in the winter scene, standing solo in the corral in the snow, its eyes slightly off-centred and misaligned—and back to his clients. "And if I don't drop a little change, or even a small bill or two, to buy that beautiful painting from that there so-called 'drunk bum,' now how's he going to be able to buy himself a little warmth, some small comfort? Something to take him back to Éire, if only for a few hours. And he's a good paying client, too."

Jingle, creak, screech, clatter, jingle.

Bill snuck out of the barber's chair, still donning the bib and all, going out to his truck to get the samples and regular orders.

"Now that is charitable of you, indeed, good sir," said George, sneering. "My kudos and apologies for thinking anything else. You own yourself a beautiful piece of art. And his blood got a little warmer as a result. I hope you bought that from him in the winter months, making your purchases after the snow flies and cold sets in. That moonshine would make him boil in this month; especially Bill's there... Oh, good, he's going out to get it, and even with his hairy bib still on!" The sheriff was contemplating all of this as he slowed down his speech even further while trying to gauge the reactions of Cal and Greg. "But if he's a client, why do you keep complaining to me then about him sitting out there when you're feeding that habit? You're keeping him about his ways. You are now, Cal. And why are you taking him in as a customer? I hope to God you clean up after, like hose this place down in disinfectant and cleaner and alcohol, and all that equipment—Christ, you use that same stuff on us, Cal."

"Well, that's a fair point. True enough, George. But Jesus, not on the cleaning thing—I can't believe you'd question my impeccable cleanliness around here, as everything gets the full alcohol treatment, my tools and my customers. You well know that. What a diversion—nice try. But yeah, I guess my love of horses and my love of a respectable drink now and then, well... And it is a nice painting, you all agreed, right?" said Cal, again seeking confirmation and an endorsement with a quick glance at his patron pals. "And he isn't really doing any harm out there. I just wish he'd sleep around the corner or somewhere else, out of town or at least off the main drag and out of the park... Anyways, we weren't talking about horses, George—you keep on changing the channel here. We were talking about perogies. Cheesy plump potato man, was he your doughy accused on the lam, your unctuous escapee? I saw Fred the Skunk, Johnny Johann, and the new soldier Dwight working with the purple puke monster—I saw all of them and more out on the course this morning, so it couldn't have been any of them, not from that lot of loony lifers."

Jingle, creak, screech, clatter, jingle.

"Well, there're the beverages we've been longing for—thank you, Bill. Good man. Now you can get your trim finished up in comfort," said George, in genuine need of a splash of something, anything from Bill's truck would suffice. "Oh, Calvin. Your horses and your booze. And not only one kind of booze—classic Mr. Cal. Nope, you sure wouldn't want the chicken-lover out. You don't want Mr. Sanders anywhere near decent folks. Not the ghost of the Colonel neither, although I guess we don't really get much of a say on that one. Nor perogies, I suppose. He wiped out ten in the family of eleven... That's the worst thing

I've ever seen in my many years on the force, and I pray to Christ I never see anything like that one again, certainly not on the scale of what he did, and how he did it. Sickening methods, that proxy of the devil himself.

"But, speaking of today... No, he's still safe and sound, locked away in those shackles you spoke of," said George, breaking out in a laugh as though he was disgusted but still wanting to amuse himself somehow. "I guess Greg leaked the info on his actual state, his freedom about the institution grounds, as we just discussed. If that twisted justice was not the case, if I was the judge, or if I was a shrink rather than the sheriff, Yuri's muscles would be too atrophied to run anywhere. And too weak to be pushing wheelbarrows about. While that's not the case, as obviously he is walking about picking apples and carting them around, it should go without saying that he's far too stout and aged to run much, if he could even run anywhere at all that is, what with all those perogies and what have you. No, it wasn't our grand perogy champ who made an escape this morning. Nope, not him."

Yum! Yum! Great!

O ur man is... Any last guesses?" said the sheriff, scanning the eyes of the room like watching a tennis match of reactions. With his own clownish but firm grin locked in, George looked around the barbershop and saw one smirk, one non-reaction, and one 'for Christ's sake, get on with it' type of a scowl. "OK, alright then. Gentlemen, our winner is... Drumroll, please:

"Mr. Campbell, he's our man; if he can't do it, no one can.

"With a cursed can; a fucking soup can. Wholesome as he is good, he is not—not good, nor wholesome, not at all. But... We got him back inside, safe and sound. Nothing some rolled up wet pants and a little billy-clubbing couldn't fix back up and right proper."

George continued to lean against the buffet with the coffee, allowing the others a free moment to let the news sink in for each one of them, knowing this news he had delivered was, indeed, disturbing news.

Cal stood to near attention like a soldier, breaking briefly from the home-stretch part of the trim he was giving Bill.

Greg sat back down in a waiting chair, slouching into the seat as if he were melting away like a snowman in May.

Bill sat straight up in the barber's chair, leaning forward and spilling some of the snips of clipped hair from the bib onto the floor.

Each of the individuals was jogging their minds to recall

who it was that George was referencing, if only for the shortest of the barely a millisecond it took for their brains to kick into high gear. They were somewhat stunned, trying to remember him with precision, but of course it took the briefest of moments to recollect the specific events... It was a hearty meal, with an actual heart as the entrée, with a first course of an organ-based chunky broth, as their minds were for the most part in the same place: It was death, a death by and for the soup can. They were all realizing that Leon (aka Soupy, aka Tin Can Man, aka Mr. Campbell) had been on the outside again this morning, right here outside of town, however brief it might have been; however full his belly might have already been on the beach.

Soup du jour

It was about five or so years earlier when a young boy went missing from his neighbourhood in a remote mill town a few hours north of the institution. This child, an eight-year-old, had been seen a short time before the disappearance, playing ball with Leon. Leon was himself a young man, if not quite still a child. When questioned, Leon confirmed to the police: The two of them were playing an innocent game of catch in the park on the edge of town. In trying to find the boy, search parties looked everywhere in and out of town, turning up sweet nothing during the initial stages. When the search became serious, a full-bore sleuthing, a police dog soon sniffed out the young boy's bloodied shirt, finding it chucked away with some other evidence in an industrial garbage dumpster between the park and town. In a second follow-up police interview one day later, Leon opened up as they went about squeezing the gory details from him, in the figurative sense; unlike Leon, who had squeezed the guts and gore and life out of the young boy, in the most literal one.

As a young fifteen-year-old lad himself, and from the same neighbourhood, Leon overthrew the ball on purpose, into the evergreen woods on the fringe of the unmanicured playground, a wild pitch from the southpaw in the outfield. Having no chance of catching it, the young victim gave chase, encouraged by and followed close behind by the older kid, Leon, the errant ball tosser. The ball landed around where Leon had set his trap in advance, as if he were preparing a snare to catch a rabbit. As the little boy crouched down by a spruce tree to retrieve the overthrown ball in this otherwise enjoyable game of catch, Leon pounced on him like a pride of starving lions hunting a baby impala in a pen. Leon used a pre-placed rock to smash the kid's skull, in repetition, crushing it, killing him. The basic mystery of the disappearance was solved in good time, but that unhappy ending was not the end, at least not all of it. Placed next to the rock was a staged open fire pit, a lighter, knife, can opener, and... A can of brand name tomato soup. There were also fresh tomatoes set about, two full vines of the juicy red nightshades uprooted and set next to the other supplies; it was learned by the police that Leon convinced the young chap to steal them himself, for Leon and him at some future point of a nice picnic break during catch, their own private seventh inning stretch in the woods. And so, the boy ripped the ripe plants right out from his kind mother's own potted garden at home, as if any further salt was needed to rub in the open wound, in a kind of act of ultimate insult to injury. When the local police had the essentials of the case down and were done vomiting in the interview room and throughout the station, they turned young Leon (the wannabe sous chef) over to the psychiatrists at the mental hospital.

What the doctors learned from Leon was already a legend, as the newspapers had reported on during the expedited trial of an in absentia perpetrator, and it was sure to go down in the annals of madhouse history, well afar from their town and far beyond their time. In a nutshell—or in a small can: Leon flayed his victim, built the campfire, and cooked the flesh in the tomato soup tin vessel. By creating a potion from this recipe received from the demons who spoke to him, the soupy elixir would provide him with many special powers and gifts, which would in turn allow him to fight off other rival devils and demons on their behalf. Superman had super-human strength, the power of flight, and x-ray vision; Leon would gain these powers and more. It was well known that lead poisoning from cans caused insanity—as used by the likes of pirates of old and more recent sailors such as Franklin, eliciting those wrong turns made throughout the maze of the Arctic Archipelago—but it was as if each container Leon had eaten from, right up to this point in his life now in his should-be innocent-ish teenage years, was from a lead can of old, and then he had eaten the can for dessert, for good measure. *Something along those lines was true of Leon*, each of them thought, at one time or another. *As well as with many other residents of the grand institution, in the can and off their nut...*

"You just had to look for the red and white label, no?" said Bill, offering his barbershop chums a great example of his signature deadpan tone, sitting in the trimming throne and wanting to remind these guys of his clever wit and of his living, breathing, sitting presence among them. "If you can follow the trail of the salty soda cracker crumbs, they'll lead you right to him, like the path that Hansel and Gretel knew so well."

"Yeah, he was a bit red, that's for sure—in a few different places, at least," said George, pondering on Leon's situation then and now. "Not much else there, I don't think, as he's pretty torn up. He took a few spills, I think past that stone wall on the road in. He must've rolled down in the scrub. The boys saw him stagger and stumble as he tried to climb up the cliff on the island a few times before he made it up and over and through those willows. Bruised and cut to hell on those rocks, bloodied and covered himself in burrs as they dragged him out of the valley and back up top. And he was all sandy, let me tell you... Looked like he got in a fight at a sandcastle building contest or something. Maybe had to wrestle a sturgeon on the way over. Incredible."

"Island?" said Cal, perplexed, unfocused, and not feeling the bother nor need to clarify his short one-word question he directed at George.

"Island. In the river," said George, explaining it as if Cal had never even heard the word before. Cal still stood deer-in-headlights stunned, so the sheriff proceeded with his enlightening education of an explanation to the barber. "A piece of land in the middle of some water is called an island. That might not be quite up to the standards of the Oxford dictionary or some such similar other august book, but I'm not too sure how else to define it beyond that."

"In the river?" said Cal, still appearing to not understand the description or definition of 'island' as provided by George.

"Jesus, Calvin," said George, rolling his eyes while pausing. "A river is water that flows…"

"Buzz off, I know what a river is. And a doggone island. How did Tin Can Man get all the way down to the river? And then he went through the river and its currents—how'd he manage that? And to what island? You mean one of those little sand bars? I'd hardly call that an island, and there certainly aren't any cliffs for Soupy to fall from," said Cal, turning around his initial slow and speechless reaction, clarifying it now and also moving to segue, bridging further to obtain additional details and a more complete understanding of the entire incident.

"There is a decent-sized island out there. Especially around this time of year. Where the creek flows out into the river on the other side—right down the hill, across from the hospital. There's not much of one in spring, during the run-off or heavy rains, but it's a pretty good size now. A bit of water flowing there, but he ran on through the sand over to it, then on over to the other side. No need to swim or boat, really—have to trudge through those little rapids maybe some, but wouldn't get more than your ankles or calves wet… Anyways, he wasn't tied down right and wasn't drugged up enough, so he ran right off—decided he'd found an opportunity to flee, so he took it. Smart, to be honest, if you're him. Nurses saw him run through the front grounds. He went out the door and down the steps when someone came in from the outside, then he ran through them flower beds—no word if he stopped to smell the marigolds… You'd better take some notes down now, Calvin, so you get all of this. Leon went through the lilac bushes by the green on nine and jumped the stone wall along the road. They gave chase with them big butterfly nets, late to the party to some extent, but they saw him run over to the island. They gave up and called us in somewhere around that point. But, in fairness, they did try to monitor him with the binocs so as to not lose the general direction or sight of Mr. Campbell, mind you."

They all took a quiet several seconds to themselves to process the sheriff's account of the escape, from the chase out the hospital door and down into the river valley below, to the brutal and gory consequences that could have been once again—it would have been a new soup du jour, on a sand bar this time, a close to tropical first course.

"How come the butterfly police weren't able to catch up with him and nab him before he got too far afield?" said Cal, as if George had not already given a full enough explanation of how Leon had made his daring escape. "With a couple of them after him, you'd think it would be no problem at all, chasing down the zombie before he got to the beach or elsewhere. Unless they made a mistake and gave him uppers instead of downers for breakfast, the wrong pills with his porridge. It seems those nurses mightn't've had their own pick-me-up morning coffee—quite the opposite of you, George. Or maybe it was the Tin Can Man who had a surreptitious cup or two, stealing the contraband caffeine, like the Skunk does with his sickly soda pops. They shouldn't even have any of that stuff made accessible on the institution grounds for them. Coffee and cola under lock and key."

"Well, the joe or the pop, pills or not, Mr. Campbell didn't beeline anywhere before he made it to the stone wall, nor afterwards for that matter. Although, even if he had, it seems with respect to his cardio, he was in a lot better shape than those psych nurses," said George, as if in a moment of reflection. "They're a bit out of shape, no question. And Leon is still a young man, of course. Batshit crazy as he is up top, he's got him some good fresh lungs and legs—maybe all that baseball practice. Unlike some of those older nurses, with tired bodies hobbling them even if housing those right wise minds."

As each of the present chaps were also all quite out of shape themselves (to varying degrees), the barber and his clients gave an ironic consideration of this fact, imagining overweight nurses of exaggerated sizes and prehistoric ages wearing all pure white from head to toe, carrying giant butterfly nets, stopping by the flower beds to rest, panting and trying to regain their breathes as Leon danced around them with agility and energy unseen save for amongst the greatest of great running backs, and as if playing against larger yet oxygen-depleted children.

"Maybe it's because those psych nurses are in training for the next perogy-eating contest—a lot of work to do if you're going to try and take on the beast Yuri, the undisputed heavyweight champ of the world that he is," said Bill, trying to reason why they could not catch Leon, even if through his rough jokes. "Rather than what they should be training on for their jobs, they're training their gastrointestinal systems, getting them in shape for the main event. Though I guess, in fairness, some extra weight wouldn't be the most terrible thing to have in there when they need to pin down some of those most agitated of fellows. There'd be more wrestling inside the building than sprints or marathons outside, I would think. And even if a straw weight could run and catch a detached big man like Yuri, he'd still need a shotgun to put him down in the flower beds. Or at least a beefy tranq dart of some robust, near-lethal formula."

"Yep, fair point, indeed," said George, as if he had just finished listening to a speech on a new ground-breaking theory on some key matter at hand, hearing the oral arguments of Bill's dissertation. "And Mr. Campbell couldn't've been full of downers if he was running at that speed, or any speed at all beyond a slobbering stroll, or more like a creepy crawl. Leon crossed the wall at first, and then he headed out the opposite way from where he ended up. He went down out towards the old graveyard first, zig-zagging his way along pretty good, down some goat trail-looking switchbacks and on over to the riverbanks before plodding on to his final stop, where he found himself trapped."

The glowing grave: One must be brave

T he graveyard?" said Cal, flummoxed yet again. "That's out back of the greenhouses, away from the river. We were talking about Mr. Sanders, your chicken-lover fiend of a pal, going there for a good rest in peace. Now you're saying Soupy went out there, and he somehow managed to return all the way back and down to the actual river, after? Christ, he must have been playing with those guards or nurses or whatever you want to call them, toying with them on the grounds. Jesus, and I was right there then, at that exact time—had to have been. Man, I could've watched the entire show myself if I'd have known that was what all the sirens were about! I could've even helped out—I could've drove some balls at Leon with my new Wilson... Then walked over to finish the beast off with the sturdy five-iron."

"Well, it sounds like Mr. Campbell was running basic patterns around them, like at football practice. But that was out front, not in the back," said George, agreeing with Cal while offering clarity on the precise location of the select shenanigans. "I don't mean that big, numbered grave-yard, with all the unknown souls of the damned—which, by the way, I recently learned, is almost the identical size and shape of a football field, only a little longer and wider before the sidelines of the pretty thick trees and brush now. And I don't mean the new one out there neither. I mean that little one out on the hill all by itself, as you're already heading on down to the river. It's south and a bit east of the building, not straight west, as the river is. It's an isolated spot unless you're a deer or bird or porcupine or something."

"That's the one way out a ways, with the glowing grave," said Greg, piping up to be the first to state the obvious, while trying to insert some unique knowledge of his own to the ever broadening and quickening conversation. "Pa said I'll have to go mow that tomorrow or sometime in the first days, the next few days. Said he hasn't cut the grass there once yet this summer, so I imagine it's a bloody mess of a jungle by now, with a lot of thick dead grass and weeds and shit, too."

"Glowing grave?" said Cal, continuing with his questions on these most basic things of which all the others seemed to be well aware of, but of which he, for some strange and conspiratorial reason, knew nothing about. He was beginning to worry if his deserved reputation was being ruined, his long-established and great credibility in all matters of the mental hospital sullied, going to tatters and right there in his own barbershop, in the presence of his most loyal of patrons. "What's that, like when a relative puts a candle by the headstone or something, to keep their spirit alive, or some kind of folklore or mysticism, some supernatural horseshit?"

"Jesus, Calvin," said George, laughing at the barber and rolling his eyes a second time. "You're losing your way on us. Lordy, help us. You've got to keep up, man."

Bill smirked and Greg chuckled.

"You cocksuckers," said Cal, growing angry, more at

himself for slipping than at his customers for poking fun at his misunderstandings and errant follies. "So Soupy's at this candle grave thingy, and then he heads down to the river... Finish the fucking story—stop stalling on us, Sheriff. It's getting close to lunch. Giddy-on-up, now, will you, please?"

"There aren't no candles in that cemetery. You almost can't even access it anymore, with the original road being shut down years ago now—Greg, you'll have to go all the way around by my road to get in there if you want to mow it, probably why Walter hasn't done it, and I don't blame him," said Bill, providing further information on the location of the glowing grave, as he prepared to have another go at Cal. "Cal, you should go out there one night when it's real nice and dark, and you can experience it for yourself, in person. That's the best way to do it, get that first-hand view of it. It must be an evening with a clear sky. Let us know how many candles you can count."

"Yeah, and if you've got a crush on Sheriff's sexretary, you should take her out there," said Greg, giggling at Bill's joke like he was a teenage boy, while not picking up on the nuance around certain boundaries of his own jokes he was wanting to crack. "If it's a dark, clear night, you'd probably get a hug and a little kiss, maybe even get to cop a feel. Tie goes to the runner at first base."

"Gregory, go easy now," said George, steering Greg away from that topic, an uncommon example of chivalrousness in the barbershop. "I don't want to take you in for the harassment of Mary, nor for getting Cal all worked up, not right before lunch."

"Yep, my neighbour farms the quarter section next to that small burial plot," said Bill, also wanting to help channel the conversation further along and out of its current rut. "It's the last bit of farmland by the river before it slopes downwards. A bit of grain, but he runs some cattle on those hilltops, as it's decent pasture for grazing. He rents it from the hospital, who I guess still owns all that land. He clears the weeds around the roads in the area for them too, hay salvage and such, but it seems as though mowing the cemetery itself isn't in the contract. Says lots of kids go out on the weekends, I bet to try and cop that feel or steal a base, as Greg suggests. Probably more strikeouts than home runs, but who knows these days."

Cal was fuming while standing in his barbershop, holding a comb in one of his mangled hands and scissors in the other. He was angry he did not know about this so-called 'glowing grave,' whatever that meant. He was irritated with constant deviations from the core story at hand, the one that had been so cruel in stealing his attention at the golf course, his curiosity bubbling away since the end of the round, and now he realized it was even the case since his early start on the golf course, with the various new pieces of information now coming to light. Cal was livid. He remained silent, seeing no further point in asking any more questions, knowing they would not be answered, or at least they would be answered at much too slow of a pace for his current wants and needs, and with too many unfunny jokes during the sidetracking.

"Yes, it's not a numbered one, not a mass one, not a fancy town or church one," said George, detailing the specifics of the graveyard in question. "It's a bit of them all mixed together, distinct in that it's the first one out there, from day one, way back around the end of the long reign of Queen Victoria. Accepted those first customers during the Roosevelt administration—Teddy, that is. And for just the first few years was when it was active—still burying the patients there, that is. Before, during, and shortly after the Great War was the only time when they used it. It's been long since inactive now, de-commissioned, like something you might see in some ghost town in the country in Europe, like by an ancient castle or a village obliterated in one of their many wars they seem to be so keen on always having over there. One of the first patients here had a loving family of some sort, I assume, as he has quite a nice headstone in place. An ivory-coloured marble, I think. Or like a porcelain or almond alabaster. Most of the others don't even have a marker on them at all, only the few lucky souls. For some, bad brains meant bad markers—for many, or most. So much abandonment. So sad."

"It's red granite, the glowing one," said Greg, comfortable and confident with his knowledge on this subject of colours and rocks, while trying to lift the mood. "It still sparkles, or shines, I guess. Or both. Or whatever. At night, I mean."

"Oh right, so Greg, you're familiar, indeed," said George, feeling as though he ought to give Greg some basic kudos when it was due, lifting his self-esteem even if having to smack him back down when he crossed too far over the line. "I'm thinking of a different one. That's the exact one, you said it, like a light, faint red rock."

"That's where I first slipped Deb the tongue," said Greg, grinning with purpose, like Genghis Khan might have flashed a smile at his conquering comrades, after some first or another for him, for the millionth time.

"Calvin, would you say the colour of the granite headstone is more of a red, as Greg says, like an apple, or more of a pinkish or coral hue, like a blossom or even potash?" said George, baiting Cal in a more overt way.

Cal did not bite nor budge, even as in his head he was telling Sheriff, *Go fuck yourself.*

"And right behind that stone, it's grown in and around it now for the most part, those menacing thick caraganas that never stop popping up, never dying off even in a drought, almost as if they seem to thrive on it," said Bill, offering a further explanation, having his own direct experience at the abandoned cemetery to share. "But the headstone peeks out enough to still see it today, so many decades later. I went up close a few years ago and it wasn't even weathered that bad, still in a quite nice, new shape. For as old as it is, it's rather remarkable, must be sort of sheltered on the hill from the worst elements at least. Hell of a rock. Can't imagine descendants or any family are visiting it today, if they ever did after the initial putting it up back then at the burial. Some rich family embarrassed but respectful in their way. A bit moving, in a sense. But still kind of sad, wretched."

"Correct, yet again," said George, seeming pleased to talk about something other than the living patients that kept tormenting him in this life of today, even if it was on the more eerie elements on the periphery of the institution. "While on an enchanting and crystal-clear night, one with a full moon out—it's ideal if there's a harvest type of moon, or a blood moon, as some call them... Once in a blue moon, or whatnot. And at the right angle—the most precise, unadulterated field of vision—the moonlight hits the rock, and it shines, creating a natural glare that looks a lot like a glowing halo type of effect, sort of like an illusion. It's only from that certain, exact vantage point, or you'd never know the thing was even there. At night, that is. If you can find it and hit that perfect night, the stone is entrancing, utterly so."

George, Bill, and Greg could tell the anger of Cal was lessening as he was becoming mesmerized by these new and mystical descriptions of things he had yet to discover. Still not done with Bill, the barber had slowed the trimming right down, trying to focus on the haircut job at hand, while they could see in his eyes of woolgathering he was wandering through this evening graveyard scenario in his head, as if planning his own tour of the cemetery for tonight, now that he knew where it was and what it was he would be seeing—even if it was a definite guarantee that Mary would not be attending the viewing of the glowing grave with Cal this evening, alas.

"What Greg did with his true love Deb, and what my son told me about—and sounds like what the high school kids still do... It sounds like what folks have done is—except for Cal here—drive out there and they walk down into the graveyard with their girlfriends, or would-be girlfriends," said Bill, presenting the barbershop quartet with the complete contemporary legend of the surreal glowing grave, as if telling them an absurd ghost story on this sunny morning to start the week. "The boys introduce their girls to old Cecil there, show them the stone, and they make up stories about him, creating a whole narrative around him and his macabre monument. They ask and answer questions, the entire who, what, where, when, why, and how of it all. It's as if they're telling ghost stories but actually showing them—show, don't tell. And so, they ask and answer questions to flesh it out, such as:

'Who was Cecil?'

'He was just a regular farm kid like anyone else from around here, but from the days of the earliest of the very first settlers' homesteads.'

'Where was Cecil from?'

'He was from a typical prairie town like any other, not fifty miles from the institution and our town here today.'

'What did Cecil do to end up at the institution so long ago, so early on?'

'Not unlike so many others back then and after him, he had a false accusation thrown against him, saying he had committed some heinous act or another, and he was a bit of an unstable type and a loner. And so, the charge, diagnosis, and conviction... They all stuck.'

'How did Cecil die there so young?'

'He was murdered by a doctor at the asylum, one of the first to try out lobotomies on the patients, but he botched the operation, making Cecil a bloody and braindead mess, a tortured guinea pig. The crank doctor had to cover up his brutal errors, so he smothered poor Cecil with a pillow and cleaned him back up before pronouncing him dead, as if he had died of a purely natural cause of a real normal sort.'

'Why does the grave of Cecil glow?'

'His soul is trapped in there. His ghost spirit remains as a gift from God to him, so he can spend his afterlife damning and haunting the graveyard, the hospital and its grounds, staff, patients, and visitors, for all of eternity.'

"That sort of crass stuff. The polished granite in the moonlight, that faux aura of old Cecil, it scares the shit right out of them. And with their hormones running like the wild wind, the little perverts can hold their girls tight and safe, then they can go and make out—if they haven't already pissed themselves by that point."

As inane and comic as Bill's story was, the group looked as though they themselves had been frightened; grown men scared out of their wits by the legend of the glowing grave—which only boiled down to something simple like: In the nighttime, if you can make it out in the caraganas, you can make out in the car.

"Some assumed it was a farmyard light from way across the river somewheres, or maybe a trick was being played somehow, but it's only the moon beaming down on that quartz in the right light, not unlike the reflection of the moonlight on a calm lake," said George, giving further reasoning on the phenomena of the glowing grave. "Some also said seeing this marvel was a bad omen or a horrible portent of some sort, but that superstitious bullshit is just for the real stupid ones, like the aged cat ladies. Not that you'd want to make out with those mystics. Not that there's anything wrong with that, Cal. But you be sure to leave Mary out of it all though, including out of your dirty mind."

With the lightest of laughs, a pause was maintained for a quiet moment, considering the myth of the glowing grave, hidden away in the first ancient cemetery of the mental asylum grounds, now long abandoned to the caraganas off a near-abandoned road somewhere on a hill close to the thick bush of the river valley.

Breaking the silence, his steam having burnt off, asking a question to his group of regulars while trying to keep as straight and emotionless a face as he could put on, the struggle that it was, Cal said, "Who's Cecil?"

"OK, OK. So you followed his tracks in the sand," said Cal, segueing from the ghost stories of the glowing grave back to the more immediate affair of the great escape of the hungry patient with the powers of Superman and more. "And once your butterfly deputies passed out in the begonias, you let some dogs out—I imagine Johann would have appreciated seeing the barking shepherds in action again, if he weren't already preoccupied with his wasp-related troubles, or busy retreating from the menacing water bomber... Why all the commotion, then? Why'd you need all your pals from towns over, from jurisdictions beyond, all that effort to put one little bowl of tomato soup back in the secure tin can?"

"Well, Calvin," said George, giving the barber a look as if he were a dumb child with another stupid question that had an obvious answer, as the sheriff believed the meticulous examination of the morning's events was now concluded. "As you're not even aware of the island there, nor the glowing grave... It's obvious you're unaware of those sand bars—not your sand bar islands, but the wide-open sand sitting in those channels now. The riverbeds are almost dry, with only tiny trickles of a stream flowing through at this point in the year, or certain sections of it at least. All the kids go down there and have parties, bonfires and dancing, some staying overnight, as if camping, plus some fishing and fighting, and fucking, no doubt. Half the town goes down there to sunbathe in the daytime—there are a million footprints out there, all seeking a tan, looking to gain some bronze while soaking up that essential vitamin D. If Leon crossed right over to the other side, he's already in another jurisdiction. Our towns and police forces, we've got to work together to put that son of a bitch down before he got hungry and needed to eat again—soup or not. We were trying to avoid an unplanned picnic at the beach. We can't do much to prevent the spontaneous picnics the wolves and cougars sometimes enjoy as they trek through the valley, but we've got to work hard to prevent any Leon-instigated picnics. It wouldn't have been the watermelon or strawberries young Leon was looking for, not competing with the picnic ants. No, not with his love of tomatoes, his obsession with the broth, or his culinary fetish, I suppose. Then him trying to fly away, for some other fatty dessert down the road, or down the river..."

As disgusting as George's last explanation sounded, Cal was becoming hungry from his busy morning, and it only reminded him of his gurgling, growling stomach, now cramping up a bit with hunger pains, if also somewhat sore from the arduous round of golf. Cal was not a cannibal; he was a civilized human being. And it had already been a long, hot and active morning without food, save for the sole browning banana he ate on his way out the door in town, finishing it as he headed down towards the pastoral golf course at the crack of dawn.

"Good Lord and thank God," said Cal in a congratulatory tone. "Well, Sheriff, you know I want to make sure it's all good, that's all. And you and your team, and those other deputies from elsewhere—hell of a job and well done, sir! Sirs! But still, if it was my call, you should've put him down and left him out there on the island or in the valley. Crack some ribs and break his legs, then the coyotes and crows would move in and take care of him in no time at all. Then who's eating whom, am I right? I guess the scavenger birds are already flying well enough but watch out for those flying coyotes and foxes if they got their wings! There'd be nothing wrong with that type of a picnic on the beach, as long as it was out of sight of the kids and the sunbathers on the far side east end of your so-called island."

"Sick. Although a good point, Cal. Sick, sick, sick," said

Bill, beginning on a soft tone, muttering, and ending the final 'sick' with a clearer and louder emphasis. He said this as he leaned forward in the barber's chair, using his hands to push up from the arm rests for leverage, as he was getting up from his own trim, Cal brushed his neck off in a hurry before Bill had vacated the seat. While using his hands to brush away any loose hair left on his shirt, having escaped from the bib, Bill walked over to the box that contained the jars of hooch he had gone out to retrieve from his truck earlier. "You guys got him, George. So, a big cheers to that," said Bill, as he opened a large Mason jar of blackberry mead, taking a first whiff and a small sip before offering a sip to the others with a delicate passing motion using both hands like it was an ancient Greek kylix, a gesture that could not, should not, would not be refused by the others. The proprietor and patrons were only too happy to oblige Bill. They each took the necessary swig as if they, too, all parched, had all well-earned it.

Here, *fishy kitty, fishy kitty…*

The morning had taken a significant toll. The heat of the early day, the sweat, the exhaustion. The effort of waking up so early for the once-a-week golf exercise and exercise of golf, back into town to open the shop a bit late—at least late for the first customer, the eminent Doctor Putnam—several trims, the bullshitting, stories, phony and real drama, the act as entertainer, the profession as barber. Cal felt like someone was doing gymnastics in his stomach as it was gurgling and grumbling. It was now past eleven o'clock in the a.m., and while not ten minutes had passed with the fruity, sweet and refreshing blackberry mead of Bill's having made its last pass around the barber's circle, it was Cal gaining the final drop into his cavernous gut as he patted the bottom of the jar, holding it upside-down to ensure there was no wasted nourishing goodness left within, allowing the final teardrop of the potent honey concoction—and a tiny crick of sediment—to drop onto the tip of his tongue.

"Who's ready for lunch then?" said Cal, licking his lips and rubbing his stomach in a circle, using his palm as if he were ironing his shirt. "Anyone else here also starving? This heat and my nine holes earlier there—I tell you, I'm right famished. I'd eat the filthy asshole right out of a dead and dusty old maggoty horse laying right out there on the road. No, wait, not a horse—check that, sorry. But a cow—yeah, I'd eat a decaying and festering cow right now I'm so goddamn hungry. Even a German cow—I'd eat that kind, too. Especially, in fact."

"Yes, I'm getting hungry, for sure. But you're saying you're going to go get a hot dog? I don't know if I'm quite up for that—I mean, I'm hungry, but jeez," said George, querying and qualifying Cal's comments, as he had heard that same line or close variations of it many times around lunchtime, or whenever that time of necessary feasting might be for an unfed Cal.

"Nope, not hotdog, as it's much too hot out for that, even as ravenous as I am," said Cal, knowing what game George was playing, so trying to counter him. "Thank you, though—good idea for next time. No dog anus, no canine tonsils, no Rufus mutt organs for this cowboy today—no thank you, sir. Myself, I'm after some other meat—much tastier. Tender, juicy, whiskers—mewy mew, glurg glurp."

"Cat! A hot-feline, or a... A feline-dog? Feline filet?" said Bill, asking the genuine questions, as he was indeed confused with Cal's brainteaser and feeling the need to get in on this conversation once again before it got in on him.

"Good guess, Bill, nice try," said George, wanting to commend anyone who could even attempt to catch up with the somewhat witty if filthy riddles of Cal's. "No, what Cal's looking for, for lunch now, is not an actual cat—it's a metaphor, or it's that slang, that limey slang thing, you know? It's pussy. You want pussy for lunch, right, Cal? But where in the hell are you going to find that at this hour, and in this fine and proper town of ours?"

"Your secretary," said Cal, punching right back. "Jesus, and I thought the Sun had wiped me out, put me down. You guys need to lay down here. Or no, not here—out in the shade in the park. You've got the heat stroke, or the exhaustion, or something, from all the heat haze. Go and rest with my drunken pal, Leonardo McFitzO' da Vinci, out there. Christ, listen to yourselves. You're sick. Should put you pricks in the nuthouse, not the other way around, George. Ice cold baths for all of you!"

As Cal went on and on with the wise cracks, he felt they were lobbing him softballs to hit out of the park. If it were any other day of the week or time of the year, he would have kept lighting them up, reveling in it. But he was of an unquestionable and legitimate hunger, too hungry for any further games of ribbing—he wanted ribs or something of like sustenance and substance before he got sick and shriveled away, his hollow self becoming dust.

"It's a light joke, but apparently too complex for you. Catfish! Our good friend, you morons," said Cal, as if it was obvious what he wanted for lunch. "Let's go to Ming's. He'll be open by now. I want my favourite seafood dish, not George's picnic with the pumas. You know, Ming had the weirdest veg there last week with the catfish. He was excited about getting them here because he said they're better than the broccoli he normally uses in the recipe. They had these deep and dark green leaves, but with a lighter green stem that was hard, like if celery was bred with Swiss chard or something. The colour of honeydew, the flesh. But this veg was Asian—Chinese, I guess. He said it was like a Chinese cabbage of sorts. First bite's this god-awful stuff, quite bland and even bitter, but it's pretty tasty when you get going into it, with the sauce and rice and the other veg on the plate. And the bamboo things—wait, wait, the uh, the—the zhu sun. Ha! How's that? I'm even learning to speak Chinese—Ming's a great tutor, beyond being a great cook."

"Christ, how often do you eat there?" said Bill, with

George and Greg also both turning their focus back to Cal, looking like they had the same question, now awaiting the answer.

"Who are you, my doc? No, Putnam was just in here for a trim first thing, as George saw, before you two clowns walked in. You my dietician, Bill? For your information, since you're ever so curious and concerned, I lunch with Ming about twice a week. Different days, but twice. Not once, not thrice—twice. That OK by you? How often do you not drink your moonshine?" said Cal, shooting back at Bill with his phony and comic rage, even though the question was not meant as pejorative, only as a basic curiosity, as Bill ate there a fair bit himself, which Cal was, of course, most aware of, the two often dining at Ming's together.

"Twice is good, Cal. It's a decent amount. About the same as me," said Bill, agreeing on the appropriate regularity of Chinese food intake. "On my moonshine, well, Calvin... I have a little snort at least once a day, and at least twice on Sundays. Sometimes more, whatever the day, the farming season. Harvest, winter; seeding, weeding. Whatever the mood, whatever the mood of the wife, and so on. And based on your orders, Calvin—including that bottle I brought in today, in fact—about the same as you, don't you think? But if you'd like, I can stop the supply from flowing your way from here on out. No problem on my end in reducing the shipments—I have many gracious customers in some serious need of the product. It's true that demand does outstrip supply, I'm quite happy to report. Unlike the spring wheat, alas. The economics are in my favour, no question. And no problem, Sheriff, as those economics don't apply to you and your boys. There's some inelasticity, but no real price hikes coming your way in any event, so no worries on that front, rest assured, and case closed on that one."

"No, no—no! Fair enough. Yes, a most brilliant product you come up with, Bill—always top shelf stuff, without a doubt," said Cal, now beaming and toning it down a couple of notches, not wanting to jeopardize his precious rations of the life-sustaining drink. "Yeah, it's kind of funny, as we eat at Ming's and tipple at about the same rate, you and I do, Bill. It's all good, bud."

"That's all swell, just swell," said George, re-intervening and hoping to re-focus the conversation away from the booze, as he knew he was already walking a fine line on allowing the distribution to move the way it did and also not wanting to jeopardize the operations, not because of something as stupid as the silly willy nilly talk of it all. "I enjoy that food myself on occasion, though I must admit I do hope those chicken balls ain't some other kind of protein, some mystery meat of some other type of fowl. You know, I hope they're real chickens, especially with Mr. Sanders now out of the picture. But, then again, not his tender birds. Nor the real balls of the chicken either. Testicles, that is—probably too small for the batter. Yet I try not to think about it too much... I love my meat, but when I think about Leon's homemade soup, and now Cal's idea of the coyote lunch on the beach... Ugh."

"You think there're really wolves and mountain lions walking around the river valley?" said Greg, in some disbelief and worry as his mind seemed paused on the reference from the conversation some minutes ago. "I know there're coyotes for sure on those trails, and foxes. But I've never seen those bigger dogs and cats."

"Oh, for sure there're wandering around there. But they're really smart—they're never seen, only very rarely.

Covering huge distances by day and night. The odd time some cattle or swine will get taken out, and then you know when you see the animal tracks," said George, confirming the reality and range of the large predators of an otherwise apparent apparition. "Speaking of the existence of animals, as it is, I'm still getting calls at least once a week about missing pets in town, little girls crying, their mamas crying, too. I tell them the cats probably got themselves up into some trees or something, but they'll come back down. If it's pups, I say maybe they just got lost is all. It's their instinct and they need some time alone, and they figure it out. Most of the time."

"Wait, what do you say when the pets don't come back? Or you never hear back from the owner? Wait. Or the cats do make it back down the trees?" said Greg, confused, and a bit buzzed from the fermented blackberry concoction, but keen on this topic while trying to remain relevant and present in the stuffy barbershop. "Is it the big cats sneaking into town and eating the little pussies? Are cats cannibals?"

"Well, it's a bit of all of the above: A little of column A, a little of column B. Some return, I'm certain. Some don't come back, but they don't call back neither. When they do call a second time... It's tough. You need to feel them out a bit—who's calling, what did they ask the first time, what did they sound like back then during the original report? And what do they sound like now, today? What's the situation is what you need to know. You've got to grasp that," said George, warming up into a full-fledged drama by the end of the extended explanation and re-enactment, as if he was teaching a course on police investigations, even if only on missing cat-related detective work. "If they're truly gone from town and been eaten, it's by the coyotes, not cougars.

"If it's a nice little girl for real and she's missing her furry companion, you might say something like, 'well, I'm so sad and sorry to hear your dear poor kitty hasn't come home yet, but I did hear from a pleasant farm family the other day, and they seen some new kitties out there, so it could be sweet Cuddles wanted to live in the country, you know, headed out there where it's beautiful and peaceful for her, and they're having a great time catching mice and playing in the flowers and whatnot, away from the busy town life.'

"If you know the cat is dead and you're so-so on the caller, but you still want to sound reasonable and business-like, then it's something such as, 'oh, yes, I'm sorry to say, but old Furball has passed on, I'm afraid, quite afraid, he met his end at the end of Elm Street this morning, but, you know, the garbage man didn't even see him, the poor ole puss puss must've been on life number nine.'

"Then there often comes a time when you have the same call, but it's a crazy old cat broad, or people who don't care for their yard, or cold hard criminals—or deviants, delinquents at least. And so, in those cases you can tell a noble truth and be done with it, for a time at least, or you can let them down not so gentle like by explaining the cold hard facts of it—that's life, suckers. Karma. Fate."

"Jesus figure-skating Christ. What in the hell are you going on and on about this pet detective business for? I'm beyond starving!" said Cal, confronting George and his other guests as he was done with the talking and wanting to move past anything that was not going to fill his stomach and in short order. "Ming's probably cooking my fish dish right now—and your chicken one, George. And all those great veg and the rice. I'm so hungry. And I'll tell you what: You eat everything on your plate and have a cup of that scented tea—the green stuff with the flowers... You'll never shit better in your life. Twice a week at that kitchen, that's all you need. Great and solid, hard and perfectly formed shits is what they are—don't even need to wipe your ass. That's what that stuff does to you. And the food tastes great, no dishes at home. Now let me close up here and we'll head on over to Ming's right now."

"Never truer," said Bill, reacting as if Cal had told him of a palpable fact in polite company. "But I'm sorry, Cal, and I'd love to, as I do enjoy lunch there myself. I'd come any other time, but I've got to get back to the farm, load up, and get dropping at the elevator. These prices right now won't last long with all the crop coming off, even as it burns in the field. I guess that could drive the price up longer-term, but it won't help if I can't get that last bit off—the rest of that crop won't last long standing in the heat like she is right now, dew-free. You boys go and enjoy the fine Chinese and let me know if you like that special new batch for you. After the sampler, I brought in an odd five bottles, so say two for the trim, two for the law, and one for the new hospital man here—especially since he's not a price-gouging grain handler prick no more. Is that about fair to all for today?"

Cal, George, and Greg all stood smiling and nodding to Bill in unison, giving him a look of great thanks and encouragement.

"Bill, I know you, and if these new batches are anything like this sample, and like the last batch, we're all good—and fair, more than fair, in fact," said George, extending the sentiment of the nod with some verbal support.

"Keep your production levels up, though, if you can, as these won't last long, not unlike your crop prices and frying fields in this here brutal heat."

"Nor will those short lines in the driveway last, Bill—you're bang on, sir," said Greg, offering his rudimentary if inside knowledge of the grain handling business. "I have to head back home myself—I have to get home and do some chores first, then... The afternoon and later shift tonight at the hospital are coming on quick. First day on the job with my old man today. The next few days and couple of weeks look to be busy on the grounds—hectic even. This bottle will come in mighty handy," said Greg, still buzzed and slurring a bit, yet cracking the lid to take a sample sip as if to ensure Bill knew just how thankful he was and how important the unordered gift of the drink was to him, some rare, thoughtful present.

Greg was interested in going to lunch with the group at the shop—not with Cal alone, not anything to do with Cal himself—but the thorough peer group camaraderie was now lost with Bill taking his leave back to the farm. Greg felt a bit awkward—as per normal with him—yet most thankful and refreshed from his morning trim and drink with this crew. And Greg knew this was what his new normal should be, which was to go home and then head to work—this must be his routine in his new life turned around, this positive step forward and out of the range of those grain elevator folks who made his blood boil just thinking about them. And out of the range of all the others who also pissed him off. As Deb popped in and out of this head, he became angrier. He took another hard swig from Bill's bottle...

From beside his crate of swill bottles, Bill took a slow

step towards the door while Greg took a quick jump forward from beside the waiting chair. Bill set his fee down by the coffee pot, which triggered a reversal in Greg's slippage of the mind. Greg took a couple of rapid paces to the shelf as if he were some skittish jackrabbit, tossing his fare down next to Bill's, doing it in a near-throwing motion so the money landed with an accurate spin-free thud on the counter, this one small bill and some change.

"OK, gents," said Cal, working to usher everyone out the front door, almost shooing them out at this point. "Well, thanks for your business, and thanks for the enjoyable discussion, the banter. And Bill, thanks for some more of that wonderful apple stuff from before, if it works—it's a beautiful drink, and I became dry again the other day, so great timing. Next time you pop by town, later in the week perhaps, could you bring a little jug of that other stuff I so love, the barley-corn mix one? And good luck at the new job there, Greg—your old man's real proud of you now, so you keep him proud of Gregory, alright? Sorry you boys can't make it to Ming's with us, but you go and count on it for next time, you hear?" Cal smiled and winked as he funneled them out the door, down the steps, out onto the sidewalk.

"Alright then, George, let's roll."

Jingle, creak, screech, clatter, jingle.

As the four individuals arrived on the sidewalk, they noticed the great painter Les was back in the park, having returned after believing the threat from Corb had lessened, and where he appeared to be organizing his painting apparatus to get back to work, sobering up in the sunshine then setting up in the shade.

"Well, you should go over there before we eat lunch,

Cal," said George, looking to elicit a final laugh from the present company before Bill and Greg departed. "I'll give you my sheriff's badge and he can paint your portrait, maybe work in you sitting atop a big carob brown horse, like your favourite next to the mirror. You could hang that great work of new art in your shop, on the empty wall by the window. An almost sort of replacement for your broken horse Hummel toy thing from earlier, after the tragic demise."

"Not a bad idea, Sheriff," said Cal, stroking his chin, thinking quickly on his feet. "Then I can sell my own portrait for millions one day, and it'll hang in the grand galleries of Europe, framed in ornate brass. However, the picture painted of you riding a little mule of a jackass, well... I don't know that anyone in London or Paris really wants to see that, you crushing a donkey like in a cartoon, weighting the poor thing down, George. You won't make it to Florence like that."

Les was continuing to organize himself in the park, setting up to paint what looked like might be a scene with the historic brick building in the background, a beautiful and classic Carnegie library, which was nestled in amongst the green canopies of mature lindens, ashes, beeches, and elms throughout the park. As he finished setting out his brushes and paints on the tray below the canvas, Les bent over next to his easel and vomited. Still in quite rough shape, as he stumbled and tried to sit down next to the easel on the other side of the puke, he bumped the stand, knocking it over along with all of his artistic infrastructure. The works toppled over with Les, who laid back down in the fetal position to pass out yet again, laying there like a drunken Color Kitten, Hush with no Brush, no green but the green as green grass in his face, a taste of Éire as he kept calm and carried on dreaming.

"Gross," said Greg, giggling again in an uncomfortable position this time, not able to offer much more than the obvious.

"Drunken da Vinci," said Bill, staring at the park in disgust. "Indeed."

"It's a good idea, Calvin—I do like it," said George, in a foolproof deadpan tone. "However, it looks like I'll have to take a rain check for today, as any puke on my jackass portrait would not work for those fine curators abroad of whom you speak, even if it might reek no different than some of their foul-smelling cheeses... Well, I don't want to break my lunch plans at this point, and not for anything other than the most heinous and gravest of events, so I'll leave this one to Corb as he'll be strolling back in through the park soon enough, his routine midday shift downtown."

Cal was nodding his head throughout as he listened to the comments of the other three, agreeing with them as he looked at the park, engrossed on the state of Les. "I don't know much about da Vinci," Cal said, "but van Gogh was a masterful drunk, and look at his amazing legacy today." The barber could not understand what was wrong with Les and why he continued to fall off the wagon, not with all the current and past treatments he was aware of at the institution, knowing Les was not crazy in the true mental health sort of a sense, but he needed real help of some kind, something to pull him from the poison, and Corb pushing him around would not do it. Cal was convinced Les needed help now, before something terrible and perhaps irreversible happened to this great local artist, or the side effects hurting someone else in town, the collegial collateral damage done. Cal continued nodding his head, as if to the beat of a song he was listening to, then ceased the repetitive bobbing to give one deeper gesture of a nod to each of the three, then spun his heels to turn around and began walking the one block down to Ming's Dynasty to have the overdue lunch he was longing for.

Book III

Chinese and Psychedelics

The Ming Dynasty I:
Saunas, shocks; pots and woks

By the time Bill and Greg had each headed off in their own directions, returning to their vehicles to drive down Main Street and away from town altogether, Cal and George were already entering Ming's Dynasty. Cal was grumbling down the sidewalk, pouting about the sorry state of Les until they entered the Chinese restaurant, which brightened his mood. The restaurant was given the eponymous name by the proprietor's father, Ming Sr., for the Ming Dynasty of hundreds of years ago in China. It was a clever play on words, if not quite a double entendre, whether the original Ming was aiming for that or if something got lost in the first translation.

Some folks in town called Ming Jr. 'The Great Ming,' including Cal, who guessed the name was based on one of the real emperors of said dynasties of old, or maybe some related play after The Great Wall. When asked about it or not, Ming would explain the restaurant name to his regular guests and so the fun nickname was obvious, sticking to him from the get-go and would remain so for the long-term now as well. It was a basic and humble café, not unlike the many others in every prairie town dotting the flat map. It was as good a Chinese or any type of Asian or ethnic cuisine as was able to be had in these landlocked rural areas for the time, and select western food was also on the menu for those so inclined to not stray too far from the familiar and ordinary meals of hamburgers, roast beef sandwiches and the like. Next door was Ming's laundromat and dry-cleaning business, and upstairs above that—where Ming grew up, the family accommodations when he was a child—now housed an office where he and his wife also had a small but burgeoning bookkeeping and accounting endeavour. His father was the pioneer who had founded and run the restaurant at first, and on returning from a self-imposed hiatus or exile in the city was when Ming Jr. came back to town, along with his new urbane bride, taking over the restaurant and re-branding it, all the while expanding his diverse portfolio of other important small-town businesses of moderate but growing success.

Cal and George stepped in past the twin golden dragon statues manning the doorway, walking towards the one table with the earliest of customers. With three of the seats taken at the table for four, George dragged the adjacent table over, pulling it together with the one where Willy, Ronny, and Terry were sitting. As Cal sat down in the existing vacant chair, George pulled a fifth chair over to the new table he had created, joining Cal and the hospital workers who were well into their lunchtime meals, even if they had only been there for the few minutes that Ming had been open.

"I thought you'd still be down by the river or out at the grounds, investigating the scene of the would-be crime?" said Willy, directing his question to George while chewing a mouthful of rice. "Taping the valley off and such, yellows ribbons rippling through the willows and whatnot."

"If I was the sheriff, the only witnesses would be coyotes, and they'd be too busy licking their bloody lips to talk," said Cal, wanting to set the tone himself with a first clever joke. "Did you hear the whole story? George enlightened us on the incident. I heard the commotion golfing this morning, but I had no idea he got out till George told us at the shop just now. I was preoccupied with some other potential escapees on the final hole, the Nazi nut on nine."

"Yeah, we heard Leon ran away," said Ronny, trying to pluck a string of celery from his teeth as he pierced another piece of it with his fork. "That's all we know. And we got him back. Or you guys got him back, anyways. What the hell happened?"

"Well, something like he wasn't on enough meds, or not the right ones. And your rotund nurses couldn't chase him down when he made the decision to cut loose," said George, too exhausted from the heat and stressed out from the general situation to want to go through the whole story again, even with these mates. "You guys are letting all those staff, those nurses and doctors... Well, they're getting too lazy and losing control. Maybe it would be easier next time for everyone to do as Cal says."

"And if he doesn't get put down, plain and simple, you have to wonder what good he'll do in the hospital now," said Cal, sharing some of his ideas through what he felt were legitimate questions. "I mean, can they use him as a guinea pig on new experiments, doing something for the greater good, for the public? Practice on him to improve future treatments for others, maybe?"

"We always get called out to the chase, and we always bring the bad folks back to the institution," said George, showing his frustration. "But what about when they're in there now, whether as research or even keeping them under control? How can they ensure the safety of our citizens? That's my main concern—maybe my lone worry. The frequency and scale of these events, even with fewer of them in there today. It's all getting to be too much."

As the table of five ruminated on this, Willy, Ronny, and Terry continued eating their lunches, slowing down their chewing and the maneuvering of their utensils, while George and Cal listened to their own empty stomachs growl. The brief silence at the table was broken by the sounds and sights coming from the kitchen in the back of the restaurant, where, through a square window-like hole in the wall, they were able to view the steam rising as if out of a volcano from where Ming was cooking over the giant rhino grey pots and huge woks on his stovetop.

"What about that steaming thing they used to do," said George, directing the open question to Willy and Ronny. "I know many of those previous treatments were terrible and inhumane—and baseless. But with characters like our Mr. Campbell, I'd be more than open to see them try anything, including some of the brutal past ways, to either work at fixing him up a little or at least keep him from running off again—no more picking those juicy, ripe tomatoes for him. Whatever they can do to prevent him from making another bowl of soup, and I don't think many folks around here, or anywheres, would disagree with me on that point."

"You got that right, damn straight and hear, hear, Sheriff. And our fine chef could've been a master back then, boiling the rice and vegetables for lunch, as well as harnessing the steam for the patients when they got all crusty and crabby like," said Willy, watching the constant steam rise and churn behind the little open window above the back counter and adjacent to the kitchen door. "If this were the olden days, they'd be flogging Leon nonstop right now, at best for him. With anything else, he'd be begging for the misty blowtorch treatment."

"I said they should've left Soupy on the riverbanks after beating the shit out of him, let the mangy coyotes finish him off," said Cal, reiterating his earlier suggestion on how to best deal with such violent escapees. "But what are you talking about steaming him? What the hell does that mean?"

"Coyotes isn't a bad idea, and the crows and magpies would take care of the little bits, too," said Ronny, as though he had planned this method through at one recent point himself, perhaps even this morning. "Quite early on, I mean right back to when the institution opened, even back before the Great War started, they didn't know what the hell they were ever doing with much of anything, but one thing they used to use was what were like these cabinets. They built them from the floor up, like a wardrobe or as if to store formal dishes in the dining room, where they would stick the patients in this tiny cloakroom and lock them in. It was kind of like a dining room buffet or an armoire with a more vertical bent, where only the heads of those getting steamed would pop out on top, maybe like a lamp sticking out atop the buffet. Willy would know this more than me, as he's seen them as they were, and taken them apart and whatnot, reverse engineered them and all. But it more often had flat panels with these utilitarian sheets of wood, while some were designed in a curvy serpentine way to show a little style and class as the mental patients would sweat out their evil. The genius doctors of the day piped hot steam into the chamber, which was to calm them down if they were agitated or got fidgety. As I understand it, the problem was when the influx of those so many hundreds of shell-shocked veterans returned from France, Belgium, Italy—they were all beyond stressed out from the war. And so, so many of them were sent here, to this one grand extra-regional institution, which is as great an understatement as one can make. You'd have had more than you can imagine, each of them taking their turns being stuck in there steaming away into prunes. In hindsight, if there was some value, they might've simply created an enormous sauna room to put them in a bunch at a time, if they were able to couple that with any decent drugs, and if there was a way to monitor them so they were certain to not kill themselves or each other as they relaxed in the steam. With too many patients and not much creative thinking, they abandoned the steam cabinet idea and decommissioned it. They closed them up, shut them down altogether."

"I have to say, that does sound pretty relaxing," said Cal, caressing his left forearm with the knackered-looking fingers of his right hand, as though he were channeling the experience of sitting in a sauna on vacation. "I'm not too sure of its effectiveness, though, as I guess they weren't either. This whole hot air idea could have only been dreamed up by some doctor specialist from Finland. But that said, I can already say, and with great certainty, the world would be a better place, at least our hospital and town sure would be, if we had more of those fine Finn folks, maybe even helping to run the joint, and fewer of those despicable Germans like Johann around. I guess they're all kind of Nordic nuts in their own way, aren't they? But I don't even know how that John is still alive. And I mean, I don't know how they haven't caught on to his bullshit story. And... I also mean, I don't know how he's still living in his natural state either—the guy's got to be as old as Bismarck."

"I took a bunch of those apart years ago," said Willy, reverting to the original conversation on the steam cabinets as though Cal had not even said a word. "Burned most of it all, as kindling in the stove. But I did take a bit home and used them to build some new shelving and cabinets in my garage, for tools and stuff. The wood panels and whatnot. When they were used, they did look a lot like that, but the inside was a whole series of guts where the patient could sit down and the mechanics of the steam getting piped in. A complex unit and rather an ingenious idea if you think about it. Even if it didn't solve all the problems the inventor might have intended it to, it couldn't have much hurt anyone too bad.

"And there was another gem of a treatment they used for those with the same conditions and about the same time, in the real early days, where some masterminds had the idea of locking patients in a crib or a chest drawer type of thing," said Willy, pouring extra soy sauce on his rice for the fourth time since Cal and George had joined them. "I've used wood from those as well, cleaner and less rot because it was a dry method—the industrial shop used to take some of it to make birdhouses with the patients. The drawer was also supposed to calm them down, giving them some nice quiet alone time, without light or movement or noise, some solitude for peace, and maybe reflection as the stresses dissipated and the brain began re-circuiting itself. With no distractions, many of them panicked even more than outside the box! Which, I presume, is because of their original condition coupled with an unknown dash of claustrophobia, and some would drop dead in the box from a heart attack or some such, a first unintended consequence—first of many."

"Imagine wanting to calm down a wounded soldier, one who had been trapped in a tunnel during a battle, or even stuck in a trench during an assault, hunkering down below the strands and tangles of barbed wire, laying in the mud to avoid artillery fire from the Germans... Then he comes home and needs treatment because he's been traumatized, and some doctor says, 'I've got it: Let's stick him in a box, that'll calm him down!'" said George, baffled and disgusted. "That, right there, is insanity. One couldn't define the supposed treatment any better."

"They called it the Utica Crib," said Willy, imparting further historic and etymological knowledge. "I think the name of it was from the hospital out east that invented it. And a crib sounds rather pleasant, but really it was more like a coffin, created as an alternative to the iron chains in the cellar. And, in fact, they stopped me from taking them out of storage to reclaim the wood at home—oh, back maybe ten or so years ago... Because they told me they could save some money by using those things as actual coffins. If they'd have thought of that back then, then when someone got scared during that treatment and croaked within it, they could've just rolled you out to the cemetery and dumped you right off into the hole, as simple as that, no funerary middlemen required."

"A coffin is what Leon needs," said Cal, with a blunt emphasis. "Garbage scrap wood—some shitty plywood with irreparable defects, just like Leon. No silken finery. Same with Yuri. And Johnny Johann. Dwight, too. Most of them, really. Although, in fairness, Fred, the Skunk, well... He thinks they burn the bad patients in the power plant and then vent them out through the smokestack, so the concept of a crib for naughty nuts might work in placating someone like him after giving him an icy polar bath or two first, though."

Terry ate as quietly as a hare and with the pace of a tortoise. Willy and Ronny were continuing to chomp about as if piranhas devouring the kill, even as they were the ones managing to speak more often. Cal and George were famished, the sensation being exacerbated as they watched between the three fellows eating at their table and Ming cooking away back in his kitchen; aromas of the meat and vegetables stir-frying in sundry sauces abound as it fanned across the main room of the Dynasty.

"Baths were almost a new version of the steam boxes, with the same kind of thinking, the extreme heat sensations redux, with the frigid version added on as an innovation to that type of supposed therapy," said Ronny, carrying on the conversation concerning past treatments. "The rumour is they would put them in a bath for some time—hours and hours on end, in some cases. Patients were strapped in with a piece of sheet metal or something over top of them, below their necks. Only allowed out to use the facilities, if even that. Then right back into the tub. And those baths were exceptional. They could be the most frigid and icy cold you've ever felt, like picture ice-fishing in the Arctic, in January, without a cozy igloo, and naked. Or they could be a nearly lava-level of boiling hot, not unlike the heat today but all moist and wet, like picture fishing in Africa or on Venus in the summer. They'd turn the faucet on in the correct direction of desired temperature, based on whatever condition you had: If your condition saw you moping about all lethargic and in a depressed sort of disposition, they'd throw you in the ice-cold bath to get you moving again, your nerves racing once more. However, if you presented a more manic or hyperactive type of demeanour, being locked in the warm bath would calm you right down to acceptable levels in a more sedate manner. That's what it was all supposed to do. The theories all had something to do with the blood flow of a person, how it would course through to the head and how it was supposed to affect your mental state, jolting your brain either way, in the correct direction, bringing you some equilibrium via your circulatory system. They started those baths at the beginning and have done it for a long time, and they still do it today but not as an emergency or acute treatment method itself, but rather in addition to whatever drugs they're injecting them with, whatever pills they're pushing on them, and whatever else they do."

"Sitting in a cold or hot bath for hours on end might sound like a bit much," said Willy, looking for a debate on the efficacy of the practices they did not really know much of anything about. "But you would beg for it if the alternative was turning the fire hose on you, or even less powerful sprays, as they would employ for days and days. Or Chinese water torture, with the drips and drops over your head—we should ask Ming if he knows anything about that method, for real or cultural folklore or whatever. I can't imagine they use those baths like that anymore, as you say, Ronny. And I guess that's real torture with the drops, not a treatment per se, so probably never employed here. What sort of information would you expect to elicit anyhow, even if the patient was in for some crime? But speaking of the different techniques, Terry and I know they're still using the electric shocks on them, as we got called in to fix one of those galvanic machines up the other day, didn't we, Terry?"

"Yeah, they're still using the voltaic contraption, but it's more for research now, I believe," said Terry, quieter and more introverted than the rest of the boisterous assembled crowd. "Although they say they're having more success as they've refined their processes over time. They used to shock anyone and everyone, which proved not effective at all, save for the odd freak who might have seen some improvement. Otherwise, most people only got burned and singed, scarred and whatnot. This new guy told Willy and I the electroshock method was being used for those with depression—he called them depressives. And like I say, the one shrink I talked to said it's a skill that's been improved over the recent years as they're learning more about it, studying what happens. I wouldn't doubt the procedure gets some lazy wires going again for some, you would think. I would think it would for me—I mean, how could it not? Even a little static shock from dragging your socks through the carpet in winter jolts you enough sometimes to wake you up, but a higher voltage entering your nerves would shake the shit of almost anyone. What does it do for the true depressive, however? Or what would it do to a real hard criminal, like Leon? The big shock is supposed to make him feel happy or good instead of sad or down. Maybe the belief is the brain becomes stuck in the mud in the parts that govern your mood, and the theory being the shock gets that section going again, like turning a stagnant slough into a running brook, if not a waterfall, making the water flow as it must rather than being all murky and scummy and dead, like the shock is to your brain as some shotgun slugs or buckshot is to a minor beaver dam—the blast breaks things up nicely, getting it going again, proper like... On second thought, maybe make it cannon fire on the beavers."

"That's a great analogy, Terry. Well done," said Cal, knowing his brain was all well and flowing fine on hearing Terry explain the electroshock. "I don't think that's Soupy's problem though, or any of these other clowns I ran into today on the course. Not for the psychos. Depression, maybe, like for the purple puking man. But a good zapping couldn't hurt them. Might shake something loose with the marbles up top, and who knows? Try, try again. With the worst of the worst, maybe they shouldn't be abandoning treatments so quickly. Don't do it on sane people or when you know there's a better and real treatment that works, but use it and modify it and keep it going for the Leons of the world, the Yuris of the hospital, Fred, Johann... Hell, even Lester, might jolt him free of his boozy demons downtown, lifting his spirits, bringing him a more peaceful temperament for painting in the park. Shit, even Walter and Greg, straighten those nuts out," said Cal, encouraged as the table all laughed. "Even you, George. It might help you to reduce your massive intake of coffee, mitigate against those tummy troubles you've been having."

"They do try the damnedest things and then about-face over a little public outcry, or peer pressure from colleagues trying to discredit one another, each wanting glory for some negligible finding, even if it's total horseshit. But George, if the shocking does not work for them, or did not work for them back a few years or even decades ago, then they'd go to the next option, which was spinning the individual in a chair," said Terry, trying to think his story through, using a preface to bide himself some time. "They'd sit you in a chair like a swing, with the ropes attached to beams in the ceiling. Then they'd twist the ropes up top as much as they could, releasing you with such a twirl it would give you a hell of a dizzying effect, where they believed it would shake you up and straighten the psychotic right out of you through the spin. And that's not even the best of it: If the patient was already in a dizzy disposition in their daily lives, they'd spin them out of it in a reverse motion, as if that backwards method would work. Think about it: They'd take that chair and suspend it way up in the air, tying the ropes in the rafters, contorting it right up as tight as it would go in a lengthy Rapunzel-like braid almost and they'd sit the patient in the seat of the swing—which was kind of like a small hammock as a sitting chair—buckle them in, and let it go. It's such a stupid idea. It's truly amazing it's been used in a clinical setting at all, and not even that long ago, really. They used it for such an awful long time and to no apparent avail whatsoever, while thinking it would unjumble the head while also causing sleepiness and rest in the patients, which is good for them, too, of course. And so, it may fix the brain and body in more ways than one."

"Jesus, what an insane thing," said George, with a careful shake of his own head. "And it's supposed to cure the insane. Christ. It's no wonder we're where we are here today like this, with stuff like that. Those phony bums, bullshit head doctors."

"You're not wrong, George," said Willy in concurrence. "While there are a few true medical doctors working at the hospital, only those to deal with the unfortunate incidents of trauma and shock from the treatments gone bad. They're also there to ensure the patients are in good shape, in as good of physical health as they can be, for further treatments, and maybe nasty experiments. Many of the doctors at the institution are psychiatrists and psychologists, as we know. Psychologists study the mind by looking at behaviour, which they do through lots of talking. Psychiatrists are more like medical doctors, physicians focusing on brain chemistry, and they can give out medications. They have different training and education. I don't know how much they really do anyways, but I'm sure they're making some progress on some fronts. But the ones who talk and talk, and listen and listen, and take lots of notes while clicking away with their fancy pens, scribbling out notes, or maybe drawing, at the doodling... I don't know. They do the observations, defining the conditions of patients, and then they try and come up with regimes for managing them, the treatments. That's how we've had all these brutal past methods we're talking about here that don't make a lick of sense, not even a pinch of a dry ounce. Although, like everything else is the world, technology and inventions and whatnot, it does all seem to improve over time, from equipment to tools to you name it."

As the sheriff, barber, plumber, electrician, and carpenter all recollected past matters of the mental hospital while they were watching the cook work away at his process in the kitchen—which they knew the steam was coming from the rice in the boiling pot of water, the vegetables in the stir-frying wok, and the meat searing on the grill—the chimes on the front door of the restaurant gave off a soft ring and into Ming's Dynasty walked the senior clinical psychiatrist of the institution, Doctor Oxenham...

Anger, cigarettes; a case of the sweats

Greg picked up a pack of Camels at the pharmacy near Cal's barbershop and headed straight home, trying to relax along the route, smoking and taking another few sips and slurps of the jar he had received from Bill. At the end of the drive on the highway, turning the corner where their mobile home lot was set on a bend on the road for local traffic, he pulled up in front of their unit to park on the gravel street, at first not noticing the somewhat foreign truck parked in the driveway. The navy-blue half-ton was reversed into their narrow dirt spot with the nose poking out of the shade created by the tops of a row of towering poplar trees in the adjacent yard.

Greg got out of his car and walked up the driveway into his yard, hearing a variety of noises as he was trying to process what the story might be with this truck. The first faint sounds he heard were those of a wailing note. The subtle crying became stronger to even overpower the loud music being played somewhere also inside the trailer. And then the yelling began, or at least that was what the sound seemed to be, assuming it was her about to scream directly at him as he approached the steps to the door, that common visceral din. However, as Greg got closer to the structure and stepped onto the first wooden step, he heard the next and real wave of sounds emanating from the open window, it now overwhelming the babies crying and the music blasting: Moaning, groaning, howling, and indeed a certain type of screaming was coming from Deb. She had not heard him pull up and so was not screaming at Greg—nor did the shrill barks have anything to do with him. It dawned on Greg, this now-familiar truck, looking at it from the side. The shrieks of Deb were with respect to a nemesis of the grain elevator, the enemy in the bedroom with Deb, conspiring to undertake certain untoward and improper activities.

Greg was already at risk of being late to meet with his old man and now boss on this first day of the new job at the hospital. He did not want to deal with any of this domestic squabble—not that he could deal with it—so he made an instinctive move to turn right around and bail on his dirty, cheating Deb, and those crying kids also forgotten by her. Between the walk from his car door to his trailer door and back to his vehicle again—a good thirty or so seconds in total—Greg's mind was lit aflame. His anger was raging, even if he was already suspecting—even if he did not know with a concrete certainty that this grubby affair was happening. Catching them in the act—in such a blatant and climactic position, at this specific time of day—only incensed him further. More thoughts raced through Greg's head in that tiny span than had ever done so before, his brain bubbling like a pot of gruel sitting on the high heat burner. In a sense, he was impressed by the productiveness of his imagination, which was of an organic nature, as he could not have conjured them up if he had tried or wanted to in a regular proactive circumstance—not that he had wanted to process these horrendous thoughts of rage.

Back in his car, with a prolific number of sweat droplets cascading from his head, he took another big swig from Bill's jar and sped away down the gravel trailer park road. Only several trailers over, his car slowed down as his mind shifted towards the aesthetic arrangement in the front yard of a neighbouring mobile home resident. He noticed the red geranium and white petunias set to grow and bloom in an old oak barrel in the yard. He was observing the antique cast iron well water pump next to the barrel; it painted a ridiculous violet colour as if to ensure the entire flower bed resembled a Valentine's Day bouquet in late summer. He was noting the two bricks in the dirt framing the little flower garden of love—he was sighting the regular bricks more than anything else, these silica bricks in classic vermilion red.

Getting out of his car to grab a single brick, returning to the vehicle, and driving back to his lot while taking his foot off the accelerator to crawl past his own driveway, he reached out his window with the brick in his hand, lobbing the sun-dried clay block of an ornament towards the front windshield of the nose-out truck of the cheater grain elevator prick. Greg took good aim and had good speed on the toss from his car, but he was so far from the windshield that it did not have quite enough oomph to make it there, nor enough of the vim required for breaking through the glass should the throw have been on a better trajectory. The brick hit the top of the hood and slammed down onto the front bumper, rolling off with a clean, sad landing in the dirt driveway.

Greg put his foot on the brake, sticking his head out the window to stare at the mostly failed effort of the brick toss, a possible minor scratch to the paint notwithstanding—he was bamboozled yet again. However, it was not a complete failure, as the noise created when hitting the hood and bumper disrupted the adulterous state of affairs occurring within his mobile home master bedroom. Deb came storming through the door in an awkward gait, wearing only an extra-large and frayed t-shirt to cover up. She stood on the top step screaming at Greg as she waved her finger at him, suggesting violence, pumping her fist and arm in a rhythmic manner. Greg was about to yell back when the fornicator had the gall to come outside as well, wearing nothing at all as he stood behind Deb, who was wearing his shirt as if to shield himself from any neighbours who might be watching on. As Greg's blood reached peak boil, he hammered his foot on the gas, peeling out of the trailer park and back again onto the paved asphalt highway, this time heading the other direction, further away out of town.

Can't even break a fucking window with a giant brick. I should leave this shithole right now and never come back. Greg's emotions were whipping around in his head like a bad windstorm on Neptune. *Go live in Mexico or the Yukon or somewheres else. South or north—those people couldn't be any worse than this dump and these assholes here. That stupid whore. See how she does then, yelling to herself all the time, all day long.*

As difficult as it was in attempting to settle himself down, Greg took another swig of the grand potion from Bill and kept trying to think it through with some reason: *I've got a new job with Dad. I know how to do it, and I'll do it well. It's not so bad. I've got to support my family, the kids. Even if she's a terrible dumb bitch.* The tangents in his mind were firing in every direction like some vicious lightning storm. *I'm going to drive to the elevator and shoot those cocksuckers right now. Then go back to get him, take care of them all. Bird gun's already in the car here. That'll do just fine. Or force them into an empty hopper and fill it right up over them. Cover them in some shitty oats. Bury them in that ergotty rye they force-fed me that one time. Smother them in oily green rape. Since you don't like them, no hulls in this car for you, bastards. Only scabby wheat—the grade won't matter this time. They'd get crushed or suffocate, for sure. Both, I guess. Then send the train on its way. Shit, no one would never even notice till it hit the mill. Or the port. Or Japan.*

As he drove off the opposite way from town, the options wrestled one another in Greg's head as he was hoping for some clarity brought to him via another cigarette and another swig of the poison. *Leave, stay, or kill? Or is there another option—a new way, a fourth way, or more? Leave for a while—even for a day or a few extra hours. A few more drinks to unwind by myself. Go to work and focus on that. Pop's waiting for me. He's the only one I really got—I can't let him down, not now. Stop by and bust up one of the shitheads' windshields and do it right proper like this time, with a cinderblock from above. Do it at night when I can't get chased down, and they'll never even know. I can hit each of them in turn, a tactical smash, one after the other. A perfect plan!*

From the second he drove away in his car—spinning off in front of his lot, out of the trailer park and down the road, to full speed ahead on the highway—the notions continued zipping around in Greg's head like a hurricane as beads of sweat were simmering on his forehead. His entire skull felt like it was on fire as his brain was already overloaded before the physical heat outside could only intensify it, further fanning the wildfire in his mind. *Maybe I do need more help. Some real help. And it's just so crazy hot.* Greg's full-on meltdown seemed to be commencing, a dizzying view from his eyes being created then exacerbated by the blackberry booze of an unknown proof. It was for these exact white-hot situations when he needed a major cooling down to kick into gear, an outlet or exercise to channel his fury, halting the breakdown. *Maybe I could get some help on breaks. Meet some of the doctors and have some casual chats on the grounds at work with Dad. That wouldn't be so bad the more I think about it. I'll become more productive for him, more useful to the hospital and everyone—for years to come.*

With his head in another space and realizing he was almost in the next town several miles away, Greg stopped and turned his car around while trying to slow down his thoughts, attempting to bring them back to a crawl, as he had been sprinting ahead on the highway full-on and going east for no apparent reason. Making a dangerous U-turn in the middle of the road, turning the car around to drive back in the correct direction of west, he could see the grain elevator off in the distance; having passed it by going the other way, this structure of a most recent and egregious bane. Greg saw his town further on, and the smokestack of the hospital signaling the grounds behind and beyond the elevator, but before the town limits. There was a goat trail of a back road up ahead, which he could take, the quickest and most direct way...

I don't need no help. It's all a bunch of bullshit. Greg's mind changed again as he flicked a cigarette butt out the window. *Those fucking loonies. Crackpot doctors. Christ. I get pissed off sometimes, like my old man. And Mom, too, if you think about it. That's it. And those assholes only make it worse, egging me on all the time. Cunts. Relax, Greg. Jesus, relax man. Calm down, settle...*

Greg could not find the pack of cigarettes he had just bought, had with him, and had been smoking from—his vital calming sticks of truth. They were not in his front shirt pocket where they should be and where he usually put them. They were not on the seat, or at least not on top of all the junk sitting there. They were not in his back pants pocket, not that he could feel through the ass end of these trousers underneath him on the seat, nor touch when reaching thereunder to check. There was not even a lone single dart lying in wait in the open ashtray.

"Argh! I had the pack right here five fucking minutes ago," said Greg, shouting at himself, feeling unable to find much solace in anything on this short, stressful stroll of a drive. "For Christ's sake."

Already back speeding along, Greg opened his glove box to find a less recent half pack sitting on top of an old and tattered Rand McNally map of the country roads in the area and to the north. Reaching in to get it without looking where he was on the road in front of him, he stretched forward and leaned over to the right to try and grab the pack, pulling the wheel with him in a natural motion. Grabbing the pack as he retreated to his safe driving position, Greg realized he was on the shoulder heading straight into the ditch to the right. He swerved away the same second as he hit the border line of grass and gravel between the road and the dusty ditch, where he surely would have totaled off the front end of his car on the bit of a depression in the ground, scraping and busting it up before careening further into the wood and barbed wire-laced fence of the pasture. Greg felt a minor tremble go up his spine and through his core, causing a slight difficulty in obtaining a cigarette, but able to work through it, placing it in his mouth, grabbing the ashtray lighter, and firing it up.

"Oh, man," said Greg, which was all he could muster as he shook himself out of whatever was sending him into the ditch. He took another sweet swig of the liquid blackberry and honey tonic he was so enjoying, the only thing settling him down the tiniest bit.

In an odd irony, the near-miss of a car crash faintly relaxed him as it took his mind off the trailer park and the grain elevator for a moment. Greg picked up his pace to get back to his regular cruising speed: A normal fifty or so per cent faster than whatever the given posted speed limit was set at on the given road.

He watched the dashboard rattle as his speed climbed

higher. Greg drove faster and faster. Everything shook. *How is this old jalopy piece of crap not falling apart? How has it not already crumbled into pieces at this point in its well overused, rode rough and hard life?*

Now well into his third smoke—but first from the glove box pack—Greg hit a bump on the road, dislodging the still-hot lighter from the loose panel while at the same time spilling a pile of fiery ashes from the burning cigarette onto his hand, arm, and lap, followed by dropping the soft butt of the scalding smoke itself.

He saw the smoke and felt the burn from the cigarette and ashes in several spots at the same time, realizing he needed to get the dysfunctional torch-like lighter from the floor, visible as it was searing the mat down between his feet. Greg looked between his hand, arm, lap, and the floor, back and forth a few times in instant succession, brushing off the smouldering embers while bending down at a wild angle, reaching for both the cigarette and the red-hot lighter, at full speed ahead...

The Ming Dynasty II:
Insulin and ice picks

Doc Oxenham," said Cal, offering a pleasant wave towards the door and pointing to an open spot at their table, notwithstanding there being no free chair. "Come and join us, sir."

Doctor Oxenham was reluctant to join them and sit down in the restaurant, as he had an important meeting to soon attend and as the regular punch-card lunch crowd would be filing into Ming's in short order. However, he had to order his food and wait a few minutes for it in any event, so he could visit for that brief time and then use his meeting or any number of medical emergency excuses to bail out on them in a swift retreat back to the mental hospital.

"Gentlemen, a very good day to you all," said Doctor Oxenham, smiling while taking off his olive-green tweed jacket, hanging it over the chair from an adjacent table that he had dragged over for himself. "Sheriff, I am sorry on this morning, and thank you so much for your efforts there. I imagine, George, you have worked yourself up a big and deserving appetite, but we do offer our sincerest apologies for that most unnecessary event."

"Of course, at your service, as always," said George, giving the doctor a courtesy nod. "No worries, and that is true about my hunger though, so I'm going to eat like Yuri for lunch. A similar quantity but of a much better quality here at Ming's, goes without saying really."

"Sheriff was telling us about the incident this morning, and we got to talking about all the old ways and then some of these new treatments and whatnot. We were wondering about the new drugs you're giving out to those patients that we hear are starting to work out so well for some of them, even if some of their conditions are already a bit extreme for pretty much anything useful," said Cal, wanting to dive right in on the questions that Doctor Oxenham was in a unique position to answer, if he was so willing. "It seems if you can use chemistry to alter some of them, you won't need to do all the electrical stuff and polar baths, ice pick brain surgeries, and that sort of thing. So, what's the deal with these new drugs? Are they working good for some, or is that propaganda from your bosses and the chemists who want more of the government cash for their projects, that sweet gravy? More money for the melancholia. Heh."

"Yes, as Calvin mentions, our conversation was around some of these more violent animals," said George, clarifying and focusing the question for the psychiatrist so as not to allow Cal an unfettered tangent of questions that Doctor Oxenham might not be privy to answering. "With new medicines and whatnot, do you think we have a chance with some of them, like Mr. Campbell, Soupy the sprinter out there today?"

Settling down, the lunch group turned each of their full attentions to Doctor Oxenham, as if he were about to reveal some great mysteries, ones that only he was aware of, divulging the cutting-edge inventions in some code and only to this specific group now assembled at Ming's Dynasty.

"Yes, there is still substantial investigation ongoing

on many of the older treatments, and modern research methods are helping us to come up with many new ones as well, all of the time," said Doctor Oxenham, offering some high-level points and a bit of extra flavour on some of his exciting new projects, believing it harmless to share such news with this local crowd who he knew, including colleagues from the hospital. "Among those new ones are many of the drugs given to patients today—regardless of whether they have schizophrenia or manic-depression, which I should say we are moving to use the term bipolar disorder... They are called psychotropic drugs. Chemists are continuing to create different versions for the many different conditions, as technology is advancing so fast in these times one can barely keep up some days. You may hear some call them psychoactive drugs, but that is the same thing with the terms being basically synonymous as they are."

"Psycho drugs, for the psycho, psycho, psychos," said Willy, widening his eyes and mouth as he spoke, as if pretending to be insane, looking to elicit a laugh.

"You're right, Willy," said Ronny, chuckling and nodding. "Psycho, psycho, psycho. No question. Especially the Tin Can Man."

"Indeed," said the psychiatrist, trying not to show his irritation with Willy's crude interruption. "Well, these modern marvels, they enter the system and go into the brain of the patient, working to alter their moods. They affect your mental state, engineering it: Your feelings, emotions, sensations. Some of them look like they do have great promise, and we are no doubt only in the embryonic stages today of this revolution using psychoactive drugs to treat patients—tip of the iceberg."

"To break it down, what you're saying is: The chemicals in the pill or needle, they go into the brain like to try and make it normal again, or better than it was in any event, like how you need put thyme in your stew, or chili peppers in your chili?" said Terry, trying to sum up the complex scientific points in a much more lay manner, in the form of an analogy and a question, in order to learn more in the hallowed presence of Doctor Oxenham. "Kind of like how coffee wakes you up?"

"Or whatever the hell weird spice mix Ming puts in these vegetables, it makes them perfect; the little manipulation is all you need," said Ronny, still eating away as he spoke. "Chinese five-spice powder, for the flavour and the cure. A bit of black pepper to top it off."

"Something like that, sure," said Doctor Oxenham, lightening up and laughing along with the silly group. "Sugar and spice; all that is nice. It might be as effective as any medical method, and no question more so than some of those old ones my primitive predecessors employed, like what you good folks were perhaps talking about."

As Ming was still busy preparing the various items he would be serving for lunch today, he looked up through the steaming hole of a window in the kitchen and realized three new customers had now joined the first three who he had already served.

"Well, speak of the devil on the topic of spices and sauces," said Cal, leaning back and tilting his chair on the back two legs to greet the proprietor. "Ming, it smells great as always, and while I enjoy visiting my friends here, watching these pricks eat while I'm already starving is really making me faint, so I'll go ahead and get a rush order on my usual dish, as always. Please."

"Of course, Mr. Calvin," said Ming, giving a polite bow. "I wouldn't have expected anything less, Mr. Cal, and in fact, the fish is already steaming back there for you—I could read your mind from the kitchen, sensing your aura. However, and full disclosure, I couldn't get the catfish in for this week, but I do have some lovely pike fillets that will do just as well in your dish. And you as well, Sheriff, and Doctor, the regulars, unless I can interest you in anything else?"

"You know me. Same as always, Ming," said George, nodding in agreement. "Winner winner; chicken dinner. Thank you, kindly."

"The same as always for me as well, Ming," said Doctor Oxenham. "But I do have an important meeting back at the hospital, and we are still dealing with the mop up from earlier, so I will have to take mine to go today. Thanks Ming."

"Certainly," said Ming, pleased enough with the regular orders. "Consider each order cooking already, and I'll bring some tea out in the interim..."

"Doc, talking about sugar and spice," said George, returning to an even more focused question. "As Cal and I mentioned, we were talking about what should happen to Leon and about all those old treatments. To be serious, though, for just a minute, what's the latest? Your psycho drugs, but I've also been hearing something about insulin, like that's used on diabetes patients?"

"Yes, although I am not using it myself on treatments or research, as we all try to create teams or clusters around our own research interests, clustering folks to focus on a given area of conditions or specialty, which should give us better odds on finding some successes for patients in all the various work being done," said Doctor Oxenham, realizing he was going to have to somehow explain it to the most interested men at the table while doing so in their language, as they were all giving him their full attention and complete focus. "But my colleagues have been using insulin in research, and I have seen what they are up to and the effects. It is a treatment they used early on some time age, but not for too long. And then it made a brief comeback and some doctors around the world are trying it out again, at least for research purposes. It is what they call the insulin shock therapy. The opinion was, or is, that giving a schizophrenic a shot of insulin puts them in a coma or deep sleep, which thereafter, combined with convulsive treatment, would shock them out of their terrible mental state, jolting them back into some sort of greater sanity.

"You all know and love Yuri, of course, your grand perogy champion hero. Well, he was one of the first to take that in the encore round. And he survived it, whereas many from those sessions stayed in their coma—never waking up, passing away. It might have even been right away as far as the brain dying, it shorting out rather than some transformative shocking out as they were hoping for. The resurgence in its use today is because, with further experiments back in the lab, several well-respected doctors are claiming new success with it, no doubt to varying degrees.

"I should say, too, that in all fairness, the early practitioners did not follow what we now regard as proper methods of diagnosis, then right through to the levels of treatment and care, and monitoring those results, evaluating them. Studying the patients with consistent observation and recording the outcomes to tweak them, continuing to improve on them, and refining the process in future rounds. And there were and are significant side effects to consider. For example: for those who woke up and lived beyond the experiment, the dose caused many of them to become obese during their comas and thereafter, and some became massive giants like Yuri, allowing him the capacity to pack away all those perogies today. Pioneer doctors claimed they were having breakthrough successes with this method elsewhere, so like so many other things of the times—at the hospital and in everyday life—we follow, we lag behind, and we copycat them. This is unlike some of the newer innovative methods such as psychedelia, which we will see where that takes us. Of course, it was not that long ago doctors here were proud to have advanced what was also considered a great modern method in performing lobotomies, which has since fallen out of favour as well. Lots of research, often two steps forward and one step back—or even one step forward and two steps back... But we do believe new treatments are seeing many positive outcomes and will only continue to improve as we move forward with the science of it all...

"But on insulin, it is interesting to ponder whether there was ever any basis for doing it, giving them that sugar needle or not. It seems to knock them right out, and the patient wakes up with no issues other than they have turned into an elephant, becoming an atrophying blob in the bed. And on your point about diabetes, George, often they become diabetic because of the insulin shock treatment, and then they end up losing a toe and a foot, and then they keel over due to direct complications of gangrene and whatnot. And so, the renaissance of the usage of insulin is an interesting study, and like I say, some still claim this works for some patients, but they do not know exactly how and at what success rate it is working as opposed to not bothering to do it at all and trying something else. As risk becomes an issue, the treatment seems to be waning yet again, while some cling to its value and want to continue on, even if for research purposes and experiments on those worst long-gone cases where it might make more sense or value by doing it than not doing it. It is a tough case and one fraught with academic bickering, let me tell you."

"Like Mr. Campbell. Maybe it did help Yuri or others, but they get those side effects, too," said George, as he and the other four sat gripped by the doctor's explanation of the insulin shock therapy. "You'd think it would be clear cut on whether it fixed up their heads or not, or if it messed them up all the same, or even worse... If they didn't pull out of the coma and drop dead, that is. Nuance in improvement versus, say, an explicit losing of the leg, which I wouldn't want myself."

"You are right, George, and it comes down to the brain," said Doctor Oxenham, wanting to reiterate and leave them with his key point as he would also try and wrap up his near-filibuster. "There are many theories and practices related to the coma. One, not dissimilar to the insulin shock treatment, is the idea of creating a so-called deep sleep in a patient. The individual is knocked out with various drugs into a coma they induce, but beyond the short shock from the insulin, these ones have them leaving them there for prolonged periods—days or weeks at a time, giving the brain some apparent real rest and the opportunity to re-charge itself, re-circuiting so they should be as good as new when they are awoken, or so the theory goes. Again, some slip away in their narcosis and do not return, so they must be disposed of with little knowledge gained beyond perhaps what dosage it takes to overdo it and kill certain types of patients based on their weights, ages, and whatnot. The hypothesis is not unlike when one is so tired from overwork and lack of sleep that you start hallucinating on some minimal scale like a disturbed person, but then once you rest, it was like it never even occurred, as you are all fine and back to normal. And so, if you are indeed batshit crazy and you have a real long sleep in a coma, it will—as expected in a parallel method—turn you back to normal through allowing your brain an equivalent rest."

"That's where the next champion will come from," said Ronny, in a futurist tone of certainty, as confident as if he were Nostradamus. "Mark my words, the reigning champ will go down one day, and it will be another bigger-bellied creation from the insulin shock program. That will shock Yuri himself and all his loyal fans here in town. Then the runners-up will want to join that program so they can bulk up for the following season, the next eating tournament."

"Heh, but that'd be cheating, like using a peculiar new growth formula some mad scientist creates, probably in Russia. To let you run a mile a minute or allow you to weightlift a thousand pounds," said Willy, snickering in agreement with his colleague Ronny. "Not like Frankenstein, mind you, but more like Superman. And who knows, maybe one day down the road, they'll make eating a real competitive sport, like football and hockey. Who can eat the most perogies, pieces of pie, hot dogs, and that sort of stuff. Make it an Olympic event even. 'And the gold medal in cheeseburger eating goes to...'"

Ming arrived with two small ceramic pots of tea for the table, which he explained was some special and excellent new product he had received from his supplier in San Francisco, which came from Hong Kong but which was grown in the mountains of Taiwan. Having overheard parts of their conversation in the small restaurant, he assured his six patrons this green tea would not make any of them fat; it was wholesome and healthy for your entire body and mind, and if they gave some to Yuri, it might even help the hefty fellow shed a few pounds and clear the cobwebs.

"Well, we don't want that," said Cal in an ersatz disbelief. "I already have my money on him again next year, and I'm betting he'll smash his own current record. The over/under odds are he'll eat one hundred perogies next year in one short go. On the other hand, if this tea sheds a few pounds like Ming says, well... George, Willy, bottoms up!"

As Cal landed the joke that he believed was an objective kind of funny, hitting his humour with great precision and timing, the six customers and the restauranteur all had a good laugh together, including and especially George and Willy, who in a fine spirit of self-deprecation, each grabbed one of the floral-patterned pots to pour their own tea then poured for their nearest tablemates, offering a gentle clank and a verbal 'cheers' across the table, taking a first sip even though it was still of a scalding hot temperature.

"The brain is so complex," said Ronny, not wanting to lose his own train of thought while still tittering away. "I look at it from the eyes of a plumber, and I'm sure these guys all do in their own way with unique vantage points, but so many of these recent and even current methods seem so primitive. And yet I know technology and everything keeps getting better and better, so we will get there soon enough. But imagine those in the not too far off future who will look back at us today and think we were like pre-human monkeys still stuck in the Stone Age with what we were trying to do to help our mentally ill folks."

"That's just like how Cal feels now about his knowledge with respect to the clitoris," said George, with everyone cackling louder than before. "No, Calvin, it's not only you—it's all of us men, fine men that we are."

"Not with these special fingers," said Cal, in an odd mix of modesty and arrogance, wiggling his mangled hands around to make his fingers look like a hobbled crab or limp spider. "Magical in here, designed for them, from God's mind to my hands. Ladies love Cal's powers."

The group had yet another good, hearty laugh and then sipped their cups of green tea in a quiet unison.

"It seems with most methods, whether they work or not, it is always about trying to control the blood flow throughout the body and to the brain, or similar in efforts manipulating and managing the activity in the muscles or nerves," said Doctor Oxenham, considering that if he went off on another playful monologue for them he could rag the puck, thus running out the clock until his take-out lunch had arrived and he could leave this table and go back to work. "This is because they assume it is a mechanical thing in the body, and with the brain chemical, but in a mechanical sense, some equation is maybe a bit off. And then the doctor-researchers are off onto the next thing as though the first tries and other things were nothing that could be controlled in that way, but can be harnessed in some new way, so they try that one out next...

"Another invented analogy was that people thought for so long—and some idiots still do—that the condition of epilepsy is the same thing as what affects the unhinged folks, but it is clear to me it is not the same thing at all, save for some basic electrical commonalities. Some epileptics feel sleepy and tired after they shake it out, cuts and bruises notwithstanding. There was a cohort of physicians who believed if you shock a troubled soul into a seizure, it will rattle the chemicals and wires in the brain, bringing them to, creating a more pleasant state than prior. And so, they would instigate them and try and find the solution there. But some would swallow their tongues and die, or it would trigger something else causing untold terrible side effects, injuring themselves in many other awful ways."

"What about the lobotomy," said Willy, interjecting in an antsy way. "I know it's still used, or at least it was not too long ago now, but I can't for the life of me see how it's supposed to be effective. It seems like even today our methods are, like Ronny says, from the Stone Age or way back, or it's like a twisted torture with no effect. Or does it do something, for real? I assume it does, or there's no way the government or public would allow it to keep going at this point, or at least to a few years ago or whenever. Or am I wrong? Maybe everyone is next-level ignorant."

"You are not wrong in those respects, no," said Doctor Oxenham, happy to move on and take whatever lightning round questions came at him, as he looked back to the kitchen window and knew that Ming would have his take-out bag here at the table any minute now. "Boring a hole into peoples' heads was a prehistoric thing they did to allow demons to escape. We would do this back when, for the most part, we were still monkeys swinging in the trees or eventually wandering around the savanna. Well, much more recent than that, but say early *Homo sapiens*, Neanderthals—we are still the primates we are today. Imagine the crude tools they would have used thousands of years ago, or only hundreds... Or even a few decades ago, actually: They would have used some rudimentary tools, but also sticks and stones, like with Leon, smashing away at a skull without any semblance of precision. Even today you can stabilize the device and whatnot, but you are still boring in like an auger through the thick ice to create a hole for ice-fishing. At least there you hit water is all, but if you overcompensate, you will hit the brain, and then what do you end up with when it gets all pierced and mashed up like that?"

"Like the purple puke monster I saw on hole five today," said Cal, interrupting once again. "He picked and ate all these cherries, then vomited them up all over himself. He's another one who could use almost any treatment—it's worth trying whatever you have at your disposal on that fellow, that zombie, as you guys might learn some new stuff along the way, too, to help others."

"Jesus, Cal," said Willy, disgusted. "Some of us are well into our meals here, even if yours hasn't arrived yet. And let the good doctor finish his important story, will you?"

"No problem at all," said Doctor Oxenham, intervening to avoid any further deviations. "We still need to do everything we can to try and find what is wrong with the brain, what is causing all this mental illness. But the lobotomy is not it, and so the method has been suspended here and across the country, I am quite pleased to report."

"There's some digging around in there, fishing for answers, in blindness in most cases, shooting in the dark," said George, thinking it through aloud. "Removing the evil spirits within, while allowing germs and dirt and all kinds of pollution and shit in, which would kill them fast, or by suffering if not from the immediate shock or first trauma to the brain. The infection would do it."

"How would they cover it up before they had hats?" said Terry, figuring chiming in with a tame wisecrack would be appropriate enough. "Without some post-surgical sombrero, wouldn't the demons seep right back on inside?"

"With lobotomies..." said Doctor Oxenham, smiling and playing along while trying to steer the discussion at least somewhat straight. "As with some of the other treatments, it was reckoned your brain needs kicking into gear, as though it is stagnant like an old slough in the country. Those with certain conditions of mental illness need waking up with a thrusting stab into the brain, using a pick to lance right through the nose or tear ducts of the eye and hammered into your head with a little mallet. Then they twisted it and sawed it around in there until your circuits got working again. It calmed patients down because it turned them into total zombies—to use your term, Calvin. It is like using your fist to punch the car hood or engine parts, as though that will put it back into shape and make it work again. Or slapping the radio around to tune it in if it is on the fritz."

"You know, I bet Leon likes this method," said Ronny, having been thinking about this for several minutes. "And with the drilling part, the boring... He could pour in some hot water and take the spoon to scoop the soup du jour right out, like drinking out of a coconut husk or cored pineapple on a tropical vacation, or how you eat a crab or lobster with the little sterling fork and tools, but with the skull and brain. He'd take flight just thinking about that exciting mealtime possibility."

"Or Soupy would invent his own, custom-made," said Willy, feeding off Ronny's idea. "A special eating utensil for a bored-out head, his own line of kitchen tools. Although not a major market for that sort of item, you sure wouldn't hope, anyways. He'd need to create secondary markets for it, other uses."

"Mr. Campbell isn't inventing shit," said Terry, wanting to re-enter the discussion after his hat joke, but he was becoming grossed out and disinterested in the current direction of the conversation. "Doc, what about all that bullshit you mentioned to me when we were fixing the electroshock apparatus, about those colleague quacks and their magnets?"

"Yes, that is a good one, Terry," said Doctor Oxenham, as he began to feel as though he had been sitting with these five folks for several hours rather than a mere few minutes. "Some frauds in our profession—as I must admit, we have many of them in the world of psychiatry, psychology, and pharmacology, not unlike every other vocation, including each of yours, as you would well know from certain colleagues in your fields, useless and corrupt contractors and the like, no doubt... They have been testing magnets and gravity, like the strong magnetic pull from the forces and what that does to the rippling wavelengths of brainwaves, as if trying to place metal in the head with that powerful a force will somehow manipulate their minds and actions, trying to create a proper balance with a gravitational pull. It is such horseshit, like astrology and the old snake-oil folklore doctor charlatans who used to come to town in their wagons to sell mystical phony tonics and supernatural potions back in the day. Terry, you are bang on: They are frauds, even if some are well-intentioned enough to do anything they can to suggest new options to cure the insane while seeking the glory. And some get the buy-in that they have even seen enough change in a patient or two—which is almost always anecdotal and coincidental—to suggest some level of success, and thus they continue the treatment for some time before eventually the jig is ultimately up. And then they leave town and are gone for good, with no real change having occurred, or often leaving negative change behind in their wild wake."

"I left some change for the Skunk this morning," said Cal, feeling the need to insert himself and his humour into the serious talk on inventive quacks and their impotent magnets. "Not that I even need to say it, but Fred bought a pop and then went and right pissed himself afterwards, I do believe, so I guess that's even some negative change left behind. I thought I was helping him, too. Next time maybe I'll give him a toy with a magnet in it, see if he can fix himself with that method. He can shove it up his ass and beam his brains somehow."

"I see you are in favour of the insulin shock as well, Calvin," said Doctor Oxenham, offering up his own joke for the guys. "Perhaps you are baiting us with your prediction on Yuri, but you are secretly training Fred to take the trophy next year, giving him all that sugar in the soda, trying to beef him up, as it were."

"Yeah, well, the Skunk could sure use some extra layers of body mass on him, always wearing the winter gear on scorching days like today, sweating away behind the down fill comfort," said Cal, shaking his head in reflection. "Although the outright coma might've been more effective for him than anything else."

"Another crooked doctor they ran out of town quite a while ago now. He was working on a cockamamie theory around making patients sweat by inducing fevers in them, which he was doing by administering injections full of blood filled with parasites," said Doctor Oxenham, presenting this information as if he himself was baffled, and so these folks should, in turn, also be mystified if not floored. "That doctor claimed if you could heat them up like that, it would work to overcome and kill off bad parasitic and disease-causing insanity, which he then began extrapolating on with all kinds of other ideas around blood transfusions, where the blood then seemed to be causing other problems. For example, he was giving malaria to some patients to try and cure their syphilis, which was causing their mental illness... But then, either way, what about the malaria?"

As Doctor Oxenham went on with his explanation, Cal's mind turned to his original ask of Doctor Putnam this morning when he was soliciting him for some penicillin. As soon as Doctor Oxenham mentioned syphilis as causing insanity, Cal thought about his upcoming planned trip to the city, where he might get crabs, the clap, or this, the great imitator. His eyes glazed over as he heard Doctor Oxenham start talking about the many writers and famous others who had the affliction through history, and who had it in such a public manner.

Ming arrived with fresh tea and said the three outstanding orders would be coming right up. In the meantime, he was excited to give the table of regulars a proud sample dish of something none of them had ever before seen. There were six purple items that had been sautéed in something. There was one for each of the assembled gentlemen, and each one with a toothpick stabbed into the centre for easy taking, for trying.

"It's delicious Chinese eggplant, the main product, along with some red cabbage and Chinese radish, with some unique spices and my own special homemade sauce," said Ming, pre-empting the inevitable looks and questions on what this was they would be eating, or at least taste-testing for him. "It's the best for you and a rare item. I can only get it from my suppliers in San Francisco or Vancouver, and even then only once a year or so, at best. These arrived in the same shipment as that special green tea. Please, enjoy."

Cal sported a noticeable excitement with respect to this new exotic dish from his friend Ming. At that, George rolled his eyes yet again while the others each took a toothpick, trying something else—as presented to them—with reluctance, if only out of courtesy and respect, and as a slight deviation from their chosen regular and individual main lunch dishes of: Fried rice, stir-fried mixed veg, an eggroll, and the BBQ-ish-style meat of the day—and fish for Cal. The automatic lunch meals desired and coming to them such that Ming never really had to ask what they wanted, nor even offer up a menu, even if he did confirm said predictable orders for show.

"Ming, good lord," said Cal, chewing away more than necessary to savour the flavour. "This is incredible. What a unique taste. Amazing."

"That is without question, bloody brilliant," said George, lapping up any last drippy remnants of the sauce from his mouth as the others all nibbled and licked their own lips in accord. "Ming, your new items never fail us, no question. Thank you."

"That is excellent, Ming," said Doctor Oxenham, starting

to stand up. "Sweet and sour flavours in there, yet in a nice compliment with one another. Impressive.

"But Ming, while I am sorry, I do have to get going, as there is this one senior government bureaucrat in town I must speak with before he heads back to the capital later this afternoon," said Doctor Oxenham, looking between Ming and the hospital workers. "Would one of you gents be kind enough to bring my lunch out for me when you come back down? Just my main office, up above reception in the forensic unit?"

"Of course," said Willy, with Ronny and Terry nodding their heads in rapid concurrence, in full agreement, even if with mild disappointment in that Willy was quick enough to pull the trigger first. "We'll be right behind you, so it'll still be good and warm when we get it to you. No problem, Doc."

"That is great, thank you," said Doctor Oxenham as he wiped the plum residue off his lips with the length of his left index finger. "I have got to run, but was about to mention, thinking about that purple colour, I was going to give you some detail on our newest discovery we have engineered, the method I mentioned where we are trying out some drugs to manipulate moods. In fact, we're using grain as the basis for it. I should say the grain is almost black like obsidian, a quite dark colour but with hints of deep purple, perhaps like a raisin. And I was going to say, I have already mentioned it to you in further detail, George, and I think you were there, Willy, when we were working on it one day, so you might all already know a bit about it. The psychedelics. At the very least the hope is this new class of drugs will help the more minor afflictions while possibly doing more to control those with the most extreme of deep troubles and conditions, in terms of their moods and behaviours, their emotions... Anyway, I do apologize, but I must run. Thank you again, Sheriff. Thanks, gentlemen. Have a wonderful afternoon."

Excessive rain = purple grain = purple rainfall in the brain

"'Manipulate moods,' he says," said Cal once Doctor Oxenham had taken his leave, blathering on as if he were still on his home turf at the barbershop only a few buildings away. "I guess if he says 'engineer' it means they're doing it with great accuracy, with precision. They've got a hypothesis, they've done the math, crossing the 't's and dotting the 'i's, drawing the raisin triangle. Anyways, they're doing all that stuff right here by the sounds of it, making new drugs and testing them out in experiments on our patients, lucky or as unlucky as they might be, for the good of the world. That's why we keep getting all these different foreign doctors and specialists from all over, moving in from abroad. They're coming here to manipulate our surroundings, our feelings. He said it, not me."

"How does that make you feel, Cal?" said Terry, trying to pretend to talk like a shrink, but failing as he slurped up his final spoonful of a side wonton soup, clanking the bowl as he was tipping it and leveraging the angle to get the last drop of the chicken broth. "Manipulating your feelings."

"Calvin doesn't have any feelings," said Ronny, jumping in as he continued to eat, munching away on his last bite of crispy egg roll, sprinkling crumbs of batter about his place setting and lap. "They might give him some feelings though, some emotion, grow his sense of empathy. I guess that's kind of their point in some respects. Making it happen in a synthetic way."

Everyone chuckled as Ming arrived with the regular lunch plates for George and Calvin, telling the hospital workers that he would keep Doctor Oxenham's warm in the back until they were ready to head back to work at the mental institution.

"Yes, in fact, that's the most interesting thing I've heard of late. I was talking to Doc Oxenham about it a couple weeks back and again this morning with one of his new young research doctors there from the university. Once we had Mr. Campbell back in the can, his own can, I was asking him some these same questions," said George, looking down to his steaming dish that was too hot to eat, gazing at Cal doing the same, and peering at Ronny, Terry, and Willy, who were each nearing their last bites. "This nerdy kid, he said they're using this new drug, this chemical formula they've invented. It changes your head in a big way, makes you see in colours, where you're all happy and calm, going into this fantasy world of a prism for a while. When it does that it all works out real good. But the pretty colours can become a full kaleidoscope, creating these delusions, making them even crazier. It's quite early in the lab stage of investigation, where they're doing the research and testing on these patients, but they say if they can get it right, the protocols in dosages and whatnot, it might be real useful to some of them, from mild right through to severe cases. There's those psychoactive or psychotropic drugs the doctors said, but they call this specific type a psychedelic, like Doc Oxenham just said to us now."

"Yeah, I heard all about this from some workers there,

and Bill was telling me about something the other day when I went to pick up some, er, blackberries from him," said Willy, winking at the sheriff. "Someone told him that, too, and he explained it like it was an artificial process, you know how a chemist does whatever they do in mixing stuff. But it's natural for grain or from grains. That's the source of it. Bill said when it's real wet out, like super-moist, the wheat and rye get a fungus growing right on the grains—it happens if the soil and plants all get too wet, then it grows on like that. It's obvious we don't have any worries of that this year in this heat and dryness, but when it does do that rare rain all summer, some kernels in the heads of grain turn a dark purple, kind of a deep red wine. Bill said it can poison you and even kill you, suffocating you from within, the toxicity making you convulse and such. Hallucinations from it are a certainty, which no doubt some doctor noticed, and that's the origin of these drugs, the genesis in a nutshell. These doctors or chemists and pharmacists—or whoever are taking it and making it in their labs now—they're using it on the patients to see what happens to them, all trial and error like."

"They say they're trying to help the patients, to get them better, but it seems to me they might be messing them up even more than ever," said Terry, uncertain of himself. "Although all the attractive colours might be kind of fun and make you happy. Maybe that's not all bad, I guess."

"Yeah, that sounds superb, a true prism in your eye," said George, voicing his skepticism. "I imagine the rainbow's rather fun if you don't mind it also making you sick, vomiting and convulsing, gangrene setting in..."

"The purple grain potion turns you purple, and not

only in your head with all your violet colour thoughts," said Cal, finally beginning to dive in on his lunch dish. "Nature sure has a way, doesn't she? Amazing stuff."

"Bill said he'd never tried it out himself, but that got me thinking," said Willy, sharing his creative marketing idea aloud. "Maybe Bill could find a new market for his shitty dark grain gone bad, so I asked him if, in those bad years with all the moisture in the fields, he couldn't find that new market right down the little dirt road to the hospital. That's where he could sell them his poor-quality fungus grain for their lab experiments. It's even closer a market for him than the elevator, as the crow flies at least, and the grain traders wouldn't buy the poison grain anyhow."

"That's right," said Terry, approving of Willy's concept. "He could sell it to them, and those chemists could harness it somehow, and even then they could cook it up and feed it to the patients anyway. They wouldn't even notice if it was in their sloppy rations, would they? Oatmeal cut with some dark, fresh bramble berries, rancid or not. Botulism? Bullshit!"

"Well, if what they saw turned colours on them one day, I guess they would," said Ronny, thinking through the steps. "Although many of them can't communicate it to the doctors and nurses in there, and who knows what with all the garble of visions going through those heads at the best of times, if they'd even notice a difference from their regular ones, bland versus vibrant."

"The one thing Bill did say was that he's been playing around with some of his recipes, hand-picking and using the ergot pieces of the grain—that's the poisonous purple stuff, with the ergot fungus—to make a special brew," said

Willy, teasing them without lying. "This is one which he only gives his closest of friends and neighbours."

"Cal, look at your ear there, the left one," said Ronny, pointing at it. "It's a bit red, like dark red, and it's been changing colour ever since you walked in here with George. No wait, it's mauve now, or violet."

"That's gross, Cal," said Terry, trying not to smile, feigning seriousness. "Disgusting. You've got to go see Doc Putnam and get that festering shit checked out. Can you hear us OK, Calvin? And what do you see—is it blurry or spinning?"

"You silly, stupid cocksuckers, all of you," said Cal, chortling. "We all know if Bill was really doing that, Greg was the one who got the jar with the special purple potion in it, even if to test it out and see what happens. Then we'd get it after, if it was a true premium product, if Greg survived the slurry of a drink."

"Heh," said George, talking through his first full mouthful of food. "Now isn't that the damn truth of it all. Poor bastard."

Willy, Ronny, and Terry got up, each leaving a bill and sundry change on the table at their respective places, bidding adieu and a pleasant afternoon to George and Cal, waving with a smile and verbal thanks to Ming on taking their leave as they approached the exit. Ming flagged them down to ensure they took Doctor Oxenham's take-out lunch along with them, to him, telling the group to relay to the doctor that Ming would put it on his, Doctor Oxenham's, tab, to which they each nodded in concurrence and set off. For good luck, as Ming had told them years ago, each gave a gentle pat on the heads of the golden dragons as they left, the mythical beasts as custodians, watching out for them on their journeys, for luck and safety back to the hospital, and beyond.

"Alright, enough of all this BS foreplay. Let's eat," said George, digging in hard on his chicken fried rice, raking it in search of a little bit of scrambled egg for each bite.

"Indeed, let's chow on down," said Cal, getting the nutrient-dense vegetables into him first, those most important items before the even more essential meat.

Having said not another word to each other in the less than two minutes it took to get in a few solid bites, if barely a couple of mouthfuls, the sheriff's deputy, Corb, came storming into Ming's Dynasty in a visible sweat, his panting drowning out the frantic chime juddering on the door.

"Sheriff, there's been a…" said Corb, leaning on one of the vacated chairs with a free hand, trying to catch his breath while wiping his forehead with his other palm to eliminate any obvious drips. "There's been another… There's been a terrible incident. You'll have to come. We've got to get going. Now!"

Farm redux and a parting:
One half-ton down; half a one-ton up

Bill got back to the farm and did not waste any time like earlier in the morning, focusing instead on his sole mission of the afternoon. The greatest intensity of the midday heat was approaching. He thought about Rose on his drive up the farmyard road as he was viewing the house. Rather than going inside now, he figured it best to take away the one load that was already set to go out; then he would come back and make her a late lunch or early dinner, do some chores, finish up on taking off the last rows standing in the remaining field of a few dozen acres on a quarter section of land nearby—minus some scrub and a modest slough in the way, shedding a wasted acre or so, here and there. He would then haul a final late evening load into the elevator. *That's an epic day if ever there was one.* Bill was delighting himself with his farmyard fantasy of heroism.

Bill pulled the half-ton truck parallel to the grain truck and swapped vehicles, changing seats. Loaded with grain to the maximum volumetric capacity—not so much that it spilled out and over the canvas top, but nearly at that level of a precipice—Bill put the old one-ton truck in gear and at an austere speed of almost still idling it, he advanced in a slow roll out his yard drive, past the red barn, the not exactly flourishing garden, weathered house, caraganas and willows, and onward towards the 'T' at the exit of the road.

As he coasted the old beast away from the yard, he reached over to grab a fresh smoke stored in his ashtray and realized he had forgotten to deliver one standard jug of the good stuff to his neighbour yesterday. *How'd I miss that both yesterday and this morning?* Bill was questioning his memory, wondering if his mind was starting to go on him. One quarter section across, Bill viewed the neighbour's adjacent farmhouse out the passenger window at the same time as he noticed the lid of a similar stock container in the compartment between the seats. He was not going to stop for any delivery at this stage, only the one in the back of the truck, the grain to haul and dump. A hot and thirsty Bill grabbed the premium jar, popped the top, took a solid swig of the light cloudy mauve liquid, then another, before wiping the rim and top with his shirt and re-securing the lid again, placing it back where it had been in the console. When the delivery was once made to thy fair neighbour...

Well, I'll get to it when I get to it. If I'm lucky.

Slowing down without quite stopping at the junction—there was no one visible in the half-mile seen in either direction—he rolled down the dirt path and up onto the gravel range road, straight towards the main highway, gaining speed and kicking up more dust, but a new and different form of dust from the gravel versus the dirt. Everything was dust, as if it did not matter what the substance was in this overwhelming heat wave, because it was pure dust. Bill was beyond thinking about it now, for the dirty particles had settled in and were here until winter when the white powder would bury it for months, so he decided to move on.

Bill began slowing down again as he rolled along the gravel road sloping towards the main road, the highway. *Would this paved path also be of dust?* Bill was in a daze from the heat, realizing he could not actually move on from these thoughts. Even knowing he had just returned from the barbershop down this exact same route, he could not help but consider it: One had no choice but to think about this systemic dust. *Maybe it's in part because my eyes are going on me.* As it was all he could concentrate on, Bill could not move on from the blurry and arid conditions, not for the moment, alas.

Approaching the border where the gravel merged with the asphalt to create another 'T'—just as he had approached the dirt to gravel 'T' only a couple of minutes ago—he could see nothing coming in either direction, this time with the uninhibited view of at least a mile in each direction, even if his cataracts were starting to develop a blur, or some combination of that, the overwhelming heat, the potent booze, the churning dust. Because of the nature of the dip off the gravel and up onto the pavement, a rolling stop was deemed enough as he again gave a swift glance in each direction. At about the same pace as in his farmyard drive—which was not much more than an idling speed—he hit the highway, making a move to up the power by giving the pedal a quick and gentle squeeze while clutching down with a rough punch to bring it into second gear, all in a seamless yet jittery motion.

The movement may have seemed somewhat seamless, but his raspy gear box was years beyond not only its would-be expiry date, but also beyond its last real and professional maintenance of any kind. Bill tinkered and knew how to fix anything on his farm, and more than that, but the old boy waited until something needed it in a serious way, until it was almost inoperable. While there was an aspect of procrastination, the more significant issue was on fixing priority items first, triaging the great list of chores. And if this grain hauler rust bucket of a box on wheels was still making its way between his on-farm granary bins and the inland terminal elevator, back and forth and only on these special harvesting occasions of late summer and early fall, it did not need fixed—not before the tractor, swather, combine, header, auger, all the seeding equipment needed to be in tip top shape for next spring, his own vehicular truck to drive to town each day, the household stove on the fritz, buzzing ice box, etc. What did a shakey-bakey, loosey-goosey, sticky-wicky clutch matter? Bill could just grind it on out to get the grain on in.

The movement with the greatest friction of all was from two to three, a grating of which needed to be manoeuvred in a hasty instant once second gear was in place, at least on the highway—like from the first gear to the second, or low to second, to be true. Bill was picking up speed well enough, with dust following him onto the beginning of the highway stretch, kicking up a trail of a mini storm cloud behind the truck. With his hand remaining on the worn-out shifter, giving it the perfect equilibrium of juice on the pedal, he gave a slight pull down from two to jam it up to three, using some extra emphasis from his shoulder to help get him there. He hit the middle neutral zone, and it jerked as per normal, then again down on the clutch and pedal, a thrust like never before—except since the last recent time—to the right and up, giving it this desperate attempt to put it in the pivotal and essential third gear. Shuffling the stick to the right and on the way up to its final position, Bill let out the clutch as slow as a sloth would and got ready for the...

The grinding shook his hand from the shifter, thrust him forward much harder and quicker than he had expected, and certainly not like anything he had remembered before. Bill smashed his forehead against the steering wheel, and the movement slammed him back into his seat but at an angle, thumping the back of his head against part of the hard frame on the bottom of the window, his head bouncing around like a pinball in the truck.

"Jesus Christ!" said Bill, screaming to himself from the excessive rattling.

The first reaction of Bill was how he could not believe the action that had just occurred. It had been getting worse for months, but wanting to be true and honest with himself, it was years, and this problem truck now appeared to be verging on undriveable. It was time to fix this ancient one-ton grain truck. The fix was long overdue. He determined this was going to be the last haul, or at least the last harvest, until it got some fond and firm attention, some stern loving maintenance in his steel shack of a shop.

The second thought of Bill was for the blows he felt on both the front and back of his head. His hat was obstructing his view, having had the peak crushed into the wheel, which he believed might have saved it from being much worse. When he adjusted the crooked angle back to normal, he felt the pulsating and concuss-inducing pain on the back, and so gave it a gentle rub while discovering the stinging sensation on the front. Realizing he was still in third gear, Bill made the now much simpler change over to four, gaining some more appropriate speed in the process. He grabbed the dirty green peak of his cap with the shifting hand and took it off, dabbing the area of the sting with his free forearm. Stuck on his forearm was a good spot of blood—a sizeable dollop and a larger smudge of it around the periphery of the fresh wound.

"Jesus Christ," said Bill, once again and this time moaning as he was still in disbelief, albeit with less shock and volume in his words this time, accepting it.

Bill considered turning around to head back home and take care of the injuries, this gash and lump on his forehead and this bump on the back, but where he was on the highway at this point he could already see the elevator on the other side of the road, not even three miles ahead, where the traders, handlers, and cleaners would be waiting within to retrieve his load of grain...

The delivery

Bill pulled off the highway by making a left turn across it, driving down the gravel service road and up to the base of the delivery ramp at the grain elevator. He stopped before reaching the halfway mark as there was one truck ahead of him, which was already well into the process of dumping his load. At his angle behind and beside the elevator, a few dozen grain hopper cars were lined up on the adjacent railway tracks in a position to follow behind their leader, the locomotive engine. Bill found it a bit frustrating sitting there in his truck in the heat. *But it's not a huge queue. And it should move along quick enough.* He figured there would be at least three or four trucks there at this time of day on a Monday during harvest, so he considered himself lucky that this first load of the week was already happening ahead of schedule.

Bill lit himself a cigarette, blowing smoke out his window as he rolled it down further while looking at the long train lined up next to the elevator, which would soon take on the grain as fast as the inland terminal could dump it into the hoppers, different processes and loads notwithstanding. He looked back towards the highway in the direction of his farm. Once this delivery was made, he needed to get right back in the field for the afternoon, where he would stay working all night. Then he would come back to the elevator again tomorrow for sure, if not even later this evening, he continued to tell himself. Prices were hovering somewhere between decent and good in the area, and Bill was tired of the hassle of storing his grain on the farm if it did not need to have some time in the bins in his yard, and not if he could have the cash in his pocket and the grain off his farm, out of sight and out of mind, money in his jeans.

Thinking all of this through made great sense to Bill. As he continued to sit waiting in line, he noticed the bigger trucks at the elevator now, the one that had pulled in behind him and the one in front of him, the latter of which would be almost finished with the dumping of his load, the driver manning the hatch. Bill reminisced further, paying attention to these modern trucks that he had never thought much about before now, or not beyond his having paid attention to the general situation of the larger modern farmer. These grain trucks were all clean and with what looked like fresh coats of paint, as if they had pulled right off the new truck lot and were already hauling grain directly out here to the elevator. *They wouldn't have clutches that jam on you, or at least not where you smash your head into the steering wheel while shifting gears. They'd be real nice for an easy haul, a smooth delivery to elevator.* If he kept farming, Bill knew he would have to modernize and scale up like the rest of them. *Maybe I should keep farming right till I drop. Just like my grandparents, those hardy pioneers.* Bill took another good swig from his jar of fruity hooch as he considered what he would do in retirement should he trend that way, being frank with himself about his advancing age. It was obvious: If he quit, which he would, he would ramp up production of his on-farm value-added processing plant, increasing capacity so there would be no shortages, no rationing for his friends and customers, all the while maintaining his monopoly on his niche and local, even if illicit, artisanal beverage products.

As the growing line of trucks behind him were becoming antsy to move ahead, the present reality smothered his daydreaming. *Goddamned gears in this shitty old thing.* Whatever he decided to do, for whatever longer-term might be left, he would still need to deal with this truck at some point, and soon. He took off his hat and put his palm to his forehead this time, feeling that the damp line of blood across his forehead was already starting to dry, the swelling section still moist but crusting over. Looking at the inside of his hand, it looked like about a two-inch gash. He pushed himself up for a clearer survey in the rear-view mirror, confirming the extent of the damage: Bleeding, but at the end of the day it was a minor scrape with a slight cut along the line of shredded skin. It did not look as bad as it felt, but that would soon change with the ballooning later in the day and tomorrow with the bruising, as most of the full pink to red to purple to black and blue to yellowy green and back to normal peachy skin tones transformation still lay ahead in the days, and probably couple weeks, to come.

As he put his grubby green John Deere ball cap back on, the sounds of a fresh siren could be heard in the distance towards town. It grew louder. It was followed by a second distinct siren. The first sound screamed from behind him out on the highway, heading towards the direction of his farm, which could also turn into a back way out to the river and the hospital, near the cemetery with the glowing grave. A police car. *A lot of action today*, Bill thought, focusing and becoming concerned again for Rose, remembering her chronic pain troubles and realizing he had not gone in to check on her as he had first planned on doing before making this delivery. Accompanied by a second police car, an ambulance sped by on the highway, as if they were chasing the first cop as they were all traveling east.

The emergency vehicles disappeared, and as the sounds dissipated the driver in front of him rolled forward and out the down ramp on the opposite side of the elevator, exiting to the highway and heading back to his own farm to continue his own harvest, if he was not already finished up. Two elevator workers waved Bill ahead. He put his truck in gear, jerking forward a bit as he inched it up the ramp, jolting forward every few feet until he could stop on top of the grates to unload his grain. Bill—and the one-ton truck, the struggling beast—had made it in.

Bill put it in park, turned off the engine, and disembarked, looking back as the truck behind him had taken his place just off the ramp as he had so done himself. Two other trucks had now pulled into the queue behind that one, highlighting for Bill the good fortune he had on his timing. *What luck!*

"Howdy," said the younger grain worker, Larry, greeting Bill as they moved together to unlock and open the hatches.

"Well, hi there," said Bill, too exhausted for pleasantries but pleased to be dumping his load. "It's a real hot son of a bitch out there." Bill felt it was all he had left, in a repeat performance from earlier, but with less energy and enthusiasm than he had mustered in the barbershop of the morning. As the Sun climbed, it was further draining him empty, drying him out with each sizzling hour passing on by.

"It's as hot as a hungry Mexican's asshole," said the other and older grain worker, Art, who had jumped in with a greater zest than Bill was able, even though it was obvious Art had used this refrain many times before, probably of late and maybe having even cracked it several times today. Bill remembered Art using it on him during similar sort of warm deliveries in years past.

"Sure is now, isn't she?" said Larry, chiming in, covering the back of his mentor. "How're things looking down the road your way there, Bill? How much you got left to get in?"

"She's looking not too bad at the present moment. But what's left—it's got to come off right away or she'll bake out there, turn to dust. I'm going to turn around and head back to work, then I'll bring you chaps another load tonight, and a couple more this week. Then I'm done with the last quarter, God willing. And maybe done forever, just been considering that, in fact..."

Another siren could now be heard as they stood inside the elevator having their little meteorological chat of business pleasantries. The initial noise was growing louder, seeming to move even closer.

"Jeez, that's a lot of action out there today, like we're living in the big city or something," said Bill, considering it aloud and maintaining the tiring small talk, the collegial if banal banter of the transaction.

Before the elevator staff could respond or move to begin his unloading process, the most recent siren appeared on the highway for only the few seconds you could see it at that angle out the open truck door of the elevator, before it turned onto the grain company gravel road, following the little path up and stopping behind the now three trucks waiting in the growing line off the entrance ramp.

George got out of his police car, walking a brisk pace up the ramp towards them, kicking up dust from each boot while dabbing the sweat from his brow.

"Christ," said Bill, aloud again but talking to himself this time more than to Larry and Art. "It must be another escape."

"Could it be two in one day?" said Larry, his eyes darting between Bill, Art, and the sheriff.

"Jesus," said Art, shaking his head as he stared at the police car. "Brutal if it is."

Just another meeting

"Hi there, fellas," said George, acknowledging the two grain handlers. "Bill, good to see you again too, and so soon."

"Well, nice to see you as well, Sheriff," said Bill, still tired but realizing George was no doubt more exhausted and stressed out than he was, the crime and the asylum versus the harvest and the wife. "You eat your pussy for lunch already?"

"Heh. No, I was interrupted over at Ming's, as business called again, unfortunately. And we'd just dove into our tasty plates also, alas," said George, removing his western hat to give a gentle scratch at the top of his head. "And... Well, I'm afraid we got us a bit of a new problem this here time now."

"I hear you, George. We got us several problems," said Bill, responding but not understanding nor caring about the sheriff's problem, regardless of whatever it might be. "It's hotter than hell out here, crop has got to come off, wife and dog are sick again, gears in my truck here are broken to shit. Problems everywhere, but it'd make a damn good country and western song, don't you think?" said Bill, gaining a second wind, trying as best as he could to repeat the refrain from earlier at the barbershop, while adding a rare glimmer of a smile towards George, who was in on the first version, and to the two grain elevator workers, who were not in on it but knowing they loved a simple and punchy joke like that one.

Art and Larry both smiled along, chuckling away.

"Heh, well true enough there, Bill, and our problem includes your truck here, indeed it does," said George, attempting to converse in his normal and calm demeanour, but he could not stop dancing and fidgeting about.

"I'll be honest though, I don't care if she's broken, as sorry as I am with your plight though. But what I do care about—what concerns me, I should say, as it must concern me, professionally speaking... What concerns me is the guy you left dead back out there on the highway. That's our problem we got us now. A real and serious problem of a legal nature, if I do say."

Art and Larry both froze, aghast.

Bill also froze, still unsure if this was the serious or joking version of the sheriff. "Dead guy?" said Bill, flabbergasted nonetheless. "Huh?"

George took a calculated slow walk around the side of Bill's truck, doing a full scan along the panels and the wheels until he reached the back end of the old beast.

"Bingo, there it is," said George, waving them all over to the back, pointing at the apparent marks on Bill's truck. "See this right here?"

They all hesitated for a second, but Art went first with Larry in tow like a puppy or a cub following their mama. Bill shuffled along at last, almost indifferent, even if he held an understandable curiosity and confusion by whatever it was George was on about.

The three parties to the grain transaction stood still, looking down while the sheriff did a measured squat, pointing straight towards the spot, touching it. With a slow extension of his index finger, he pressed at the mark right in the middle of the timeworn and rusty back bumper, circling out from a slight radius of fresh damage around it with the tip of his finger.

"A solid dent there. Cobalt blue paint scuffed on here. And shit, there's even some shattered glass here, wedged right into your gate. No doubt about it," said George, confident in his investigation and seeming conclusion thereof, now keeping a cooler disposition—after all, it was apparent that a man was dead. At present, only the sheriff had the full understanding of this incident culminating in some deceased person—the complete details on the late driver of the little blue car, still sitting in his wreckage on the road not quite in their current line of sight from the open elevator door, but not more than only a few miles down the highway.

"Now, Bill, are you bleeding?" said George, looking at Bill's askew cap with fresh blood leaking from behind the hat down towards his eyebrow, with dried blood mixed with grit, sweat, and dust crusted over in a couple of patches of skin. "What's that under your hat there, on your forehead? What in the hell happened to you? I mean, what has happened since I just saw you at Cal's shop in town, not much more than an hour ago!"

Bill knew he was bleeding from smashing his face on the steering wheel during the difficult shifting of gears, but he was still unable to comprehend the situation being laid out by George—the heat, the drink, and the mild concussion not helping with his current cognitive abilities. He looked up at the sheriff, and with a measured reaching up, he removed his cap, taking it off to show his forehead wound from the slamming action as if worried about his guilt, even as he knew nothing of the particulars, nor caring in any sort of general nor specific way.

"George, I'm at a total loss here," said Bill, being honest in his confusion. "I drove straight here from the farm without stopping. I don't understand what you're talking about."

"Maybe that's the problem, your driving without stopping," said George, as if his words were a series of blunt jabs. "You just ripped right onto the highway without stopping then, did you now, not even wanting to yield one teeny tiny itty-bitty bit, as per the traffic sign there? Christ, that's your own range road!"

"Huh? No, I stopped at the end of the road," said Bill, defending himself even as he was becoming an abnormal level of defensive in the process. "This truck's full of grain. How could I not stop? She'd tip and flip, maybe roll right over into the ditch or onto the highway. Jesus, George."

There was a quiet pause while everyone considered the current facts as known, to survey this new and unique situation before them, as if brainstorming while they looked down to continue inspecting the alleged damage on the back of the truck.

"Well... And either way, the car hit him straight into the rear ass-end right here, clear as day," said Art, wanting in on the chat and to join the investigation, as he could see what had happened and so felt the need to present his own evidence as well as to help out his long-time customer, Bill, during this seeming pickle he found himself in. "Bill must've already been on the highway when some jackass flew right into him. Smack! Right there. That ain't Bill's fault, getting hit from behind."

"Why didn't you stop when he hit you?" said George, as if he already knew Art's comments to be the exact description of what had indeed happened. "When you bashed your head there? Why'd you keep on driving up here, bleeding and all? These boys aren't going anywheres."

"George, Christ," said Bill, growing angry. "I still don't get it. What you're talking about? I never got hit. This doesn't make a lick of sense."

"Bill, come on now. Don't bullshit a bullshitter. Look

right here," said the sheriff, pointing to the same spot again, growing frustrated himself, as much from the heat, his hunger, and general annoyance as from the traffic investigation and crime scene situation at hand. "You can't escape this one, not like Leon anyways."

Bill looked down again, his hands on his hips, with Art and Larry doing the same thing on each side of him, standing right behind him as if they were Bill's supportive sentries.

"Well, I don't get it. I don't know how that could've happened in any scenario, getting hit. I felt a jerk when I shifted, but it always does that, this giant old piece of shit here, the gears stick and it pushes you around is all," said Bill, kicking the corner of the back bumper with his roper boot. "I told you that earlier today even at Cal's shop. Christ's sake. Well... So, are you going to arrest me or something then, Sheriff?" said Bill, half-joking and half-threatening George, showing his explicit confusion and irritation through this range of his own unique and direct verbal and physical mannerisms now on full display.

Art looked at Bill and then at the sheriff, while Larry looked at Art and then shifted his gaze between Bill and the sheriff, as if watching some strange three-way triangular game of tennis on their grain elevator delivery floor.

George looked up from the bumper again, scanning the faces of the three others, with Bill getting the last and longer glare. The sheriff wiped his brow with his forearm sleeve, again trying to sop up the effluence of sweat from the heat.

"Arrest? No," said George, shaking his head as though it was a stupid question Bill had asked. "Heh, hardly. What could I get you for? Driving on the highway the right way?

I don't think so, no. Any witness would be with you on this one, too. The judge would toss that one out in short order. Eating up too much valuable court time, which is better spent on the likes of Mr. Campbell, Mr. Sanders, and their types of wicked ilk—Corporal Dwight, the perogy boss, the real criminals. Taking you in would be like... It'd be like taking in the railing on the bridge or the poplar tree that took out the jerk-off kid this morning. No mea culpa for the tree. No mens rea for you, Bill."

Bill was feeling sort of relieved, remaining somewhat baffled as the circumstance overwhelmed his other emotions, his own thoughts still racing, processing this mystery event, whatever might have happened back out on the highway, who might be dead, maybe others injured. And he was still thinking about his Rose, needing to see her and to hold her.

"I'm sorry to say, for it is an unfortunate circumstance," said George, thinking through the scenario. "But that Greg... He was a crazy son of a bitch that one. Always driving like a complete maniac, had a good stiff drink before, even earlier this morning, I'd suspect. Well... Anyways, something was not right with him. We all knew that. He was heading to work with his old man today. Christ, he really should've been committed there long ago himself. The whole thing's real sad, it is. Tragic, I suppose. And poor Deb and the kids."

"Greg?" said Bill, still seeming confused and seeking further clarification.

"Yep. His little peacock blue piece of shit car, that's what hit you there," said George, confirming the event. "See that paint, and glass—that's from his jalopy. It does make some sense, though, that you wouldn't've even felt it. It's so light. Of course, minus your nice handsome gash you got. Although he was moving a serious clip in it, real race car-like fast. Oh well. I better get back out there as we've got to get that road opened up again. Deputy Corb's most likely cooking out on that sweltering asphalt, spreading some sand on the fluids from the car. And the body."

With that, the sheriff walked back to his cruiser and spun it around, driving down the grain elevator road. However, when he reached the highway, he went heading the other way, opposite of where his deputy would have been at the scene of the crash—George appeared to be heading back towards town. Bill, Art, and Larry all stood at the edge of the ramp in silence, watching until George's car and resulting trail of dust were out of sight.

Due to the circumstances, Bill's emotions and mind ran as much as they could, which was not even a slight jog compared to most others in any semblance of the same grotesque situation.

"Are you going to unload me then, or do I have to do it myself? I've got less than twenty more acres on the home quarter field I intend to take off this afternoon and bring in later tonight, but before that I'm going to haul my last bin load back here right away, and she ain't going to do it herself now is she?" said Bill, changing his plans for the day on the fly, deciding to move quicker with harvest, asking Art and Larry as if he was scolding naughty children who were addressed as though they were now equal partners in this important effort.

The Ming Dynasty III:
Zhu sun, green tea; fortune cookie

Eating his last few delicious bites slower than ever and in a rare total silence by himself—at least so far on this hot summer day—Cal looked at George's almost untouched plate, which had lost its warmth, cooling off as he had noticed while eating the last few bites left on his own dish. The sheriff had only begun chowing down with Cal, excited as his warm lunch plate was delivered by their good friend Ming, the proprietor of this finest café in town and in all the area. Those first few bites brought on an ecstasy level of taste sensations in George's mouth and down in his empty stomach. But then Corb had come along with some purported critical emergency to which the sheriff ran off to attend to, to take charge of the grave situation. Cal's money—his smarter than smart, hair-cutting, all-knowing barbershop money—was on another cat gone climbed up the tree and could not understand gravity, some venerable want-to-be flying pussy, sans parachute. Or maybe it was another stupid kid jacking off while drinking and driving, crashing his car while wanking it, hitting a deer or moose or something more exciting this time, perhaps a near rigor mortis vehicular orgasm to ensure going out on top. *Although the bear part beats the juniper part. As prairie Gothic as that sounds.*

However, in a most intense lunch-time daydreaming session—induced by this sudden self-dismissal of the sheriff's—Cal's imagination took off on him, out into some other galaxy or dimension...

Leon had gotten out yet again, on the same darn day, within a few mere hours, the epic episode of teasing the officials and authorities;

or, the Tin Can Man was chained inside, getting tortured and punished (and 'treated') for his escaping and other sundry soupy shenanigans;

or, they found a casualty or some victim from the earlier escape of Soupy now down on the beach, with the flesh all eaten away at on those sunny shores of the sand bars, the corpse now carrion for the crows and other scavengers;

or, they had shocked and drugged up Mr. Campbell so much that he dropped over right dead in the hospital dungeon this time;

or, the Colonel did come back as a full-fledged zombie version of Mr. Sanders, who left regular people alone in their comfort and peace, yet the Dirty Bird continued his fornication of the fowl, having sex with chickens at an extreme and more torrid a pace than when he was still alive, in a modern commercial coop, tenderizing the birds on an industrial scale;

or, they put the chicken-banger, Soupy, and Yuri the perogy champ, all in a room together, way down in the bowels of the basement, and the shrinks let them get it on, no holds barred, going to town on each other in their own unique ways, with their special crazy powers and manners—in a room with three soup cans, three chickens, three perogies.

Holy shit! What would happen there? The incited antics: The battle of the borscht with a bird! And what if when one of them died, they added in a new one, piling on skunky Fred, Nazi Johann of the axis, veteran Dwight of the allies, the purple puke monster of the cherry orchard, and each single last one of those damned and demented hordes of individual patients, cleaning out the institution, madhouse, asylum, loony bin, nuthouse, hospital... Until it was right empty like, the institution abandoned, the hospital in ruins.

"Christ, where could George have rushed off to like that?" said Calvin, speaking aloud to himself as he took his fork, stabbing it down to pierce one of the last obscure pieces of food on his lunch plate, now no longer even warm.

"How do you like it all, Mr. Cal?" said the gracious server, cook, and owner, asking with an authentic and genial wide smile. "Can I get you some more of anything, anything else at all, for this afternoon?"

Ming had been looking down at Cal for a few seconds, knowing Cal was lost in himself, in some sort of deep cogitation in a special barber world. Ming had seen Cal look like this before, and often enough. Cal snapped out of his imaginative trance with a slight jump off his seat, into a proper posture and attention to the proprietor's question.

"Oh, Ming. Jesus, you startled me there," said Cal, regaining his bearings and ceasing his mind-wandering, even if it was on his most favourite subject of crazy patient antics and related fantasies. He was done at last, even with a few bites left, having spent so much time yammering on earlier with his pals and now as if rooted in his own personal musings. "Great lunch, really. Couldn't eat another sprout there, no way, Jose—no way, no how. Great rice, tea, veg, fish, everything as always. I love the, uh... The zhu sun! Did I say that right?"

"Zhu sun. Yes, yes. That's perfect, Mr. Cal," said Ming, smiling and bowing. "I'll have to take you on my next buying trip to the coast, and you can help me out with some stuff."

"Heh. I don't know about going that far, but I sure do like that purple stuff," said Cal, deliberating on Ming's comment and thinking further about his business. "I'll have a side dish of that later in the week, if I could. But I'll stay away from Bill's purple drink, as I don't think I need any of those colourful images in my eyeballs, those violet visions then floating around in my mind. Only in my mouth and stomach is where I want that good stuff."

"Yes, I hope that treatment is successful for the patients, and I know the great Doc Oxenham has high hopes for this method," said Ming, sipping his own green tea out of a small cup emblazoned with white and fuchsia lotus flowers that he was carrying around when one free hand was otherwise unoccupied. "And I hope it doesn't cause any ill effects and turn the clock further backwards. I'll tell you, in the last century, so many people in China got hooked on opium. One hundred per cent addicted, and that garbage made it seem as though they were insane sometimes. Doc Ox said they're even looking at that again today, to further react it through chemistry and use the derivatives as pain treatments and the like. I don't know if that's a good thing. Entire wars were fought over the stuff in China for decades. I hope it doesn't turn into something like that, neither the pain medication, nor the purple grain hallucination way he's talking about. Some gentle treatments that work well and with no nasty side effects, that's the master key."

"I hear you, Ming, and we need more guys like us who think these things through a bit better, deeper," said Cal, in a moment of philosophical grandeur, however baseless it was in actual substance. "Say, Ming, what do you think about our nuthouse here? I know what you said about some of the horrible drugs, but do you think they're doing any good down there, or do you think it holds much of a future the way we're heading?"

"The past is the past, and it's not often a pretty picture looking back," said Ming, almost reminiscing as if he had already thought this through with some considerable reflection over time. "It's not so rosy. They treated soldiers and regular people so bad, so poor—those who ended up in there, whether right or wrong. All those immigrants. My father is lucky he never ended up in there, a bold and maybe too extroverted new immigrant from China back then in his day, as he often said of himself, you'll remember. But look at where we are now: My daughter's finishing all her training at medical school this year. She is going to be a fully licensed doctor this time next year! And so, all that past stuff is not good, and we can't nor shouldn't forget it, because we don't want to repeat it. And yet it is behind us—not all of it, but we're getting there. The future looks bright, and forward is the only way we have to go. The mental hospital has its place, because what else would we do with all those crazy and dangerous pricks like Leon and Yuri? Jail is no place for them, but they can't be walking the streets all alone either."

"Jesus, Ming, you said it," said Cal, impressed with his friend as he always was. "You should be running the joint and we wouldn't have all these problems any longer, I bet. And that's real exciting about your daughter, a chip off the old block, Ming—I know we're all thrilled about her great achievements, so a huge congrats is in order! And if I ever need anything, like some penicillin or something, I won't have to go to that lazy prick Doc Putnam any longer."

"Heh. Oh, classic Mr. Cal," said Ming, applauding him with a requisite light laugh. "Anyways, what about our dear sheriff? Do you think George is coming back to eat, or should I clear it away for now, maybe package this up for him?"

"Well, with the ghost-like look Corb had on him when he came running in here, I got a feeling he's probably out there for a while now. Might as well clear us away here.

Sad to waste that good food, a damn shame. I bet he's starving out there in that heat, especially after this morning… Yeah, sorry Ming, I've got to get back to the shop myself. But I'll get both lunches today. You remember that: Sheriff owes me one now, next time."

"OK, yes. Yes, very good," said Ming, as he picked up George's still full lunch plate. "Thank you, Mr. Cal. Glad you enjoyed it all."

With a few deft moves, Ming cleared the plates from the combined tables in one swift go. Cal stood up to reach for his wallet, setting one bill and some change down as his payment, when the faint chime on the front door rang and in walked George.

"Whoa, whoa there Ming. Where are you going with my lunch now?" said George, half-smiling and rubbing his stomach while taking off his cowboy hat, taking a sip from his cup of cold tea left behind as he sat back down to his place with a conviction of wanting to finish his lunch, no matter its temperature.

"Well, I'll be," said Cal, as Ming set the dishes back down on the table, including Cal's nearly empty plate. Ming smiled and bowed at George and walked back towards his kitchen at a brisk pace, with so much post-lunch clean-up and pre-supper prep work ahead.

"I just told Ming," said Cal, as Ming was still within earshot. "What a shame it'd be to waste all this great food, throwing out your lunch here, including this lovely zhu sun. Christ, what gives? Didn't beat Mr. Campbell hard enough earlier? That'd be a hell of a shame, too."

"Yeah, a shame indeed, a big shame," said George, speaking slower again in his deep monotone, even if with a bit of a rasp in his voice, while diving right back into the hodgepodge of exotic Asian greens placed back in front of him, eating away in a feverish manner as if a starving traveller without care that they had now gone cold on the plate, as they would warm up once inside. "Suppose just like a shame, a terrible shame, to waste a good haircut this morning."

"Cut?" said Cal, wiping his mouth with the crumpled napkin a final time before he picked up his fortune cookie, setting the crustacean-looking confection in a precise position in the palm of his warped left hand and punching it with his wonky right one, hammer-fisting it to smash the cookie into acceptable pieces of eatable, brittle little crumbs. Cal ate the largest chunk while shuffling off the smallest bits, all the while unfolding the tiny, rectangular paper within, as if with a genuine excitement to view his note of prophetic serendipity. "Huh, what cut?"

"Gregory," said George, crunching away with his molars, going at the juicy white end of a large piece of bok choy, grinding as if at some sinewy, lignin base. A piece of the dark pine green leafy top dangled out of his mouth while the tawny stir-fry type of sauce was dripping off the blade of the vegetable and back down onto his plate like a catarrhal discharge. "He didn't need no trim today."

About Atmosphere Press

Founded in 2015, Atmosphere Press was built on the principles of Honesty, Transparency, Professionalism, Kindness, and Making Your Book Awesome. As an ethical and author-friendly hybrid press, we stay true to that founding mission today.

If you're a reader, enter our giveaway for a free book here:

SCAN TO ENTER
BOOK GIVEAWAY

If you're a writer, submit your manuscript for consideration here:

SCAN TO SUBMIT
MANUSCRIPT

And always feel free to visit Atmosphere Press and our authors online at atmospherepress.com. See you there soon!

About the Author

R. Conrad Speer, a Saskatchewan-based writer, is known for *Saint Lazarus Day and Other Stories*, published by Atmosphere Press in 2020. With a postgraduate certificate in creative writing from the University of Edinburgh, he draws inspiration in this novel from his past experiences working on the grounds of a vast rural psychiatric hospital.